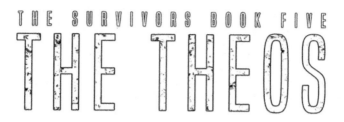

THE SURVIVORS BOOK FIVE

THE THEOS

BY

NATHAN HYSTAD

This is a work of fiction. All of the characters, names, incidents, organizations, and dialogue in this novel are either products of the author's imagination or are used fictitiously.

Cover art: Tom Edwards Design

Edited by: Scarlett R Algee

Proofed and Formatted by: BZ Hercules

ISBN-13: 9781720239987

Also By Nathan Hystad

<u>The Survivors Series</u>

The Event

New Threat

New World

The Ancients

The Theos

Old Enemy

Red Creek

PROLOGUE

The destruction was palpable. Life forces were snuffed out as the fabric of their reality was sucked into the swirling, ever-growing vortex.

Mary stood on the farthest moon in the solar system, its cold surface hard against her boots. From there, she could see the Unwinding's unforgiving power; but more than that, she could feel every ounce of energy pouring into it as entire planets were devoured.

She'd started with the system's star, and what a rush of adrenaline that had been. She felt the vortex slowly growing with every planet's addition. Each entity and consciousness it ate fed the annihilation, and Mary knew she was accomplishing the Iskios' goal even faster than they'd originally expected.

As the colorful vortex continued through the system, it came into view, and tears spilled down her mortal face inside her atmospheric bubble. Tears of joy. Of accomplishment. Of sadness.

Mary shook her head, trying to clear out the never-ceasing voice of reason that lingered in the back of her mind: a tiny pecking at her brain, telling her this wasn't right. That she could stop all of this, that she just needed to concede to the voice, to give it back control.

Images of another human mortal flashed into her mind: short dark hair, graying at the sides, a smile that made her heart warm. A name. Dean Parker.

"Begone!" she screamed. Her hand rested on her belly, where she could feel a change. The spawn was growing inside her, and she could feel its energy already spanning into her bloodstream. There was no time for this vessel's motives.

The Unwinding was upon them, and they had a lot to do.

Mary watched as the last planet in the solar system was swallowed by the gaping, swirling maw of the vortex. She floated off the small lonely moon toward the next target, staying just long enough to see the moon ripped apart before she closed her eyes and vanished.

ONE

"*I* need to see Sarlun," I said to the paisley-robed guard approaching me in the Shimmali Shandra room. As always, the stark whiteness of the chamber reminded me of a hospital room. If I closed my eyes, I could hear the soft beeping of the machines Janine had been hooked up to all those years ago.

The guard's elongated snout twitched. "He's not available." The translator I was wearing allowed us to speak to one another with ease.

"Then make him available!" I shouted, not willing to put up with any barricades today. Mary's loss was still fresh. The void left from her abduction by the Iskios had burrowed deep into my soul. Nothing was going to keep me from getting back to her.

"I'll see what I can do," he said, his tweets and chirps sung in a staccato tone. He left the room, leaving me alone in the white space, making it feel even more like a hospital waiting area.

Magnus was going to be angry I hadn't brought him along. When I'd woken up in my house alone a couple of hours earlier, I'd decided I needed to see Sarlun one-on-one. He didn't know Magnus well, and I wanted him to be as open as he could be. As a Gatekeeper, he wouldn't share any inside knowledge with someone not sworn in.

The doors slid open, and Suma came rushing forward. She wrapped her little arms around me, as had become her custom when seeing one of us. I held her tight, trying to understand the translation of the erratic noises she was making.

"Calm down, Suma. What is it?" I asked.

She separated from me and stood back. I noticed how much taller she was, and that her eyes were damp. She was nearing adulthood for a Shimmal, and I was proud of how smart and caring she was.

"Is it true?" she asked.

Word had somehow gotten around. That was interesting. I nodded. "It's true. They took her."

"How? I don't understand."

We moved into the hallway, and she led me toward her father's office. "I was told he wasn't available."

"He's here. They're always told to say that to any unscheduled visitors." Suma was greeted by a few other Shimmali people as we wound our way around the building.

We arrived at his office doors, and Suma typed in a code on a panel; the doors slid open after the console beeped and turned green. Sarlun sat behind his desk, staring out a window at the lush landscape below.

He jumped when I cleared my throat, like he hadn't even known someone had entered his space. When he saw us, he stood, his snout drooping low.

"Dean. I'm surprised to see you," he said, motioning for me to have a seat. "Suma, can you leave us, please?"

"Father, I want to stay. I can help."

"Suma…"

I cut him off. "Let her stay. She's old enough, and she's one of the few I actually trust around here."

Sarlun cringed and twitched before speaking. "Fine. Suma, remain silent."

"Yes, Father." She sat in a chair, her legs just long enough for her feet to touch the ground.

"Why didn't you tell me?" I asked.

Sarlun watched me closely, and I could see his brain calculating what I was leaving out.

"Damn it, Sarlun, we're on the same team. Why didn't you tell me about the Iskios?"

He'd been holding a glass, and he dramatically let it slip from his grip, shards shattering against the stone-lined floor. We all watched as the red liquid rolled toward the edge of the room.

"Iskios!" he shouted, standing up once again. He turned his back to us and looked out the window. His hands flicked open and closed. "This can't be. You must be mistaken."

It was my turn to stand up. Blood boiled throughout my body, and every inch of me flushed in an instant. "Must I? Must I be mistaken?" I crossed the room in seconds, grabbing the Gatekeeper by the short collar, and I shoved him harder than I intended against the wall. "Tell that to Mary! Tell that to my wife, who's now possessed by them!"

"Dean! Stop!" Suma was at my side, trying to pull me off her father.

I looked to her worried face and back to Sarlun, who was staring at me with wide black eyes. He didn't try to fight back or yell at me; he just stood there, taking the abuse.

I loosened my grip, and he slumped away from the wall. Suma was gaping at me with fear, and she backed away. "I'm sorry. I don't know what to do," I said.

"Dean, tell me what happened." Sarlun had come forward, and he set a hand on my forearm.

The fight drained out of me and I sat back down, elbows on my knees, hands on my face. "They took her, Sarlun. It was them all along. The artifacts, the challenges. It was them, not the Theos. They were looking for a vessel.

They found her."

Sarlun leaned against the front of his desk. "No."

"Yes. We were so blinded by the idea of finding the Theos, we didn't even think there could be anyone else behind it," I said.

Suma crossed the room and grabbed me a glass of red liquid, bringing it back in two hands. I accepted it with a forced smile and took a long drink. The fruity sensation hit me, and I perked up as the natural sugars flowed into my bloodstream.

"The Iskios..." Sarlun said quietly.

"I assume you've heard of them." I knew he would have, and initially my anger at not knowing about them was directed at him for withholding the information. As I sat talking with him, I was no longer mad. He likely hadn't thought discussing them was important at the time. Now it was a matter of life and death.

"I have. Long ago, and I mean *long* ago, before the modern expansion of the universe, there were two races. They lived in separate corners of that chartered galaxy, and it's said they didn't even know of one another for a millennium." Sarlun got himself another beverage and settled in behind his desk to tell the tale. "Eventually, one of the races became advanced enough to begin exploring space. Rumors say the Theos learned it first, but other texts claim it was the Iskios. No one really knows."

I made a mental note to take every file, book, or drawing Sarlun had access to on the topic.

He continued. "They worked together, the races similar, yet so different. Eventually, the Theos found out their new expanded family was to be feared. As they explored the universe together and came across newly-evolved races, the Iskios only wanted to exploit them, to mutilate and adapt the beings to their needs. It went against

6

everything the peace-loving Theos had built their history on. One particular time, it's said, the Iskios enslaved a race in secret and forcefully adapted them to become a food source for the rich. The Theos found out and abolished their treaty, and warned the Iskios to cease their destruction. They threatened war against the other side if they so much as interfered with another race."

Suma sat forward, listening intently to a story she hadn't heard before. I was on the edge of my seat too, wondering where it was all going.

"Years passed, and centuries turned to millennia. The Theos lost communication with the Iskios as they set forth and colonized countless worlds, leaving the strange beings to their own devices. The Theos were tactful and tried to not interfere with new races. Eventually, they heard more terrible tales of the Iskios destroying worlds and trying to harness the power of the black hole in order to threaten entire solar systems. That was it. The Theos were powerful. They had technology unlike anyone had ever imagined. Humans would consider them magic wielders, but it was not trickery. It was pure science and energy manipulation that they dealt in.

"The story goes like this: the Theos created the portals, or Shandra, on any known world the Iskios had set foot on. They then manufactured a device that would identify every Iskios in the universe, using a functional DNA detector. From there, they roamed for centuries, capturing each and every Iskios out there. It took the Theos countless years, but they did it, and from there, no one knows what happened."

He took another swig from his glass, and his snout rose as he kept talking. Suma and I sat in silence, letting the Gatekeeper convey his story.

"The Theos themselves disappeared after that. No sign

of them either. Rumors say they destroyed each other in an epic battle of all battles. The Ancients, they called them: Theos versus Iskios. The Ancients destroyed one another, leaving the universe without the first two races that ever existed."

I leaned back, trying to take it all in. "So the Iskios knew what was coming? They had time to make this crazy plan of finding a vessel?"

"I suppose anything is possible," he said before adding, "I can't believe I hadn't considered the Iskios being behind this. Especially after seeing that shadow. They were known for their theatrics." His tweets and chirps were slowing down, and I could see the strain on him as he sat there, slumping in his chair. "Dean, I'm sorry about Mary. We'll do anything we can to help find her."

"Thanks, Sarlun. And I'm sorry about…" I paused, and he just waved a hand in the air, dismissing it.

"There's something else I have for you." He flipped the screen on his wall from artwork to a map. With a few taps of his hand, he inputted coordinates into it, and the map zoomed into a faraway world. A familiar symbol appeared beneath it, identifying the planet as a portal world.

"What is it?" Curiosity raced through me, mixed with urgency to get back to the crystal planet where I'd been forced to leave Mary behind.

"This is Bazarn Five, a world of intellectuals, arts, and fine dining. It's a destination for anyone with enough means to visit," Sarlun said.

"I'm not in the mood for philosophical discussions with the galaxy's elite right now."

"It also houses the universe's largest library. There you can find… anything about anything. Scholars have spent thousands of years researching and collecting information on every corner out there, and if you're to find where the

Theos are hiding, that's the best place to start."

Suma was on her feet, interest piqued at the idea of such a place.

"Why would I be looking for the Theos? I want to find Mary." Sarlun's train of thought was veering off the track.

He stopped fidgeting with his glass and looked me in the eyes. "You think you can just find Mary and bring her back? They have her."

I gulped, my throat raw and dry. Before I could get my two cents in, he kept talking. "If you found her now, she would be nothing more than a vessel. She's now a harbinger of destruction. She wields the Unwinding."

"And just what is this Unwinding?" I asked, knowing I wasn't going to like the answer.

Sarlun paused and looked at his daughter. He reached over and grabbed her hand, pulling her into a hug. He rested his chin on the top of her head as he spoke. "It's the end of everything. It's the Iskios using the theory of the black hole to destroy all life and matter in the universe."

The idea that Mary was wielding anything like that made my skin crawl. "But I have to find her. I have to try."

He nodded. "So you do. But know there's only one way to get her back and to stop the Iskios."

I considered this. It was obvious, but I had nowhere to start. My plan had been to find the insectoids, then find the crystal planet. What if she was gone already? What if they wouldn't help me? I needed the big guns. Sarlun's story about their detection invention stuck in my mind. "I find the Theos, they find the Iskios."

His head bobbed up and down again, and Suma broke free from his embrace. "Father, I want to go with Dean to Bazarn Five. I can help research."

I was about to decline the offer, to save Sarlun from looking like an unsupportive father; then I remembered how intuitive and resourceful the small alien had been when Slate and I first met her in that abandoned city. Without her, we could still be wandering around the desolate world. "Suma, I'd love your help."

She chirped in excitement, and Sarlun's eyes went wide. "Very well. But take care of her."

"I'll be back for you, Suma. I have something to do first. I have to know."

I needed to see if Mary was still on the crystal world, or if she was gone. Then, and only then, could I start my real search for the Theos.

TWO

*M*y house had turned into a war zone. Maps covered screens, and printed papers were layered over the table with coffee-cup ring stains all over them. Leonard leaned against the kitchen island, sketching our meeting. Natalia held her baby, Patty, bouncing her on an arm while singing a Russian lullaby softly as the rest of us discussed the plan.

Magnus pushed back in his chair. "Why didn't Sarlun run this Theos quest you guys went on by the smarty pants at Bazarn before you went?"

"We've been through this. We'd likely have been killed just for having it. Then the map would have gone to the highest bidder. We couldn't trust anyone."

"And we can now?" Slate asked. Denise was there with him, though she hung at the edge of the room, uncertain what she could do to help. She glanced at her new boyfriend with loving eyes, and though it was obvious to me, I didn't think the big lug even noticed.

"No. But we aren't going to tell our contact at Bazarn anything. We're historians, nothing more," I said, imagining the likes of Magnus and Slate arriving there, muscles bulging and pulse rifles hard in their grips, looking so unlike historians. "They don't know anything about humans, so what objection will they have?"

"That may not be true. If they have the universe's largest known library, they may know everything about us." Clare finally spoke up. She'd been poking around on her tablet for the last hour, searching for something.

"Good point. Either way, it'll work. It has to." I took a sip of coffee and swallowed the cold, bitter brew.

"What's this about the hybrids?" Nat asked. Patty was resting on her chest, eyes closed, drool spilling onto Natalia's shirt.

"Terrance and Leslie will know how I can get to those insectoids' world. I need to find out how they knew where we were on our trip to find the Theos. Or Iskios. Whatever. They tried to stop us. They know where the crystal world is." It was nearly time.

"We'll dig through the datasticks Sarlun gave you. You take my husband with you, *da*?" Natalia demanded more than asked.

"What about me?" Slate asked, standing up quickly and pointing to his chest in defiance.

"Slate, you can sit this one out. You've been through a lot, and I can't ask you to be there by my side all the time. You have a life too." I glanced over at Denise, who smiled at this.

Slate wasn't smiling at me. "Is this because she was taken? I know I failed you. And I failed Mary." His big shoulders slumped forward, and I crossed the room to stand before him.

"Listen here. You did everything you could. Neither of us could have stopped what happened, and I don't trust anyone to have my back more than you, but I need you here. When it comes time to take the fight to the Iskios, I want you rested and ready for it."

He straightened at this and gave me a small grin. "Fine. But, boss?"

"Yeah?" I urged him.

"I always knew I was a more kickass sidekick than this guy over here." He hiked a thumb toward Magnus, who frowned at Slate before barking out a loud laugh.

"This kid is all right." Magnus wrapped a bulky arm around Slate's shoulder and put him in a headlock.

"Then it's settled. Magnus and I leave in the morning. You all find anything you can about the Theos, and when we get back, we're heading to Bazarn. Got it?" I asked. Everyone shouted their understanding, and I began to fold up the papers on the table.

Symbols of the worlds we'd visited on our quest were sketched out: one for Atrron; one for the world where the Picas had taken over the Apop village; and another for the planet shrouded in darkness, where the Raanna were now free from the moth.

My friends filed out. Nick stuck a fist out, and I bumped it. Clare gave me a kiss on the cheek and told me she would find some gadgets to help us. Natalia told Magnus to grab their son Dean and to take them home. I watched him pick up the boy, who was out cold. It was late at night, well past the child's bedtime. I was hesitant to bring Magnus with me on the trip, but Nat was adamant, and so was Magnus.

I'd already had an earful from him for ditching him to go to Shimmal alone. Still, I'd leave him behind if I knew I could handle finding the crystal world by myself. Something told me it wasn't going to be as easy as I wanted.

"See you tomorrow." Magnus lingered in the doorway and turned to me. "Dean, I know you're worried, but we'll see this through. Together."

"I know we will."

"And if you leave without me, I'm going to find you out there, and I'm going to make you wish you'd never met me."

I wanted to laugh at this, but his face didn't break into a smile. He turned and walked away.

My head was starting to pound, and I heard Maggie scratch to be let inside. She must have gotten out when Clare left.

"Dean," a voice said from the kitchen, and I realized Leonard hadn't left yet.

"Leonard. How're you doing?" I asked the young man. He was looking more fit since our adventure, and his hair was cut shorter, no longer shaggy and covering his eyes. Not only that, but his artwork kept getting better and better.

"I'm okay."

I glanced over at his drawings and saw the group of us huddled around the table. A speech bubble pointed to my mouth, reading, "We will find my wife!"

It hit home, and I sank onto one of the island stools. "You're so good at that."

He shrugged. "What good is it if people are in danger out there?"

"Leonard, we're all here for different things. You have a gift and telling the Survivors stories with your comics is something the people love to read." I couldn't believe just how popular the issues were, especially after the rest of Earth had moved to New Spero. The kid was basically a rock star.

"I really like Mary. I want you to bring her back." Leonard saw me looking at his stack of drawings, and I caught him tucking one away.

"Can I see it?" I asked.

He hesitated before saying yes. He passed it over to me, sliding the eight-by-ten sheet across the island. It was more detailed than his other work, done in pencil. It was a drawing of Mary embracing me, clearly right after I'd found out she hadn't been killed by the Bhlat.

He'd captured the moment, and my emotion, so well.

This wasn't one of his over-embellished comic drawings; it was a real piece of art. I held it up, not noticing the tear falling from my eye until it splashed the bottom of the page. I missed her so much.

"I'm sorry. I didn't want you to be upset," Leonard said.

"Don't apologize. This is the best thing I've ever seen. Can I keep it?"

"Of course," he stammered. "It's yours."

"Thanks." I flipped it upside down for now. I couldn't bear to see it at the moment.

"I want to help too."

"I'm sure there's something we can get you to work on. How about you collaborate with Nat on going over the books?"

He shook his head. "I've never been that kind of a nerd. I was thinking I could go out there with you." He pointed to the ceiling.

"We'll see." I didn't want to bring any danger to the kid, but I knew I'd let him help if we needed it. The more people around that cared about Mary, the higher the chance I got her home. At the same time, I didn't want to get his hopes up.

"Thanks for watching over me."

"Leonard, you helped me so much back then. You never have to thank me for anything. We're family now." I got up and lightly clapped him on the back, nodding to the comic strip. "And we *will* get my wife back."

"I know you will. If I've learned anything since the Event, it's this: Dean Parker wins. Every damn time." He grinned, and I couldn't help but smile alongside him.

Leonard gathered his drawings up and went home, leaving me alone with Maggie in the house. It felt empty without Mary.

When I turned the lights off in bed, a flash of Leonard's words hit the back of my eyelids in Comic Sans font. *Dean Parker wins.*

THREE

The portal room on the hybrids' world had changed. Since it was now being utilized, Leslie had installed a camera system to alert them when someone was arriving or departing. They also kept security nearby, ready to warn of an attack if necessary. The portals were still a secret way of travel, and few knew of their existence. The people we'd transported from Giza to New Spero via the portal system were told that it was the only one in existence, and that it was destroyed afterwards. Most had seemed to buy it.

The portal by Terran Five was under lockdown, and they'd caught several people trying to sneak into it. The Gatekeepers had done a wonderful job keeping the secret of their vast network of worlds, but as with anything, the more minds that knew about them, the higher the chance that word would spread.

Kareem's body was gone, but a gravestone marked his place of passing. I knelt by it and silently thanked him for all his help. "I wish you were here to help me figure this one out, Kareem." I said the words quietly, and Magnus left me to it, staying on the opposite side of the room.

Magnus waved at the cameras, giving a big toothy smile. "They can't hear me, can they?"

I shook my head. At least, I didn't think they could.

"Good. I sure hope they aren't going to cover up for their buddies." He cracked his knuckles.

"Mag, this isn't going to come to that. You know how

much the hybrids have dealt with. Leslie and Terrance are on our side after all we've been through. They'll help us." Inside, I knew Magnus was right. We'd pry the information from them if we had to. All that mattered was getting Mary back.

"Sure." He didn't sound convinced.

We exited to the outdoors. It was nighttime there, insects chirping their mating songs throughout the swampy landscape. Thin clouds blocked some of the starlight, but otherwise, it was a fresh evening. The smell of a recent rain hung in the air. I'd been through some crazy things on this planet, and coming back here always sent me through a flurry of memories.

Mae saving me from the swamp creature, her head resting on my shoulder in a familiar gesture, one I hadn't picked up on until it was too late. Meeting Kareem for the first time and eventually gaining his trust and help in our effort to beat the Bhlat. Bringing the hybrids to their new home and allowing them a new life. Seeing Kareem die in the portal room, hearing his final words to me: *Change the universe.*

"You okay, Dean?"

I looked up at Magnus, seeing worry crease his forehead. "Yeah. Just remembering how we got here."

Before he could reply, the sound of a lander's thrusters carried to us, and soon we spotted the lights flying toward us from the north.

"Looks like someone was watching the cameras." Magnus stepped forward, and that was when I noticed the landing pad. That was new. They were really becoming more of a colony than a hiding place for outcasts.

The small lander set down on the concrete surface, its bright lights nearly blinding us before they dimmed. I covered my eyes with a hand stuck straight out, fingers spread just enough apart to see a form jogging toward us.

"Dean! Magnus! It *is* you." Terrance was in front of us, the lights behind him casting a long shadow on the grass.

"Terrance. What are you doing making these trips?" I asked.

He smiled at the question. "We all take turns. Not many people come through the portals, so when the alert came I had them check the camera. I didn't believe them when they said it was you two."

He gestured toward the lander with his right hand and turned, Magnus and I flanking him as we headed to the transport vehicle. It was shaped much like ours, only a little wider, and it was walled with a heavy-duty black metallic material instead of our lightweight thin outer shells.

"It's good to see you. We need some help," Magnus said.

"You guys know we'll help if we can."

Terrance got in first, and Magnus gave me a look telling me he was ready for action if it should arise. It was funny knowing a friend so well that the smallest eye contact could tell a story. It was good that he wasn't trusting; he had a lot to worry about. Not only was he New Spero's highest commanding officer these days, he was also a husband and father to two children. I had to make sure no harm came to the man beside me.

He entered before me, blocking my way for a few seconds before turning his head and nodding. Terrance hopped into the pilot's seat, and we took the back bench.

"Where's Slate and Mary?" The question was so innocent, but it hit me right in the gut.

"That's why we're here. Mary's gone." The words came out of my mouth stilted.

We were in the air, already flying for their village, and the lander jolted as Terrance jumped in his seat. "What do you mean, 'gone'?"

"She's not dead. She's been taken," I said.

"Then we have to get her back. Who has her?" He was craning his head around, trying to see us and fly at the same time.

"The Iskios." I said the name with distaste in my mouth, and a gnawing at the pit of my stomach. For a second, I felt like I was going to be sick.

"The Iskios? I've never heard of them. Where are they from?" he asked.

I wasn't surprised he'd never heard of them. I hadn't either, until they ruthlessly took Mary. "They're from a long time ago. We'd better wait to tell the story to Leslie too. I don't have it in me to tell it twice."

"Sure. We'll be there soon." The lander was already lowering, making quick work of the distance. It was much faster than the time Mary and I had cruised the ground on hover scooters.

Before we knew it, we were on the ground. I hadn't been there for over a year, but I was amazed at how much the small village had grown. Even in the night, I saw streetlights going for a few blocks, as well as countless buildings with well-lit windows.

"Things have changed around here," Magnus said, nodding his approval.

"No kidding. We've worked really hard to get to this point. We have a couple thousand residents now. A mix of many races, even some humans." We touched down on the ground, and Terrance led the way out of the lander.

I'd heard that a couple hundred of us had asked to see the hybrids' world. At first, Terrance had balked at the idea, but he'd warmed up to it when we offered supplies and assistance at making some improvements to their world.

"What are you calling it here anyways? I'm sick of not

having a name for it," I said.

We were on the ground now, and I spotted a few sentries in towers near the small outdoor landing pad. A dozen various ships were parked there, and I squinted, trying to see if an insectoid ship was there. I didn't see one.

"Haven," he said, his chest rising slightly.

"Haven." I let it roll off my tongue. "I like it. The town or the planet?" That there was a whole world with only one small village tucked away on it was mindboggling, but after all the empty or dying planets I'd now visited, seeing one start from scratch was exciting. It was much like our own race's journey with New Spero.

"All of it, and our village. Easier that way." Terrance led us past the large complex where we'd first met Kareem when we'd followed him and Leslie there from Earth. It felt so long ago, and it was strange to think it had been much longer for Magnus, since he hadn't skipped over seven Earth years on that trip.

Even in the dark, we could see how much had changed. Where there had been nothing but empty ground and trees, there now stood an entire town. Houses were close enough together to feel like part of the community, but not right on each other like the old developments on Earth. Large lots spread the neighborhood out, and we passed what looked to be a main street on the right, where businesses were erected.

A faint light could be seen inside one of the buildings, and I curiously stopped to peer inside the window. A group of human men and women were playing some sort of a game with a hybrid and a few other aliens I'd never seen before. Everyone was laughing and having fun; a portable translator was perched in the middle of the table.

My heart leapt at seeing how far we'd all come. They'd truly built a haven here, and I was humbled.

"Mary would absolutely love to see this," I whispered to no one.

"What's that?" Terrance asked, not hearing my low speech.

"Nothing. This is just great to see. Everyone together, having fun. It gives us hope for the future," I said. If the Unwinding was really happening, I needed to stop it, to keep life like this going. Selfishly, my first priority was Mary, but if I got her, I knew we could stop the Iskios. She was their vessel, and without my wife and child, they couldn't accomplish anything.

We kept walking, and eventually we got to the last house. It was made of huge white logs; a front porch much like my own jutted out, and an inviting walkway led to the front door. Smoke poured from a chimney, the smell of burning wood making me long for more peaceful nights like that at my own home.

"Is this your house?" Magnus asked him.

Terrance nodded, and for the first time, I wondered what period of the night it really was. Had we woken them? He opened the door, and Leslie was standing there in sweat pants and a t-shirt. It was always hard to see her. With her hair cut short, she didn't look exactly like Janine or Mae, but it was unmistakable that they were cut from the same mould. Either way, Mae was dead, and so was the second Janine. Neither of them had really been married to me, and the only woman that mattered was Mary.

"Magnus." She hugged him before hugging me as well. We'd had a tumultuous relationship over the years, but we'd come to a mutual appreciation and respect for one another. Terrance had been the one with the hardest shell to crack, but tonight he seemed like a new man.

"What's the matter?" Leslie asked me, her chilled hands resting on my arms. She could see the pain in my eyes.

"Mary." I wanted to be strong but seeing Janine's face brought back the heartache of losing Mary – not that it had gone far over the last couple of days. It kept a permanent home in my chest and liked to remind me of its presence during the quiet times, when I couldn't distract myself any further.

"Let's sit," Terrance said, and he led us into the living room, where custom-made furniture sat in a comfortable pattern. "I'll get some coffee."

I changed the subject. "The town's really coming together. You both must be so proud."

Leslie looked ready to ask something, but she bit her tongue, feeling the room. "We are."

"How's everyone doing? The ones we found at the prison?" Magnus asked.

"They're thriving these days. They were pretty sick, malnourished, but you'd never know the amount of abuse they took, not anymore." She paused. "At least, not physically. They still have some tough days mentally, but that's to be expected."

I couldn't imagine having to go through what they had. I was glad to hear they were all healthy, and as happy as they could be.

Magnus perched on a wooden chair, with Leslie beside me on a couch, the cushions hand-sewn and filled with something soft. Terrance set cups down in front of us on the wide coffee table and poured us each a serving of steaming hot coffee.

"It smells amazing," I said, realizing I'd skipped my morning coffee at home. We'd been in a mad rush to get to Terran Five and head here.

"Tell us what happened to Mary," Leslie urged.

"You're not going to believe it. Thinking back, it seems

so unlikely, and you've seen some crazy stuff yourselves." I took a sip from my cup, noticing a slight shake in my hand. I was anxious to know something before I told them how Mary was taken. "Those insectoids. Are there any here now?"

"Insectoids?" Terrance asked. "You mean the Padlog? The few of them that were staying here have actually gone back to their home world. I haven't seen them in quite some time."

"Padlog," I said. The name sounded strange as it hit my ears. "What were they doing here in the first place?"

Terrance shrugged. "They had some sort of a deal with Kareem, I think. Come to think of it, they left shortly after he passed on."

Magnus cut in. "How do we find them?"

"We know where they live. That's not a problem," Leslie said, eyebrow raised curiously.

"Can we jump there with the portal?" I asked, hoping for a favorable response. I needed to get to Mary quickly. They were my only connection to finding the crystal world.

"No, but it's not that far from here. A week by ship," Terrance answered.

"Damn it!" I yelled, startling our hosts. "I'm sorry. I don't have a week. It could be too late. It's already been too long." I slammed my fist on the table, instantly regretting my action as the pain echoed through my wrist.

"Tell us what happened." This from Leslie.

"Dean, we'll do what we have to do. We'll go see these Padlog and get the answers we need." Magnus was the ever-reassuring voice of reason. "Tell them."

I leaned back on the couch, telling the hybrids about the artifact Sarlun had shown us a year ago, and subsequently, the second piece to it we'd found on the ice world.

They were on the edge of their seats as I explained each

stop on our quest to find the fabled, mysterious Theos. The sun was beginning to rise as I finished recounting the crystal world and Mary being possessed by the long-dead Iskios.

"That's...I'm speechless," Terrance said.

Leslie watched me with sorrow in her eyes. She patted my hand but didn't say anything at all.

"Now you know why I need to find these Padlog. They're my only clue, the one link that we were really on a derelict space station above a waterlogged world, and they know where to find the crystal planet Mary sent us home from, before the Iskios seized control of her mind again.

"She's still inside there. I saw it after the stones fell on her, and if I find her, I can and *will* pull them out of her. Somehow." My bravado was falling short in my own heart, because the truth was, I had no idea how to do that.

"When do you want to leave?" Terrance asked.

"Now," I said. "Now."

FOUR

Terrance had finished going over the ship tour when Leslie climbed aboard.

"Terr, I'm going with them," she said.

"What? You can't go." Terrance crossed his arms and stood up straight. "We have obligations to our town."

Magnus and I stepped back, giving them space to have their not-so-private discussion. Having Leslie around would make the trip that much easier, because she knew how to operate the ship far beyond the half-hour training we'd just been given.

"They don't need us like they used to. Everyone's just fine. Better than that, they're flourishing." Leslie glanced back at me, sadness in her eyes. "I need this as much as they need my help."

"Then I'm coming too," Terrance said forcefully.

She shook her head. "You should stay. Look, we'll be fine. I know Sergo too. He trusts me. The chances they'll be forthright with two humans who let the Iskios out, after killing two Padlogs the day before, are slim to none."

She had a good point, one I hadn't really considered. I stepped forward, directly beside the two of them, who were facing one another. "She's not wrong. And we'd love your help, Leslie."

"Terrance, we'll make sure she gets home safely. You have my word on it," Magnus said. The two of them hadn't always been fast friends, nearly coming to blows under the pyramid of Giza, but they did respect each other.

Terrance's mouth went rigid in a straight line, and I saw his jaw muscles clench. He was holding something back but kept it to himself. With a bob of his Adam's apple, he resigned himself to the fact he wasn't going to win this battle. "Fine. But be careful. We need you here." His hands reached for hers, and I saw her give it a light squeeze. "I need you."

Magnus and I walked away from the bridge and toward the open galley. The ship was larger than any we'd been used to. Here on Haven, the options were limited, and Terrance reminded us that the cost of a fleet wasn't easy to come by. They only had what had been gifted or loaned to them from visitors, or from newly colonized races finding respite on the secret world.

This ship had once belonged to a smuggler. He hadn't made it as far as Haven, but they'd found his vessel dead in space on one of their trips to a nearby system. His ship had been patched up and made to run again and, as Terrance pointed out, the blood on the bridge had been scrubbed clean.

"You cool with her coming along?" Magnus asked me in private.

"Sure. The more help the better, and she made some good points. They might shoot on sight otherwise."

Terrance walked past us, saying his goodbyes and good lucks. He walked down the smooth-floored hall to the cargo bay, where the ramp was lowered to the ground at Haven's outdoor hangar. Leslie came to stand behind us and waved at Terrance as the ramp lifted, a soft beep notifying us that the ship was sealed.

"Thanks for coming," I said.

"Glad to help. I like Mary."

"Let's go find your pal Sergo." Magnus led the way to

the bridge. After being on that tiny ship on the way to the crystal world with Slate and Mary, this felt like going from a canoe to a yacht. Two separate consoles sat two meters apart, facing a large viewscreen, where we could see the other ships idly lined on the landing pad.

What could only be called a captain's chair sat back and center, with other standing stations along the walls to either side.

"How large of a crew would this ship have?" I asked.

Magnus answered. "We have ones like this now, or a variation of it. Not quite as big, but you'd have seven people on the bridge at any given time, in shifts, and then there's engineering. A lot can go wrong on a vessel like this, especially when you're cruising through uncharted territory. I'd estimate with a cook and support staff, you'd be looking at twenty to twenty-five people."

"I'd have thought more," I said. There were ten cabins with bunks, four in each, and a captain's cabin, along with what could only be the first officer's slightly smaller quarters.

"Wait until you see what we've been working on at Spero," Magnus said as Leslie took the pilot's console and fired up the engines.

The vessels they'd made and tested as they journeyed from New Spero to Earth during the Bhlat threat were immense, with thousands of crew and space for a hundred fighters in each. Fortunately, it hadn't come to war with the Bhlat, but Magnus said it never hurt to have them ready, just in case.

"I can only imagine, after seeing what you already have," I said, not probing him further.

"Ready?" Leslie asked and lifted off the ground, raising us up slowly.

In no time, we were out of Haven's atmosphere and

starting our trek to Volim, the home world of the Padlog.

I was becoming accustomed to being part of a small crew on a larger ship. Everyone had to do their share of tasks, and that meant cooking, cleaning, and maintenance, as well as shifts in the pilot's chair. When the filter alerts popped up, Leslie explained where they were kept, and I meandered to the engineering room, happy to do something different with my time.

Any distraction from thinking about Mary was a good one. Otherwise, all I could see was her eyes clouding with black mist, and an unfamiliar voice speaking through her.

I walked the hall in socked feet, wearing jeans and a gray hoodie like the world's worst-dressed spaceship officer. I passed the crew quarters to the right and saw Magnus stretched out on a bunk, his light snores telling me he was finally asleep. He joked that it was a vacation for him, since being at home meant dealing with a four-year-old and a newborn. I knew he missed them, though. For some reason, he'd taken to sleeping down here, instead of on one of the larger beds on the higher floor.

A week. It was going to take a whole damn week to get to Volim, and that was if everything went smoothly. Filter failure wouldn't kill us, at least not quickly, but I set to the task in hopes it would somehow expedite our progress. We'd been gone for four days, and we were over the hump, sliding down my seven-day countdown, looking for the homestretch.

The doors slid open at my approach. The ceilings here were eight feet tall, and to my left was an elevator leading to the officer's quarters above; below was storage. I imagined the storage area had seen its share of illegal objects, since the previous owner had been a self-proclaimed smuggler.

I was impressed with the décor as well. The Kraski ships had been so bland – purely slick, modern, and functional – but this vessel had color, with walls painted and artwork from around the universe displayed in cases, as well as screens showing images from various planets. I'd watched the full loop on the second day, and Magnus and I had been amazed at the landscapes shown.

I'd seen a lot out there, but evidently, there was so much more to witness. I already felt like a speck in the galaxy, but I felt even more so now.

"What do we have here?" I asked myself, making my way into the engineering room. It was nothing like the movies I used to watch. There was no giant power source fueling the hyperdrive. Instead, it was all behind closed walls, but I could feel the heat rise, and everything vibrated heavily inside the space.

To my left was a large metal unit, ranging from floor to ceiling. That was where the filter system was. Per Leslie's instruction, I found a replacement cartridge near the floor in a cupboard. It was cylindrical and the size of a water cooler bottle. I pulled the casing off of it and carried it over to the right side, where I looked for the fan icon Leslie had told me about.

I tapped it on the computer screen, and a door opened to my right. Inside, I found the handle for the old filter, and I turned it to the left, twisting the locking mechanism. With a tug, it came free, and I cringed at the dirty cartridge. No wonder it needed to be replaced. It looked like it had been a while since anyone had done this.

With a push, the new pristine-white filter slid into place, and I locked it back, shutting the door. As I did, the computer screen dimmed and shut down. I tapped it, but it stayed dark. Crap.

The floor stopped humming, and the lights flickered in the room before going dark. Emergency pucks lit up along the floor, giving me just enough light to see where I was going. The door didn't slide open, but I found the manual handle, turning it and heaving it to the side.

"What the hell's going on?" I called down the hall. Had I broken something with the filter?

I ran in the dim hall, waking Magnus along the way.

"What is it?" he asked groggily.

"Something's wrong."

He followed me to the bridge, where Leslie was fidgeting with her dead console.

"Leslie, what's happening?" I asked, discomfort crawling up my spine as I took in her pale, frightened face.

She pointed to the viewscreen. "The ship's dead."

I stepped forward, trying to see what she was pointing at. Then I saw them. Three ships were slowly flying toward our unmoving vessel.

"Pirates," Leslie whispered.

FIVE

"*P*irates?" Magnus was already sitting down at the helm position, trying to get the computer activated.

"It's no use. Weapons aren't working. Hell, everything's offline." Leslie stood and walked to my side. The ships were getting closer in the viewscreen. "I zoomed as soon as the sensors picked them up, right before our power went down."

The ships weren't large; they were smaller than the one we stood in. The middle one was in rough shape on the outside, a mismatched mess of spare parts and panels, making it all the more intimidating. Like a sewn monster, stitched together from different creatures.

"I've never heard of space pirates," Magnus said, and he slammed his hand down on the console, maybe hoping it would kick the computer into functionality. It didn't.

"They exist, but we haven't found them on this particular pathway. Maybe their regular routes were discovered. I can only assume what goes on in their collective mind, but I'm guessing attacking at random locations would increase the chances of happening by unsuspecting prey." Leslie backed away from the screen slowly. I didn't even think she knew she was doing it.

"What do we do?" I asked, not happy to sit like a target at the range for them. I didn't have time for this, and if I was killed now, Mary would never be safe. Blood rushed through my veins. I was angry. Mad that anyone thought they could come between me and finding my wife. I answered my own question. "We get our guns."

"What will that do?" Leslie asked. "Maybe they just want our ship, and when they see we have no cargo, they'll let us go."

"I'm not willing to take that risk. How'd they kill our power?" I asked.

Leslie tapped a fingernail nervously on the back of the pilot's seat. "They had to have an ion cannon, something that would kill our engines and power."

"The backup still works," I said, thinking about the puck lights on the floor.

"No. Those are battery-charged. They'll only last so long."

"Does that mean our air?" Magnus asked, cutting his question short.

She nodded.

"Okay, which ship would have the device needed to kill our power from that far away?" I asked, watching the three approaching vessels. Two were thin and rectangular, like floating cell phones, but the larger, patched-together one had "lead villain" painted all over its gaudy exterior.

"The middle one," she said, mirroring my thoughts.

"Then we have to get on their ship and shut the device down," Magnus said.

"Easier said than done." Leslie was now pacing back and forth on the bridge. "We don't have that technology on us."

"We don't have to." Our ship bucked as a red ray from the lead ship hit us, grabbing us and pulling us in with a tractor beam. "They'll bring us to them."

A plan formulated in my head, and I sent Magnus to get the EVAs and rifles. Leslie and I talked it through, and when we were satisfied it was our only real chance of breaking free, we agreed to go ahead. Magnus was back quickly, and while we were being dragged toward the pirates, we suited up, making sure our weapons were fully charged.

"Dean, if anything goes south here, take care of them for me," Magnus said, not having to tell me who he meant.

"And if something happens to me, kill them. Destroy the Iskios. Save my wife and unborn child. Make them pay, Magnus. Make them all pay." Rage burned inside my chest like a smouldering fire. I gripped my rifle hard enough to feel each ridge through my gloved hand.

"Deal." He stuck a hand out in the air, and I gripped it. A promise made by each of us, signed and sealed.

"Leslie, go below and hide," I ordered. She had a part to play, and I hoped we could pull ours off to get power back. The Relocator sat in my pocket, and I tapped it on, saving our current location into its system.

"You sure you don't want to switch roles?" I asked Magnus. I felt like his was the most dangerous part, and I didn't want anything bad to happen to my old friend.

"If anyone can skulk around quietly on an alien pirate ship, it's you," he said, smiling through his facemask. "Can you picture *this*" – he waved a hand over his large frame – "doing anything quietly?"

"Good point. I'll stay close." I pulled the device Mary had used to hide from the Picas on the Apop world from the pack on the bridge floor. Clare would be so happy her inventions were being used to potentially save lives.

We walked to the cargo bay, knowing they'd be coming aboard there. I felt the buzz of entering a containment field and knew we were nearing the pirate ship. What did they expect to find onboard? A full crew? Would they come in with guns blazing? If they did, our plan wouldn't work.

I attached the cloaking device to my leg with the built-in strapping. Our ship shook before falling still. We were at our destination. Something banged hard against the ramp, and before the invaders could pry or cut their way in, ruining our ship, Magnus nodded to me and pushed the "ramp open" icon.

It didn't work.

"There has to be a manual way." I thought back to the door I'd been able to open back at engineering. We searched the floor and quickly found two panels, one on each side of the ramp's pivot line.

"There's two," he said, no doubt worried I wouldn't be able to cloak quickly enough.

"I'm on it." The latch was a twist and push. I tapped my cloaking device on, and I could feel it activate. "Can you see me?" I asked. Magnus looked up, his face startled to see nothing.

"You're as good as gone. Damn me if that doesn't work well. Let's turn them. On three. One. Two. Three." He twisted his, and I did the same, each of us then pressing the red button down. The ramp hissed open and lowered.

I stepped back, toward the far side of the opening, so I'd be at their backs when they walked on board.

"*Teel ooorah nhull srevla.*" The words, spoken in a tinny voice, translated through my suit and into my earpiece. "*What do we have here?*"

Multiple boots clanged on the metal ramp, and soon three bodies emerged, their backs to me. They wore thick armored suits, and each of them walked slowly, methodically, toward Magnus. "What the hell are you?" I heard Magnus ask, and I cringed. He backed up, holding his pulse rifle to his chest. They followed him, stopping a few yards from his position.

"Where is the rest of your crew?" the question translated.

"What you see is what you get," Magnus said. It was my chance to slip by. I took one last look at my buddy, silently hoping he'd be okay, and climbed down the back of the ramp, hitting the bottom of it with as little noise as I could muster.

I peeked upward and saw one of the pirates starting to look back before Magnus got his attention with an insult. Something about a rust bucket. I hoped the pirates weren't extra-sensitive about their ship, because Magnus could be unrelenting when provoked.

I left them in a standoff and crept down the ramp to the open bay door on their ship. To the side, I could see the expanse of space, and my breathing quickened. I knew I was invisible, but seeing the stars in the blackness beyond, with nothing but a pirate's containment field between us, filled me with a moment of dread. I shoved it down and kept moving. The outside of the ship before me was painted red, large rivets bolting it to a black section.

I tentatively crossed over the fifteen-foot bridge they'd laid down to connect the two ships and entered their vessel. It was poorly lit onboard, lights dimming and getting brighter, reminding me of a generator running out of gasoline.

Whatever they were using to kill our power was draining theirs, and quickly. That was a good sign.

No one met me as I stealthily moved into the back of the pirates' ship. I was still using the cloaking device, but it wasn't infallible, so the fewer of them I came across, the better. The ship was a mess, clutter and crap piled high. I had to creep through the labyrinth of junk to get out of the open room. If I met anyone in here, there'd be no way of hiding, since there wasn't enough room to get by someone in the narrow pathways amongst the garbage. A smaller ship sat inside their cargo bay. It looked like it was maybe an escape pod, made for one.

I scanned the area to see if anything would constitute a device used to cut our power off. Nothing fit the bill, from what I could see. These space pirates appeared to have a penchant for picking up anything not bolted to the ground. I tripped on a metal chair as I neared the exit and saw it had indeed been ripped off a ship somewhere. I'd spoken too soon.

Once I passed the junk, it opened up to a wide hallway. The lights continued to dim and brighten repeatedly as I walked quickly but quietly toward the first door on the left. A whirring noise snagged my attention, and I pushed my back against the wall beside the doorway. Something was rolling my way, and I looked in their direction, knowing they couldn't see me if I stayed still.

One of the pirates was coming down the hall, the same armor covering its body, only this one was rolling instead of walking. As it got closer, my stomach churned. It wasn't what I'd expected. This wasn't made of flesh and blood. Its legs were soldered together, mechanized rollers replacing feet. The rest of it was covered by the thick muted gray armor, but the face. The face was what made me recoil in horror.

It felt like a child's drawing of what a humanoid would look like, having never seen one. Skin of some sort was pulled tight over a robotic face, ripped and sagging on a cheek to reveal shiny metal behind it. Dead machinelike eyes blinked and twitched under flapping fake eyelids. A gray nose was sewn onto the material, slightly off kilter. It wasn't from a human face, but the premise was the same.

The idea that the nose might be real, stolen from one of their victims, made me shudder in disgust. It rolled closer to me, turning sharply. This was it. This pirate creature was going to see me, and the whole plan was over. My hand lowered to my Relocator, and I was ready to press the icon.

Only, it didn't turn to me; it was rotating to the door beside me. As I watched it pass me by, entering the room, I couldn't help but wonder if it was all wires under the armor, or if it was only partially synthetic. On the other hand, I decided I didn't really want to find out.

It whirred into the room, and the door slid shut behind it. I took a few deep breaths to slow my racing heart and kept moving down the corridor. Frayed wires stuck out of the walls, spliced together in intricate patterns. They might understand electronics, but these pirates didn't care about aesthetics. The whole area looked like the garbage bin of an electricians' trade school after their first week.

Careful not to trip on any loose wires, I stepped cautiously and ended up peering into two open rooms, which held nothing that I could see from the hall. The device I was looking for had to be large to be able to cut our power from that far away. None of these small rooms off the corridor would house it.

The lights dimmed the farther down the hall I made it. I was close. A double door hung at the far end of the corridor, and two robots emerged; one on wheels, the other walking with obvious mechanical steps. They didn't have fake skin on, just round heads that lacked a mouth or eyes. It was almost as creepy seeing them with no face at all.

I kept still as they moved past me with a sense of urgency I hadn't see from the others I'd encountered. I hoped Magnus was all right. How many more of these things were on the ship? The double doors slid open as I approached; the sensors knew someone had stepped by the doors, opening them.

I peeked inside and was greeted with a large room, this one free of debris and junk. A computer the size of my old master suite clung to the left side wall, and that was where I went first. It hummed with energy, and I did a three-sixty looking for any signs of nearby robo-pirates. The room lay empty.

At first, I tried to find a control panel I could understand. Fail. Next, I looked for a power source. Fail. My rifle came off my back in an instant, and I held it, deciding blowing it to pieces might be my best bet. Right before I pulled the trigger, which would undoubtedly inform them as to my location, I saw a blip on a monitor. It was an old screen, the rounded kind I used to play pixel games on my computer in the eighties. Two rectangular objects sat on the screen with a boxy ship in between them. Pixelated lightning-bolt images shot from the ship into the rectangles, which were glowing yellow.

It hit me. They weren't ships. They were the devices the pirates were using to cut our power. But how to disconnect them?

SIX

*F*rom somewhere deeper into the ship came the sound of clanking metal. A voice sang in an unknown language, and I was too far for the translator to pick up the words. Against my better judgment, I followed the sound. Pirates often took hostages. I couldn't abandon a being in good conscience if they needed my help.

I stopped. Couldn't I, though? Mary needed me, and I shouldn't be wasting my time trying to help every random alien, human, or robot, no matter how much they needed me. From the other side of the room, the voice was clearer, even beautiful, alien and imaginative.

"Damn it." I exited the room with the massive computer through the door on the adjacent wall, and the moment the door opened, the voice was much clearer.

Words and phrases hit my translator, and it relayed the song reflexively but with no rhythm. *"Here I am alone. But my love hasn't forgotten me. When I die, we will reunite. When I die, we will reunite."*

It kept going along the same lines, the words more touching in their alien tongue. One of the pirates swung into the room, and I quietly followed it, still cloaked. A short blue creature stood behind bars. Bald and skinny, it looked close to death, its collarbone jutting from taut skin, but it stood erect with pride as it finished its song.

The robot uttered something about "power down," but it kept singing, even after the pirate repeated the phrase four or five times. When the song was over, the pirate lifted a hand, and a ray of red light shot from its finger tips, shocking the creature's body with electricity. She — as I was sure it was a female now — shook in pain but kept standing.

The robot spun on wheels and left the room. The lights dimmed and brightened again; then the door slid shut behind the pirate, and the two of us were alone, me free, her behind bars. Her prison was tiny. A blanket on the floor, a bucket in the corner. It was heart-wrenching to see.

Holding my rifle, I snapped the cloaking device on my leg to the off position, revealing myself. The prisoner yelped and scrambled to the back of the cell.

"It's okay," I said quietly. My translator didn't know what language to translate, and I tapped my arm console, telling it to use the language from the song. It was identified as Molariun. The database the Gatekeepers had provided us was vast. I had no idea where this race hailed from.

"It's okay," I repeated. This time, it was translated at the same volume I'd spoken in.

"Who are you?" Her question came back to me through my earpiece in English.

"I'm Dean." I pointed to the bars. "Why are you here?"

Her shoulders slumped, and I could now see how ragged her clothing was. It hung on her skeletal body like a sail with no wind on a mast. She couldn't have been taller than four feet, and there was no hair visible on her. Her pigment was dark blue, her four eyes piercing pure white; no pupil met my gaze. Holes acted as a nose just above her slip of a mouth.

"I'm Rivo. They are gone. My love, Nico. All dead. These… *Ligros*" — the last word didn't translate, but I guessed it to mean the robot pirates — "attacked us. They took me and killed everyone else."

"How long ago?" I asked. Judging by the shape she was in, I assumed it hadn't been recently.

"I don't know." Her voice was slight but still strong.

"I'm going to get you out of here," I said.

She rushed to the bars, her tiny hands grabbing them. "My ship, is it here?"

"I saw one in their cargo bay. Is it a single passenger?"

Relief flooded her face. "It's still here."

"Is there something you're not telling me?" My intuition was sending warning bells off in my head.

"No point in hiding it. My family's very wealthy. A small fortune was hidden in the escape ship. They ripped every inch of our vessel apart, but I don't think they thought of that. They seem very single-minded, especially for artificial beings."

"Why are you telling me this?" I asked. "You don't know me."

"Because I'll pay you to get me out of here. Isn't that how this works?" I had to replay the translation to catch the quick words.

"Can't someone help because it's the right thing to do?" I asked her as I stood a foot away from the bars. I reached for them and tried to tug on the door. It wouldn't budge.

"No one I know. Either way, I appreciate it."

"Where are the keys?"

"I've never been let out, but the one with the face unlocked it when I arrived. I'd been beaten up, was dizzy and confused. At first, I thought I'd dreamt the robot with a face, a terrible nightmare. But he comes and visits me. Never says a word, just watches me. Sometimes I wake up and he's there, outside the bars, staring at me with dead eyes." She shivered, and I knew there was no time to waste. I had to make sure Magnus was okay, and I had to shut down the rectangular power cells.

"I have an idea." I told her my plan and crossed my fingers that this would work. We were running out of time.

———————

My back pressed against the wall again, my cloaking device on. Two of the pirates entered the room, and they listened as Rivo admitted she knew where the family fortune was stored. They needed to bring her to the cargo bay, and she would finally show them.

The robots turned to one another and silently discussed it, with no words needed. I imagined a series of ones and zeros flying from one data processor to the other. They didn't reply to her; instead, they moved to the side as the door slid open and the pirate with a face rolled in.

It moved to the bars, stopping just before them. "Finally," its word translated into my earpiece. It was speaking her language. "Come," it said, sticking its finger into a hole on the bars. A loud click, and her cell was open. My heart beat faster as they clanked to the side with a tug from the creepy pirate. She came just past the robot's waist, and it reached for her, pulling her arm and dragging her before it.

I nearly shot the repulsive thing there and then, but with Rivo so close, I couldn't risk it. I didn't know what effect my pulse rifle would have on their thick armored bodies, though I intended to find out. Initially, I'd only wanted to get power back to our ship and leave, but now I was going to obliterate these freaks, making sure no one else was hurt by them.

Rivo led the way, and the three pirates followed her out of the room. I kept my distance, making sure to stay at least ten yards behind them at all times. Even though they couldn't see me, I wasn't silent, and any mishap could give away my position.

We headed back to the cargo bay, sidestepping junk piles on the way to her ship. She'd claimed she just needed to get near it, and from there, she could escape. I wasn't sure how, especially with the pirates right on her, but she seemed adamant about this. All she needed, she'd said, was a distraction. That was why she hadn't attempted it before. She'd also thought her father would track her down eventually.

I looked toward the bridge leading to the ship where Leslie and Magnus were. What was happening over there? Were they okay?

I'd find out soon enough. I waited at a distance, hiding behind a stack of glass containers, each filled with electrical components. I noticed a strange triangle symbol on many of the supplies around the ship.

"Hurry," the pirate voice translated.

"Step back. I need space to show you," Rivo said, and two of the robots did as she wished. The one with the flesh face didn't obey. Instead, its monstrous face twitched in several directions, as if it was programmed to convey emotions like a dead puppeteer.

"Hurry," it repeated.

Rivo looked around the room, as if trying to spot me, and crouched to her small ship. A door hissed open on the side, and she stepped inside. The robot held the door open so she couldn't close it. It was time.

I pushed the wall of jars. Over a hundred of them went crashing down in a symphony of shattering glass. The pirates turned their attention to the noise, even Face, and Rivo had her moment. The door closed, and its small engines fired up. Before I knew what to expect, rear thrusters burned hot, scalding the nearest pirate, leaving him a scorched pile of melted metal. Her ship launched toward the opening between our two ships before racing through the energy of the containment field. With that, she was off.

I was already moving for my ship, hoping Rivo was going to keep her half of the bargain. She claimed her ship had enough firepower to destroy the amplifiers trudging along in space with this patchwork vessel. If she blew them up, we could escape.

The remaining two pirates were angry. Face bashed some junk away from him, sending a large unit heater toward the wall with a swipe of his hand. I didn't want to be on the other end of that fist.

I leapt away from them, my cover blown. I had to get back on my ship.

The bridge was thin, almost like a ladder dropped between our two ramps, giving access. I ran over it, the whirring of Face's wheels giving chase. Once I was across, I tried to push the bridge over the edge, only I couldn't. They'd attached it somehow. Spot-welded, maybe.

I swung my pulse rifle toward the oncoming robot and fired. The beam hit it square in the chest, and it slowed, a black hole showing wires beneath the armor suit. It kept coming.

I pulled the trigger again, hitting the other pirate in the head. It lifted an arm and shot an energy pulse from its hand. I ducked, and it narrowly missed striking me in the upper body. More pirates emerged into the cargo room, each of them shooting energy beams. There was no time. I had to prevent them from coming onto our ship.

Wondering why I hadn't thought of it in the first place, I shot the bridge between our vessels. It melted in the middle, collapsing with two robots in the center. They fell and passed through the containment field into the ice-cold confines of space. There was no screaming or panic from them, just digital acceptance of their situation.

The others continued to fire at me while I ran inside, hitting the manual controls for our ramp. Though they couldn't see me, more energy blasts shot at me, and I wasn't quick enough to avoid them all. I went down when one of the red rays hit me in the legs. Pain erupted in them, and as the ramp lifted, separating me from the attackers, I pulled myself forward, further into my ship, my legs hanging limp behind me.

I rolled onto my back, holding my rifle up, ready to fire at the three pirates I knew were onboard. No one else was in the room. Relief flooded me.

If all went to plan, my crew were in the belly of the vessel, showing our "guests" a surprise or two. My feet began to tingle, and I could move my toes after a minute or two of lying on the metal floor. Our ship rumbled slightly. Either Rivo had done as promised and had blown up the power grabbers out there or the pirates were still trying to get into our ship.

Before I could check our engineering room, I had to go check on my friends. Another minute passed, and I was able to get to my knees. One more and I was on my feet, the feeling coming back to my legs. I stumbled to the corridor that would lead to the stairs.

My hands bounced off the walls, helping to keep me upright, and I fell more than ran down the hall, panting by the time I found the doorway. It was closed, and I used the manual lever before pushing hard to slide it open.

Shouting exploded below, and I found my footing as I rushed down the thirty industrial stairs to the storage area below. Smoke stung my eyes as the lights came back on, telling me our power was back. I silently cheered Rivo but knew it was all for naught if Leslie or Magnus was hurt.

I saw my reflection in the smooth metal wall, and I

realized the shot to my legs must have fried my cloaking device.

"Magnus!" I shouted, already exposed.

A pulse beam shot across the room from the left to the right, and I ran for the left side, knowing that was one of our rifles firing. Red light beams shot from a pirate's finger across the room, and it mechanically kept shooting in even intervals.

"Dean." Magnus was bleeding from a cut on his forehead, blood covered his face, and he had to wipe it away from his eyes. Leslie was on the floor beside him, clearly unconscious, or worse. "You got the power back?"

I nodded to his question, not breaking my gaze from her limp form. I lifted my rifle over the edge of the containers and fired a pot shot at the pirate across the room. "What happened?"

"We did as we planned. I lured them down here with the glorious promise of treasure. They stupidly obliged our trap, and Leslie popped up from her hiding spot behind them, only we hadn't expected them to be so quick. We ended the first one, and the standoff began." We took turns firing over our heads as I filled him in.

"Is she...?" I didn't finish the question.

He shook his head, blood spilling from his wound. "No. I dragged her here, then blasted another one of the bastards. Then it was one on one."

"So there's just one left?"

Magnus smiled at me, his bloody face making a mask of horror. "Are you thinking what I'm thinking?"

"Divide and conquer?" I asked and got a curt nod in return. He got up, crouching below the top of the containers. I did the same, only I went the opposite direction. "I'll be the goat," I whispered, and it looked like he was about to argue, then decided not to.

In seconds, I was at the end of the stacked containers, with Magnus at the far end. I fired a shot across the room and stepped out with my gun in the air. "I know where the treasure is. I killed him," I shouted. The pirate turned its faceless head toward me, as if considering what I'd said, before it lifted a finger and started to fire at me. I rolled back around the crates as Magnus snuck behind it and laid down a barrage of blasts.

The room went quiet, save the noise of crackling wires, an acrid smell lingering in the air as the last remaining pirate fell to the ground with a heavy thud. Magnus fired at its head one last time for good measure and did the same to the other two fallen robots.

He shuddered and helped me to my feet.

"Let's get Leslie and get the hell out of here," I said, ready for this nightmare to be over.

SEVEN

Our ship pulled free from their tractor beam with a blast of our hyperdrive, and we spun around, firing at will on the robot pirate vessel. I watched the ship explode into hundreds of pieces with joy as our missiles and rail guns pummeled it.

"We did the universe a favor today," Magnus said, holding a rag to his forehead.

Leslie had come to, angry she'd missed the action. Her eyes had widened at the mention of Rivo. "You know who she is, right?"

"A short blue alien who saved our butts?" It was the truth.

"Her father, Garo Alnod, is one of the most wealthy and influential people in the galaxy. Rivo is something of royalty, if not by title, then by opulence. They live on Bazarn Five. Hell, her father practically funded the place at the start." Leslie tapped coordinates in on the console and paused to take a drink of water. "Damn, my head hurts."

"How do you know all this?" I asked incredulously. What were the chances I'd saved someone from Bazarn, someone whose father ran the place?

"Haven is a respite for outcasts, and many don't have a lot of means. What they do have to share is rumors and gossip," Leslie said.

I looked for Rivo's small ship on our sensors, but it was nowhere to be seen. I wondered if our paths would ever cross again.

---

*T*he space near Volim was a hive of activity. Cities were erected on the three moons over the planet, and a large space station orbited the yellow world. We'd been stopped halfway across the system and were escorted by five wasp-shaped vessels.

Leslie had done the talking, explaining who she was, and that we needed to see the church on important details involving the Ancients. We'd experienced silence for a few minutes before they replied, telling us we'd be allowed to land on their world.

"I know they're zealots of sorts, but what religion in particular do they follow?" I asked Leslie.

"They believe in the universe, first and foremost. They consider the Theos to be a race of beings, not gods, but through them, divinity was passed on, or something like that. The Padlog on Haven didn't talk about it much. I assume like any culture, some are more devoted to old ways than others." Her answer made sense.

"Do you think Sergo will have the information we need?" Magnus asked.

"If he doesn't, he'll know where to find it. He's somewhat of a spy on their world. I know he exchanged gossip for technology from Kareem on occasion." Leslie slowed our ship, and we watched as more wasp-shaped ships flew in the space before us, each moving like they had somewhere to be in a hurry.

A buzzing sound echoed through our communication system. I'd initially thought of them as the insectoids, not realizing they had different races on their world, each uniquely insect-like, with their own language. This one sounded like a hovering bee.

"Follow us," the translator repeated.

We passed the closest moon, where our zoomed-in viewscreen showed an intricate system of housing, much like a beehive. Soon we were entering Volim, and I spotted small oceans in the primarily yellow-toned landscape. As we lowered toward a sprawling city, I noticed four towers rising high into the sky, stretching through the low hanging clouds. Around the metropolis, mustard-colored hills rolled, leading toward a body of water. It was unlike any world I'd ever seen.

Four of our escorts veered off, letting a single ship lead the way toward the center of the city. We landed directly in the center of the four towers, and it wasn't until our ramp lowered, and we stepped onto the ground that I realized it wasn't the ground at all. The whole place was lifted off the surface, and we were above part of the urban sprawl.

I was the first off the ship and was greeted by armed guards. Each breath was short, and I felt like I was nearing the top of a mountain. The guards looked much like the Padlog who'd tried to stop Mary back on the crystal world: the same uniforms, the same antennas protruding from their heads; their eyes were large and black. For a second, I thought they'd know what we'd done, and we'd be mowed down by their weapons, but they just gestured us forward. One of them walked toward us and passed us each a small breathing tube.

He pointed to our noses, and I understood. Leslie helped me place it on my face, and I noticed the air become more breathable. The line tied around our heads, with two small holes allowing oxygen into our noses.

"Thank you," I said, and it translated to the buzzing sound.

"Wrong dialect," Leslie said, adjusting the settings on the translators for us. I was suddenly glad she'd insisted on coming along.

"Thank you," I repeated, the sound coming through now as more of a cricket's chirp.

"Come," he said, turning and walking away.

The sky was cloudy, muting the hills beyond the horizon, but I was in awe of the sights. The sparkling skyscrapers were taller than any buildings I'd ever seen. I hadn't expected this from the Padlog, and I knew I shouldn't have assumed that just because they looked like insects mixed with humans, they would live underground or in hives.

"Where are we going?" Magnus asked him.

"To see the Supreme." He didn't elaborate, and we didn't ask him to. With a name like that, he'd be the end of the road.

Leslie stepped close to me, waiting to make sure our host wasn't looking. She whispered in my ear, "I'm going to feign illness later and sneak out to find Sergo."

"What about the Supreme?" I asked quickly and quietly.

Leslie shook her head. "He won't give you what you want." Then she fell back, walking a yard behind me once again.

Magnus looked over with a grim face. His head still had gauze taped to it, and his eye was a little swollen. He claimed the cut was mostly superficial. A cut on the forehead wasn't often deadly, but it made for a bloody mess.

Other locals milled about, some sitting inside white gazebos. Heated discussions carried to us, and the guard told us not to worry. Theologians rarely fought, but they always spoke with passion.

A being with a long abdomen walked on four thin legs, bending at the thorax. It looked a lot like an ant, but its arms were thicker than the legs; powerful mandibles clicked as it spoke to a friend nearby. Already I'd seen at least three types of the Padlog and was happy to see their world was a blended pot of cultures. Smoke poured from a chimney on a squat building as we passed, and I saw something that looked like a two-foot-long fly rotating over a flame. Five or six Padlog lined up, waiting to place their order with the food vendor.

Perhaps the Raanna, the spider beings from our trek to find the Theos, were originally from Volim. The Iskios, I corrected myself. We hadn't really been searching for the Theos.

Magnus raised his eyebrows at the fly on a spit, and stuck out his tongue as we kept moving, heading toward the tower closest to the hills. I wondered what was beneath us. Was it housing, transportation tunnels, or something as basic as a sewer system?

We arrived at the base of the tower, and I looked up, the sheer height of the skyscraper giving me a wave of vertigo. This couldn't be called a skyscraper; it was more like a skypiercer.

"This way," the guard said, leading us through a wide-open entrance. No doors sealed the tower from visitors.

Inside, we were met with a pristine lobby. Alien script was embedded in gold lettering on the walls. Robed insectoids clicked, buzzed, and chirped amongst one another. A fountain of water gushed in the center of the white marble-like floors, its soft flow a comforting white noise in contrast to the multi-language speech around us.

A wide set of stairs rose from deep in the lobby, and our guard motioned for us to ascend them.

Magnus set a hand on my back. "I hope they don't expect us to climb to the top," he joked.

"If they do, you'll be carrying me by floor one

hundred."

We climbed the stairs, which were mostly bare of the Padlog, who seemed happy to be conversing on the main floor, sprawling out beside the fountain and beyond.

The stairs went on only a short way before we had to turn and walk up another flight in the opposite direction. By the time we'd climbed three stories, our guard had slowed. A row of Padlog similar to our host stood by large yellow doors. More gold script crossed the walls on this floor, and I thought about trying to translate it.

But I didn't have time as the doors opened simultaneously, and a small cricket-shaped man hopped out.

"Come. We have much to discuss." His voice was deeper than I would have expected, and the translation came through clearly.

The room wasn't large, the ceiling short. Inside, lights shone down on the floor, and I couldn't help but think they were there to simulate sunlight. Their glow was warm and rejuvenating.

The cricket-man was under three feet tall, and he hopped over to a table, where he sat down, motioning for us to do the same. He had a pallid green skin tone, small black eyes, and his words came out in smooth sequences. I wasn't sure, but I had to assume he was elderly. Compared to the guards, he seemed to be slower and more fragile. Dozens of tall plants sat in the room. The Supreme directly beside one with thick green leaves. For such an extreme title, I'd expected someone more imposing.

"The Ancients." He slouched slightly, and I shifted in my seat, which was directly across the table from him.

"Yes," was all I said.

"What do you know of them?" he asked. He tapped the table and whispered something to the guard who'd brought us in. The man nodded, bowed, and removed himself from the room. We were left alone around the table with the small Padlog.

I looked to Leslie, who nodded. She was supposed to warn me away from saying too much. This meant she thought it harmless to be honest. Maybe she thought we could get the information from them and save ourselves the time of tracking down Sergo. We had agreed not to mention our involvement in the Iskios being released or the part about us gunning down two of the Padlog. Somehow, I didn't think that would sit too well.

"I know there were two races in the beginning. The Theos and the Iskios." I waited for him to say something, and when he didn't, I continued. "The Iskios were a sick race, and eventually the Theos had enough of their cruelty and manic behaviour, so they executed them, hunting them down to the edges of the universe before burying their corpses on a barren world."

The cricket-man leaned forward, and his small hand cinched his priest's robe up tight as I spoke. "How do you know this?"

"I'm a Gatekeeper," I said, as if this was explanation enough. It seemed to relax him. I wondered if he would set the guards on us if I'd said anything else.

"Gatekeeper indeed. What race are you?" he asked, squinting his small black eyes at us.

"Human," Magnus answered.

"Never heard of it. Some days I think the universe is too large. Today is one of those days." He leaned back, and the guard who'd left came back with a tray carrying a bottle of a thick golden liquid and four cups.

"I'll second that," Leslie agreed.

The guard poured four equal measures of the thick liquid, and once again departed without a word. "Not very talkative, is he?" I asked.

Our host disregarded my comment. "How rude of me. We haven't even had introductions. I am the Supreme. You are?" He passed each of us a cup and waited for our replies.

Magnus took charge of answering the Supreme. "I'm Magnus, this is Leslie, and across from you is Dean."

I swore his eyes widened a touch at my name, but if he recognized it, he hid it well after that first instant. "To new friends." He lifted his cup, and we each grabbed one. It was made from an unfamiliar material, and I sniffed the drink before tasting it.

"Here goes nothing," I whispered to no one in particular, and tried it. My mouth exploded with flavor as the sweet syrup hit my taste buds.

"Our finest nectar," the Supreme said.

"I can tell why," Magnus said, wiping his mouth with his hand. "Damn me if that wasn't the best thing I've ever tasted."

"Enough," I said. Even the liquid gold wasn't enough to distract me from the purpose of traveling all the way to Volim. I needed to locate Mary. "I need to find the Theos."

His eyes went wide. This time, there was no hiding his surprise. "They are dead."

I didn't want to discuss the Iskios with him; it would open too many questions I wouldn't answer. "Then how do I bring them back?"

"We believe they were powerful beings. Not quite gods, as others' faith allows them to think; like anything else, we all die eventually." The Supreme took another sip from his cup, his small mandibles spread apart while he drank the nectar.

"Tell me where they died."

"And why do you need them so badly?" he asked, his curiosity piqued.

"The portals are failing," I lied. "The Gatekeepers

don't all know about it yet, but they're acting erratically. Sometimes they send you to the wrong location, others they don't activate at all. Sarlun has a temporary ban on using them while we look for the Theos to solve it."

The lie was a solid one. The Supreme didn't have a connection to the Gatekeepers, and if he bought my improved fib, I'd be one step closer to finding them.

"I don't want to raise them from the dead or anything like that. I just need to find their world. There has to be records there on the portals. If they created them, they'd know how to repair them." I bit my tongue as I waited for the Supreme to consider this.

"Come back tomorrow." He pressed a button under the table, and the guard raced in, firearm drawn. "Denni, put that away. I just want you to escort our friends here to some quarters for the night. Come back in one cycle of Volim. I will have an answer for you."

This was a better outcome than I'd expected.

Denni led us out of the room, but not before Magnus drank the last few drops of the nectar from his near-empty cup.

"I think it might be a little fermented or something. It has the kick of a strong port," Magnus said, hitting me lightly with his elbow. "What say we find another one of those somewhere?"

Leslie hung back from the guard, and I slowed to match pace with her. "Once we get settled in, you two ask Denni to show you to some food. I'll pretend I'm not feeling well."

I nodded. "Sergo?" I said the name quietly, but she still frowned and waved her hand for me to stop talking.

In a few minutes, we were one hundred and ten floors up, and walking into our guest suites. I hadn't known what to expect from them, but it seemed the Padlog enjoyed their luxury. Each unit was larger than my house's square footage, and all three of the rooms had panoramic views of the ocean beyond the yellow hill. The sun was beginning to set, and it majestically glared off the water.

"Everything satisfactory?" Denni asked.

"More than," Magnus said. He'd checked out his room and now found himself sitting with his feet up, looking out my window. "You guys know how to do it up."

"These are for interplanetary guests. Only those invited by the Supreme stay here." The guard turned as if to leave.

I thought back to what Leslie had said. "Is there anywhere to get some food? You know, something not made from bugs?"

"Yes, the terrace on the rooftop," Denni said, pointing up.

"How many stories is this building?" Magnus' voice was muffled while his head was stuck peeking into a closet.

"Two hundred," Denni said.

"Wow. We need to up our game back home," Magnus said, winking at me.

"Come, I'll show you to the dining terrace. Our cooks know how to prepare anything…" Denni paused. "Well, maybe not human food, but I'm sure a Ballemiol from 5R333L will satisfy one of your…stature." He looked at Magnus when he said the last bit, and I laughed, following them out of the suite.

After a gentle knock on Leslie's door, she opened it, and I could tell she'd applied a dewy moisturizer and turned her cheeks red in an effort to pull off the "sick card."

"You guys go ahead. I'm not feeling so hot. Maybe bring me back something bready." With that, she slowly shut the door, and I shrugged.

"Guess it's just us, Magnus."

EIGHT

*T*he sun was set now, and the ocean water glowed with bioluminescent life. If I thought the world was a sight during the day, nothing prepared me for its beauty at night. Insects chirped incessantly, giving a droning white noise that was surprisingly calming.

I wanted nothing more than to get the details we needed and leave, but if we were stuck there for a night, at least we were in the comfort of luxury, not camping on a beach being attacked by some unknown predators. Here the predators had guns, and they would likely stab you in the back rather than shoot you in the chest.

The Padlog gave off an air of concern, of culture and thoughtfulness, but I knew the only thing they cared about was preserving their way of life. What happened to me or Magnus didn't matter to them, unless we could provide them with something. We needed to show them value, and telling the Supreme we were Gatekeepers with a problem had planted that seed. Undoubtedly, the Supreme was sitting up right now, considering how high he could rise if he were the one to help fix the portals. Maybe he considered the task large enough to wake the sleeping Theos.

We wouldn't know until tomorrow, but at least Leslie was out making contact with Sergo now. He would find a way to get the location to the crystal world. He had to. I wasn't sure where I'd start if he failed, but I was going to stop at nothing to find Mary.

"That was something else," Magnus said, pushing his plate away. We sat on the rooftop terrace, and as the clouds dissipated, our view improved.

A Padlog resembling a beetle walked over, his body every bit a shield of armor, only he was a waiter, not a soldier. No matter how many times I told myself we were safe here, my gut was telling me otherwise.

"Anything else for you?" his clicks translated into English. We'd taken Denni's advice, and he'd been right about the Ballemiol being delectable.

"I'll have one more of these, and one for my friend." Magnus gestured for another of the golden nectar beverages he was quickly becoming enamored with, maybe even a little tipsy from. The server nodded and left us to ourselves.

I poked at a purple legume left on my plate. "I know it's quite the place, but I only want to get what we came here for and leave."

"We'll find her, Dean." Magnus gave me a tight-lipped smile. His cheeks were flushed, and there was a slight slur to his words.

I didn't know that for sure but didn't want to say it out loud. "I know."

"This is the first time I've been away since dealing with the Bhlat."

"Seriously?" I thought about that and realized I'd traveled to countless worlds and had too many adventures to count on my fingers since then. "That's what I've always wanted. To be home and make a family."

"It's great. But there's something about taking off to an alien world to make you remember what life used to be like. Being a mercenary and taking down bad guys, rescuing hostages, and just kicking some ass every now and then was my life. It all changed a little once Natalia was in my life." He looked out over the horizon pensively.

"What changed?" I asked, thanking the server when he brought new cups of nectar and cleared our plates away.

"Everything. I fell in love with her pretty quickly, you know. She was hurt. Not just physically, but mentally and emotionally. Her parents were poor, terrible people. Rumor has it, her father traded her as payment for a gambling debt."

I winced. I hadn't heard this part of the story before. "That's terrible, Mag."

He nodded, still looking out over the edge of the terrace. "When we found her, her eyes were so dead. I can hardly remember them now when I look my wife in the eyes, but sometimes, like this moment, I can picture the distant stares she gave, like nothing mattered to her anymore. I wanted to fix her but knew I couldn't. Only time could restore her wounds, and even then, I know many of them have never healed properly. A deep cut often leaves a scar, even with the best stitches."

"She's such a strong and wonderful person."

"She is. So is Mary. It's funny. All those years, and Nat wouldn't talk. All it took was to be tossed into an intergalactic crisis with you and Mary by our side, and she found her voice again."

I remembered that moment vividly.

Magnus took another drink from his cup and held it in a large hand. "You know what's crazy?"

I waved my hand toward the dark sky and illuminated ocean beneath it. "I can think of a lot of crazy things."

"I wouldn't trade any of it. I know it's selfish, and we lost a lot of people along the way, but I wouldn't have it any other way. The Event, the Bhlat, New Spero, you giving away our planet. These were all just things that needed to happen for my life to end up where it is." He turned to me, making eye contact. "I owe a lot of that to you. The good parts anyway."

I laughed lightly, knowing I was responsible for a lot of the bad parts too. "I hear you." But did I? If I could go back to before the day Mary and I had just relived in the Iskios' test, would I? If the Bhlat hadn't forced the Kraski to run, if the Deltra hadn't planted a device on Earth... there were a lot of "ifs," and one thing I knew was that there was always a larger predator. Just when I thought we'd seen all we could see, we were up against one of the Ancients, the Iskios. And they'd been resurrected through my wife.

If none of it had happened, I'd likely still be alone, watching the Yankees on Sunday matinees and combing through my clients' bookkeeping needs, wishing there was more out there for me. But Mary would be safe.

"You don't owe me anything. I'm happy for you. I need to find Mary and stop these bastards so you can keep enjoying your family and life on New Spero. And every now and then, I'll make sure you go on an adventure or two. Maybe something like rock climbing on the moons of Evello or hiking the ocean pathway on Ceenlok Four."

"That sounds perfect." He clinked my cup, and we each took another drink. The sweet nectar was thrumming through my body now. My arm console buzzed, a coded message appearing on the screen.

"It's her. Leslie sent coordinates. She's found Sergo."

———

Getting to the ground level had proven easier than I'd expected. What I hadn't counted on was how difficult it was finding a way below the faux surface the Padlog had created.

The streets were eerily empty at this late hour, and the two of us looked sorely out of place. I kept looking behind me to see if we were being followed. I doubted we could leave the tower without the Supreme knowing about it, but we didn't have a choice.

"What do you think? I don't see access anywhere," I told Magnus. Leslie's communication had gone silent after the first message, and I was worried about her safety. We'd left our rifles back in the rooms, but we each had the compact pistols tucked into our belts. There was no way we weren't going to be ready for a surprise.

Our dark jumpsuits made us hard to see in the softly-lit square between the four towers, and Magnus ducked away to the corner with the least light. "Over here," he whispered.

A Padlog leaned against the back of a food stand, its posture telling me it wasn't in the least concerned with us sneaking around. Its chirps and clicks translated to our earpieces as its antennae twitched. "What can I help you find?" The voice was lighter, different, and that was when I noticed this Padlog was thinner, curvier. It was a female.

I looked at Magnus, lifting an eyebrow in a "can we trust her" kind of message. He did the talking. "We need to get below. I hear the best nectar is down there."

"The best everything is down there. What kind of things are you two visitors into? You can do anything below…for a price." She was still leaning casually.

"You don't want to know what this one's into." Magnus jabbed a thumb back at me. Before I could say anything in defense, the Padlog spoke.

"Come with me. I'll show you the way."

"Is this a good idea?" I shut our translator down so our new friend couldn't understand me.

"What choice do we have? We need to make sure Leslie's all right, and without Sergo, we have nothing." Magnus was already following her.

"My name's Till, purveyor of dreams," she said.

"Sure. I'm Parker, and this is Tobias," I said, making something up on the spot.

"Now that we have that out of the way, we need to talk about payment." Till stopped and I bumped into her.

"Payment? For what?" I asked.

"For showing you into the Vespiary."

I paused at that. Wasn't that the name for a wasps' nest? I wasn't sure I wanted to go in there. But I had to. "We don't have anything of value."

She eyed us, trying to take inventory. "What about the weapons you're concealing?"

I coughed, but before I could say anything, she held a slim gun in her hand. Magnus wasn't far behind, and he pushed me behind him, standing his ground a couple yards away from her. "Look, Till. We have to go down there, meet a fella named Sergo, and get the hell out of here. You're going to show us the way and get on with your night."

Her gun lowered slightly. "Sergo? Why didn't you say so?" she asked, her voice lighter. The gun vanished as quickly as it had appeared, and she patted Magnus on the shoulder while walking by him. "We go way back. If you have business with him, I don't want to keep you."

I swore there was a tremor in her voice, and though she was trying to play it cool, she was scared of Sergo. This much was clear.

I looked at Magnus and shrugged. He frowned at me in return and tucked his gun away.

She led us to the far edge of the square, where shorter buildings lined the entire way between the huge towers in the four corners. At night, they were lit up in random windows, but it was hard to see just how tall they were.

We approached one of the buildings, where a business name was hardly visible in the night. She knocked on a metal door devoid of windows, and a stifled voice called from behind it. The Padlog with us said something nonsensical to our translator – a secret password, I guessed – and the door opened to reveal the largest beetle I'd ever seen. He wore a bright silver vest, because I doubted any shirt would be able to contain the tree-trunk arms he sported.

The bouncer glared at us with suspicious beady eyes, but Till slipped him something we couldn't see, and he moved out of the way. The room was wide open, dim yellow lights lining the walls, and I spotted a wooden staircase on the other end of the chamber.

The beetle didn't say anything; he just watched us walk by and toward the stairs. The room was sparsely furnished with just a few worn old chairs, but I noticed the holes in the walls and the mounted surveillance in the corners of the room. This entry was obviously being watched, probably by the Supreme or someone in power. They were a religious race, and like every culture, there would be seedy things going on under the surface. In this case, it was literal and metaphorical. I didn't glance back as we started down the steps. The world above had a sweet scent to it, almost like a field of flowers from a distance, but it was already musty indoors.

The dim yellow wall sconces continued to light our path along the steps, and we walked down them with caution, Till confidently leading us below. After a few minutes of winding stairs, we found ourselves at the end of the line. A cage with a lift behind it blocked our path.

"Going down," Till said, and a cricket-like Padlog

emerged from the shadows and slid the cage open, waving us inside.

"What floor?" his chirps translated.

He looked at me, then Magnus, and we shook our heads, before I remembered the coordinates Leslie had sent me. I read the location digits to the small insectoid and he made a noise akin to a grunt before slamming the gate shut with a clank.

"Good thing you have those guns," Till said.

"Why?" Magnus asked.

"That's Larzi's spot, where nothing remotely good goes on. It's even unusual for your friend to be there," she said, meaning Sergo. She wouldn't want to let the lift operator know who we were there to see. Word would spread down here, where gossip acted like currency.

The cage stopped, and unfamiliar smells and noises carried to us. My heart rate sped up as I heard something that sounded like gunfire in the distance.

"Don't worry. Just the games. We'll be fine; just don't look anyone in the eyes. And that will be hard, since some of them have hundreds each." When we didn't reply to her, she continued, "That's a joke. You aliens are always so dry."

The cage opened to reveal something completely expected yet unexpected at the same time. We were in a lobby of sorts, pillars added in the underground area for support. Lights flashed and Padlog of every shape, size, and color milled about. We stepped off the lift, and I tripped on something. Magnus was there to keep me from landing on my face, and I peered back to see a limp Padlog stretched out on the floor. Various tiny black legs were kicking in all directions, which wouldn't have been as disturbing if there were only two of them.

"He's not what you think. Just had a little too much of

the Ponla. See, look at his proboscis." Till kicked a foot toward the sprawled-out alien.

He had a golden powder on his face and hands. It had to be some variation of a pollen, which apparently would knock you on your butt if you took too much of it. I shuddered and moved past him, now seeing signs of the drug on many of the Padlog down here.

"Is it always like this?" I asked.

"It is on this level," Till replied.

"Why don't they do something about it?" Magnus asked this time.

"Who?" Till led us away from the lobby, toward a hallway. Storefronts were cut into the sides of the space; one was selling clothing, and an almost naked female wasp-like Padlog grabbed my arm and buzzed up beside me.

"Sorry, not interested," I said and broke free of her firm grip.

"Suit yourself, weirdo," her words translated into my earpiece. I wanted to get to Sergo and get out of here as quickly as possible.

"What were we talking about? Oh, the Supreme and his sect. Shouldn't they want to help?" I asked.

She spat on the ground, a universal gesture. "The only thing those blowhards want is prosperity for themselves. They've built their society on top of our backs and don't care what happens to us anymore. Sure, they have programs to help the needy, but it's all a show." I could hear the venom in her voice, though the translation didn't convey it.

We kept moving. The floor was stone, and bits of food, pollen, and God knew what else littered it. I had to step over a few more unconscious Padlog. No one down there seemed too concerned about them, so I tried not to be either.

Music was strumming up ahead, and various locals were loitering in the halls in front of the tavern, drinks in hand. As we approached, two of them were yelling obscenities at one another, and before we knew it, their cups were thrown down and they were in a full-on melee. The female beetle grabbed a stool from the side of the hall and smashed it at the wasp-man. The wasp's arm came up to block it, but the stool hit with a sickening crunch, and the seat broke in half, the wasp buzzing in pain.

Till stood between the fight and us, keeping her arms up, warning us not to get involved. The wasp turned and jabbed a thick black stake from its lower back at the beetle, piercing her leg, fluid oozing out. She clicked in agony, but the fight continued. They moved farther down the hall, and Till grabbed Magnus' hand and led him inside the emptying-out tavern.

The smell of sweat, rotten flowers, and sticky-sweet syrup hit me like a brick wall as we entered the bar. If I was going to picture a rundown underground sketchy bar on an alien insectoid world, it would look exactly like this. On the left, a bouncer slept on a chair, golden powder on his fingertips.

Beyond were a dozen booths, with enough space to seat six comfortably. On the right, a few Padlog were shooting targets at the end of an aisle. Images appeared on a screen, and they took turns firing their weapons, cheering as they hit peculiar-looking creatures and mocking each other's misses.

"Do you see Leslie anywhere?" Magnus asked me. I looked at all of the tables from our vantage point but couldn't see our friend among the Padlog. A few other beings were spread among the locals, and I didn't recognize any of their races. One walked by us, its skin translucent, organs beating and moving inside its hairless body.

"Nope." I swallowed and kept looking.

Something pushed into my back, and a voice whispered in my ear in broken English. "Want to see your friend alive?"

Magnus noticed the gun jammed against me, and as he was about to pull his out, Till stuffed her thin gun against his side and shook her head.

"Damn it." We'd been set up. What did they want? "Where is she?" I growled, feeling the insectoid's hot breath against my cheek.

"Come," it said and pushed me toward the dank back corner of the bar where the only light was a small red bulb hanging from a socket on the end of a rope. A Padlog sat behind a booth, his hands laid out flat on the tabletop. A large mug of nectar was parked before him, mostly untouched.

"The one and only Dean Parker," he said.

NINE

*T*he insectoid leaned back, not breaking eye contact with me. He looked familiar, and I put it together. He'd been there the night we'd first arrived at Haven all that time ago. He was there when Mae escaped in Leslie and Terrance's ship, before we gave chase with Kareem's blessing.

"Sergo," I said. "Where is she?"

He motioned for us to sit down. We obliged, not that we had a choice with two guns pointed at us.

"You are a resourceful man, aren't you? I knew it the moment I saw you all those years ago. Kareem spoke highly of you," Sergo said. His eyes were wide and black, his mouth a slim line on an oval-shaped head, highlighted by two antennae moving of their own volition, as if seeking answers to a problem.

"Kareem was a good man."

"That's right. He was." Sergo leaned forward and took his mug, taking a small sip before setting it back down. "How rude of me. Can I get you anything?"

"We're fine," I said.

"I wouldn't mind one of those," Magnus cut in, and Sergo chuckled, the sound eerily human in nature. He'd spent enough time with the hybrids to pick up a few things, as well as our language. Sergo waved the goon with a gun away from behind me. Till remained beside us, standing casually with her gun in her hand.

"You have more on your mind than just finding Leslie,

don't you?" he asked.

"You know why we're here. We need to know everything about the Supreme's latest mission." I shifted in my seat, nervous he wouldn't have any information for us. If this whole trip proved to be a waste of time, I'd lost far too many days.

"Yes, Leslie mentioned that," Sergo said.

"Where is she?" Magnus asked, his voice threatening.

"Don't worry about her. We go way back, now don't we? I have her safely tucked away in case things go wrong. Not that they will, right? Dean, your reputation precedes you. Where you go, bodies follow. Dead bodies. Just like the recent deaths of some of the Supreme's top people. They were on a secret mission and never came back. You wouldn't know anything about that, would you?" He spoke in English, and I looked around, making sure there were no prying eyes or ears. If someone overheard the fact we'd killed two of the Supreme's troops, we might not leave Volim alive.

"Keep it down, would you? Yes, we know something about that, but they came in guns blazing. We had no choice. If they'd explained why we should stop instead of tracking us, we could have prevented..." I almost said, "Mary being taken," but caught myself. "...the Iskios from escaping." I whispered the last part.

"The Unwinding. I always thought that was a crazy religious fable. I guess they do know the inner workings of the universe up there in their towers. I, for one, have to thank you guys." Sergo took another sip.

The guard approached from behind, and I jumped in my seat as he flung two mugs down at the table. The nectar spilled out, wetting the dark wooden tabletop.

"Thank us? For what?" This bug-eyed gangster was getting on my nerves.

"There's great opportunity for a man like me in times of crisis. And the Unwinding is just that: the ultimate crisis."

"Just tell me what you know, Sergo, and we'll leave you to your opportunity."

"Why so hostile, Dean?"

I started to stand up, but Magnus set a hand on my forearm. "Because I need to know where that crystal world is so I can get there and find my wife," I hissed.

Sergo leaned back once again. "You were there, weren't you? When Kareem died?"

I settled back down. "I was."

"What did he say?" Sergo asked.

I hesitated to tell him but thought he might be easier to work with if I gave him a connection to his old friend. "He told me to change the universe."

Sergo laughed again; this time, it wasn't off-putting. "For a Deltra in hiding, he sure was an idealist. I miss him, you know."

"It looks like we have something in common," I said.

Sergo smiled a thin grin and nodded. "It does. So you want to know the coordinates to this so-called crystal world you unleashed the Iskios from?"

"We didn't know. We thought they were the Theos. They fooled us," I said. This guy knew how to push my buttons. I expected it was part of his game. Make the other side uncomfortable and keep them off balance while trying to get facts. It was working, and I wanted nothing more than to expedite our transaction.

"Regardless, this is what you're after?" He knew it was, and I could see it in his smug black eyes. His left antenna twitched and gave him away.

"Yes."

"And what do you have to offer in exchange for this

information?" he asked.

Magnus looked over at me. Why hadn't Leslie anticipated this? Did we think a rogue smuggler like Sergo, who'd had to spend a few years on Haven while his crimes cooled down around him, would freely give us this information?

"We…don't have anything of value at the moment." I glanced behind me, seeing Till standing there, pretending to not pay attention to our conversation.

"I think you do have something I can use. Kareem sent you after a device. He was quite the inventor. Those Delta loved to make things. Some quite dangerous, some more for convenience."

I didn't like where he was going with this.

"This particular device would have a lot of value on the open market." Sergo set his hands on the table. "It's rumored a whole Bhlat outpost was taken down with it in an instant."

My gut churned. We needed to find Mary and stop the Unwinding, which we still didn't know much about. I didn't have the portable Kalentrek with me, but would I be willing to trade it even if I did have it? I couldn't have it fall into the wrong hands. With it, they could kill countless beings without so much as a bang. I knew. I'd killed the Kraski with the original Shield, and, as Sergo had stated, the Bhlat outpost where Mae had been shot.

"Look, we aren't here to negotiate weapons with the likes of you," Magnus snarled.

"Then I guess I have nothing for you either." He went to get up, and I shoved the table toward him, pinning him back there. In an instant my gun was in my hand and pointing at him under the table. By the look in his eyes, he knew it. Till was quickly behind me, but Magnus had already stood up, kicking his chair away and drawing on her.

"Well, well. It looks like the rumors about you are true, Parker. You aren't just a scared *Zebtron* like you appear."

"Damn right they are." I was past the point of caring what this bastard thought of me. "Now you're going to tell me how to get to the planet, or we're going to leave here with two less scumbags alive on Volim."

"If we don't come back, neither does Leslie." His words hit me hard.

"I thought you were friends," I grunted.

"We are, but what kind of friend sets up a deadly meeting like this?" he asked.

A thought occurred to me. I reached into my jumpsuit pocket and pulled out a palm-sized device. "Here. This is worth the trade."

He eyed it skeptically. "What is it?"

"Kareem gave it to me. It's called a Relocator."

Magnus interjected, "Dean, you sure you want to part with that? We could use it to get out of here, you know."

"We aren't leaving without Leslie. Not after all the help they've given us." I still held on to the device but let it rest on the table for now.

"How does it work?" he asked, eyes wide.

I had the greedy insectoid hook, line, and sinker. I explained the value of the device, and he watched me teach him the controls with vested interest.

"It's not what I'd hoped for, but it'll do in the current situation. If I can't get the right price for it, I can use it myself. Do you know how many predicaments I could have escaped from with that?" Sergo asked.

"I'd rather not know. Do we have a deal? You give me what I want, and this is yours." I slid it forward a few inches.

Sergo reached for a breast pocket on his jacket. "Hold on," Magnus said.

"It's what you came here for. I happen to have a few sets of eyes in the towers. They were able to procure it quite quickly. If the Supreme knew it was you on that world, you wouldn't be sitting here now. Just remember that. My advice is to get off Volim as fast as you can. You never know who might feel like selling you out." Sergo pushed a small datastick across the table.

I snatched it up and left the Relocator there.

"Thanks for your advice. Where's Leslie?" I asked, getting up from the seat.

"Probably sleeping in her suite by now," Sergo answered.

"You mean she wasn't ever in danger?" I asked.

"Why would she be? As you said, we're friends. Nice doing business with you." Sergo disappeared to the far corner, Till in tow. She turned back and gave us a wink before holstering her gun and stalking after her boss.

––––––––

*L*ight poured in through the windows, and I realized I'd forgotten to close the blinds last night. The sun was just beginning to peek over the horizon as we made it to our rooms. We'd found Leslie pacing in her suite, waiting for us. She'd given us each a hug when we returned.

My door buzzed now, and I rolled out of the comfortable bed feeling like I hadn't slept at all. I threw on my jumpsuit, noticing someone had been in the room and laundered it. It sat nicely folded, smelling like honey and lavender. They were a strange people, but not so different from us.

"Coming," I called, and when I opened the door, Denni stood there with Magnus and Leslie.

"Guess it's time to see the Supreme," Magnus said. He had bags under his eyes, and I wondered if I looked that terrible.

"Just a second. I'll be right there." I closed the door and used the facilities before grabbing the datastick under my pillow. I was glad I hadn't left it in my jumpsuit. That was likely why it had been cleaned. They could snoop while playing the gracious host.

We headed back down the tower and into the room where the Supreme had met with us the day before. He was already at the table, tapping on a tablet in front of him.

"Good. You made it," he chirped, and our translators did the rest. The small Padlog rubbed his hands together, looking even more like an insect as he did so.

"Can you help us?" I cut right to the chase. If we could get the details on the Theos while we were here, we'd be killing two birds with one stone. Otherwise, I was happy to have the location of the crystal world in my pocket. That was if Sergo had been honest about what the datastick contained.

The Supreme watched us for a moment. "The portals are a vital part of our society. Not the Padlog per se, but the whole of the universe. The Theos created them long ago, and there is an importance behind them you can't even begin to understand. If they are failing, this is an omen of the end."

I wasn't sure making up the lie was such a good idea. "How can I find them?"

"You won't. Many have tried. We've studied them, and countless other beings and deities from the known universe, and believe me, every world has one; some have many. They elude us. It's almost as if they never did exist, though there is ample proof from numerous worlds. But we cannot find their home world."

I wondered if he was telling us the truth. He had no reason to be honest with us, and every reason to hide information. "Can you share some of your findings on them? I have an interest in the Theos."

He chirped a command, and Denni was back with a clear tablet. "On here, we have compiled a history as we know it. It's not as elaborate as the findings at Bazarn Five, but most of that is useless information. Here we have the necessary details."

I was flabbergasted he'd share this. "Thank you, Supreme. Hopefully, we can find something of use for our mission."

"You're welcome, Dean," he said. His eyes twinkled. "I hope you had fun in the Vespiary."

TEN

I was happy to be leaving Volim. We wound our way past the busy moons and intricate space station, back out into calmer territory.

"Think we're far enough away?" I asked, flipping the datastick between my fingers.

"Yes. Let's see if Sergo was good to his word. If he isn't, then he'll have a nice surprise waiting for him on his next visit to Haven," Leslie said.

I pushed the universal stick into the helm console and held my breath as data appeared on the small screen. The text was unreadable to my human eyes.

"Here, try this," Magnus said, grabbing something from a shelf on the bridge. "Clare gave it to me. Apparently, it can translate anything."

I pulled the datastick out and plugged in the adapter from Clare. When I plugged the stick back in, the readouts came in English. "That woman never ceases to amaze me. Remind me to buy her something special when we're back home." Home. It felt so far away.

I tapped the folders open and found the one marked "Leslie." The data files inside were basic. There was just one line. Coordinates. "Got them!" I yelled. A tiny piece of anxiety broke free, but it was short-lived. The world wasn't close.

Leslie keyed in the location. "Even with the hyperdrive, it'll take us two years to get there."

"The portal. We can map this now." I went to the captain's chair and used the console to bring up images on the viewscreen. "Follow me. We know there's a world a week's trip from the crystal planet. I was there. We flew in that small ship, but by Mary's memory." I zoomed out on the map, and we found twenty habitable worlds within that rough distance.

"How do we know which one it was?" Magnus asked.

"I have a question," Leslie said. We stopped talking, waiting for her to ask it. "How did the Padlog get there so quickly?"

That made me pause. How had they? If they'd been tracking us, there was no feasible way for them to be waiting so close by.

"I don't know. Maybe they were in all corners of the galaxy, waiting for someone to arrive?" I said, but it didn't feel right.

"Wormholes," Magnus said.

"That's it. A wormhole." I leaned back in the captain's chair, the 3D map of the crystal solar system rotating on the viewscreen.

"Dean, don't…"

"What?"

"I can't. You know what happened last time you used them to travel. You came back home and missed seven years. I can't do that. I have a family. Nat…the kids." Magnus' jaw was set in a hard line.

I wanted to yell at him that my wife was gone with my unborn child, but I clenched my teeth together and stopped myself. He was right.

"What are we going to do?" Leslie asked, and no one answered. We didn't know.

I flipped through the Theos document from the Supreme, trying to grasp anything about the portals I didn't know. Apparently, that was a lot. We were heading back to Haven, with no better plan at the moment. We decided to get back home, then go as planned to Bazarn Five with everyone. We needed to find the Theos in order to counter the Iskios. I didn't like the idea but had no choice but to go along with them. I vowed to myself I'd get back to the crystal world alone once my friends were safely at home. I'd do anything to find Mary, and traversing through wormholes counted as anything.

I lay on my bed, staring at the sterile white ceiling. Every time I tried to sleep, I saw her face looking at me, black mist filling the whites of her eyes. I tried to puzzle it out. I was missing something. The portals, the symbols. I'd accessed the portal icons in the computer, but those only showed the ones visible to everyone using the portals.

There were still a large number of worlds blocked off by the mysterious Theos Collective. I had access to those worlds, being gifted the skill by Kareem before his passing, but I couldn't see the symbols, as I didn't want to store them where prying eyes might see them.

Something clicked in my mind, a clear image, and I knew it was important. I got up and fumbled for my tablet. Scrolling through my stored images, I flipped open the file on the Iskios' cube we'd found on the ice world. It was a map. On it was a symbol for the water world, where I'd first laid eyes on the Iskios shadow playing at being a Theos.

But I'd searched high and low for those icons already. They weren't in either catalog. I stared at the images long and hard. They were stretched out on the page like an unfolded cube, looking ever like a cross. I couldn't figure it out. The clue had to be there, on this image.

We were getting close to Haven again. Frustration boiled inside me, but I felt powerless to do anything about it. I was helpless when Mary needed the most help. I threw the tablet down on the bed in anger. It spun and slid to a stop as it hit the wall. From here, I could see I'd cracked the screen. Something caught my eye as I looked at the fractured tablet. The symbol on the bottom burned into my eyes.

I recognized it. I'd been looking at it the wrong way this whole time. I ran to the tablet and picked it up, sure I was right. With it now upside down, I knew I'd found the symbol.

"Guys, I need to get to the portal! How far are we from Haven?"

"*D*ean, it wasn't a waste of time. We would've had no idea how to get to the crystal world if we hadn't met with Sergo. At least now we can get to the place where you borrowed the ship. It's just another week."

Magnus was trying to help me, but it just made me angrier. Another week. A week was forever while Mary was infiltrated by the essence of the Iskios.

"Why don't you go home?" I asked Magnus. We were at Leslie and Terrance's. They'd made me go there first to get more supplies.

"I'm coming with you. Can you wait one more day?" he asked.

Could I? Everything in me wanted to rush for her, now that I knew how to get there, but I also knew I should let

Magnus see his family. Nat would kill me if anything happened to him.

"Fine. Let's go."

Terrance walked in as we were heading out the door. "Ready to go back already?"

"Yeah, we're going to go back to Spero for a few hours," I said, catching Magnus' grim reaction. A couple of hours was better than no time with his family at all. I decided I could convince him to stay once we were home.

"Great, let's get to the ship." Terrance grabbed a vest and tossed it on. "Dean, thanks for bringing Leslie back in one piece."

I was irritable and ready to be on the move. "Don't thank me. She's the only reason I got anything out of the mission."

A half hour later, we stood at the portal stones. Terrance was gone. Only Magnus and I stood before the glowing crystal. I wanted to key in my secret code to access the blocked icons and confirm my thought that the upside-down image from the map matched the planet icon I was thinking of. I looked up at the surveillance and thought better of it.

Instead, I found the symbol for New Spero and gave Magnus a forced smile before tapping the icon.

ELEVEN

"*I*t had me thinking," Clare said. "Sarlun told you the Theos used some tracking devices on the Iskios so many years ago in order to hunt them all down to bring to this crystal world. What if we could make a device like that?"

The whole gang was holed up in Terran Three. The research facility was one of two located on New Spero, and Clare was adamant we needed to visit there before going on the next leg of our trip. We stood in a brightly-lit room, with shelves and cabinets lining the north wall, and a large white smooth-topped workstation.

"How would you do that?" I asked, tapping the table with a nervous energy.

Nick rolled his eyes, telling me he'd heard this a hundred times already. Nat was there, and little Dean played with a truck on the floor near his father's leg. He hadn't left Magnus' side since his dad had returned home.

"That would be really cool." This from Leonard, who, for once, had put his pencils and paper away and was talking with us instead of being a silent witness.

"First, I'd test such a device on some known DNA. Dog, for example. And then I'd see if I could get it to locate said animal," Clare said.

"I'm assuming this isn't hypothetical. Did you find the dog?" I asked.

She nodded. "I did, but the problem is, the device only works in close range." She blew a strand of blonde hair out of her face and smiled. "But…I think I can get it to target almost anything, as long as we know what we're looking for."

"How about a long-dead, misty black Iskios?" I asked.

"That's what I was going to say next." Clare stood and passed something to me. It was the size of a paperback book and had a screen covering half the top.

"It's heavy," I said, hefting it in my hands.

"It's got a lot of *stuff* in it." Clare smiled. "Take this and see if you can find any remnants of the Iskios while you're there. Just in case…"

Clare didn't finish her thought, so I did it for her: "In case Mary isn't there. Gotcha." I frowned and felt bad for raising my voice. These were my friends, and all they wanted to do was help. "I'm sorry. It's been a trying few weeks."

Slate came over and set his hand on my shoulder. "We know, Dean. We all want to get her back."

"Any chance you've duplicated the Relocator?" Magnus asked, his eyes hopeful.

"Not yet. That was something far beyond our understanding. It's one thing to trick the eyes or track biological particles, but transporting molecules is something for gods, not mere mortals." Clare smiled thinly. "I do have another cloaking device for you, and some new weapons. Want to see those?"

I agreed, but my heart was heavy. Slate and Magnus rushed over, and I stood behind them as they excitedly played with some new guns and something that looked like a grenade. I'd leave them to it.

Slate had convinced me to come, though it really didn't take much to twist my arm. He'd been there with me when she was taken, and I was happy to have him along.

Leonard stood watching with wide eyes as Slate tested

the grenade in a containment field room. Inside, a water-melon sat on the metal floor. He lobbed it through the blue field and counted down the timer he'd set on it. Six seconds later, the watermelon exploded, but instead of spraying everywhere, an energy sphere around it contained the damage and muffled the noise.

"How did you do that?" Natalia asked.

"With a built-in containment field. Grenades and this type of weapon are usually loud and destructive, so I thought, what if you could keep the victim isolated, and the noise to a minimum? Voila." Clare stood straight-backed, and Nick wrapped an arm around her waist and kissed her on the head.

"Awesome!" Slate yelled. "Can I do that again?"

The others laughed, and I stood watching the water-melon drip inside the shield.

"Now, who wants to see…"

I cut her off. We'd been thinking about this the wrong way. "The detector you're working on. Could you use it to track a specific person instead of the Iskios?"

It caught her off-guard, and Clare stopped in her tracks, a pensive look crossing her face. "I suppose that would work. I hadn't really thought of it that way yet. I was trying to duplicate what the Theos had used the theory for. Oh, my God. Mary."

"Exactly. If you go to my house, there'll be DNA everywhere. Feel free to take her hairbrush…whatever you need." I was getting excited. If we didn't find her on the crystal world, maybe Clare could track her down.

"Dean, you know it's only working in a two-mile radius so far? I'm not sure I can stretch it to what you need," Clare said.

"I know you, and you're resourceful. Look at all of the amazing things you've been able to come up with. Find a way to boost the signal, and you have it. And if you come to Bazarn Five with us, you might find your answer." They were waiting on us to return before we made our trip to the world that Sarlun was calling "the center of their own universe."

Clare smiled widely at this. "I'll do everything I can, Dean."

"Thanks," I said. "Now who's ready to get this show on the road?"

"I wouldn't mind some lunch first," Slate said, rubbing his stomach with his left hand.

"And this is why I always hated road trips," I said, not admitting that my own belly was grumbling.

---

*T*erran Three was turning into the Mecca of New Spero. I hadn't spent more than a day there before, and that was a long time ago. Since the influx of people from Earth, the size of the city had tripled. It was on desert-like terrain; each of the Terran cities was unique in what it could produce and grow. Here they did most of our manufacturing, and it was near the warmest spot year-round on the planet.

There were textile plants, food processing facilities, and everything from coffee roasters to plumbing manufacturers. Life went on. Capitalism still existed, even after the world ended. Initially, there had been a barter system, but it was quickly evident that with this many people, a currency was needed. Everyone needed to work and get paid.

Already I'd heard about unions trying to form, but the government that Patty had begun to build had come to full fruition, and though each Terran location could set some internal municipality rules, they all had to abide by the New

Spero guidelines. That meant taxes and social programs. Earth may have been gone, but a lot of its problems had followed us.

I'd been so distracted by my own life and the things I was dealing with away from New Spero that I'd hardly noticed what was happening on our own planet. When I was in my own home, out on the acreage near Terran One, it felt like paradise. Now, walking the streets of Terran Three, it felt like another industrialized city. Mary always reminded me that it was necessary, that without all of this, society would crumble. She was probably right.

I still wished better for our new world. We were in downtown Terran Three, and Clare was leading us to her new favorite restaurant. She could tell from my glare that I didn't want to waste my time with this, but she swore it would be quick.

"Spare some credits?" I hadn't even noticed the woman curled in a ball at the base of a building.

She was haggard. Young too. The others kept going, but I stopped and crouched down in front of her.

"What's your name?" I asked.

She looked surprised someone was talking to her. "I'm...uhm...Annabelle."

"Where are you from?"

"Here, I guess. I lived in one of the compounds on the outskirts of town when I first came."

She couldn't have been over twenty. Her brown hair was greasy, matted together. Her clothes weren't much more than rags covering a skeletal frame. "Annabelle. That's a nice name. I mean, where were you before? Before it all?"

She visibly relaxed and told me, "I grew up in a suburb outside Chicago. Nice place."

"What vessel were you on?" I asked.

"Twenty-five." Her eyes broke contact with me, and I instantly knew her experience during the Event was a traumatizing one. It had been for everyone.

"Did you come to New Spero on the first influx or last year?"

She shifted in her sitting position, still not looking me in the eyes. "Last year. I'd been living in Chicago. Things weren't good for me there."

"What do you want to do?" I looked and saw track marks on her arms.

"I don't know." Tears fell down her face. "I can cook."

"My friend Nick here's going to give you some information." Nick was a doctor, and he would know of any rehab programs on New Spero.

Nick came over and softly spoke to her. While he did that, I searched for local tablet IDs and found an image of the girl, a much healthier version of herself, and tapped a hundred credits over to it.

She mouthed a "thank you" to me, and I heard Nick say my name to her. Maybe if she knew the Hero of Earth had a vested interest in her well-being, she would turn things around. I hoped so.

We walked to lunch after Nick said he'd meet us there. I looked around with a new perspective of our world.

TWELVE

*T*he lander set down near the caverns of Terran Five. The portal room was just inside, and it was becoming a spot I seemed to visit frequently. Leonard was the first to exit, with Magnus and Slate right behind him. It appeared I was bringing a full crew this time. Clare and Natalia had wanted to come as well, but they had other things they needed to do.

Clare promised she would get the tracking device perfected. Watching Magnus separate from his wife and children had been hard, so I'd turned from it, leaving them to their private moment.

We'd wasted too much time on New Spero, a full day already. A day I could have been getting to Mary. But I did have a bag full of new tools, and an ambitious assortment of characters with me.

"Lead the way, boss." Slate grabbed two packs, one full of weapons from Clare and the other full of food and water. We were in our EVAs, and excitement thrummed through me as we entered the caves in the mountainside that led to the portal room. I blinked and recalled the first time I'd set foot in here. The stones had called me, and I'd freaked Slate out.

"With any luck, we can bounce to the next world and be on a ship in less than an hour." I was walking quickly, my EVA boots kicking up dust in the corridor with each step.

"Boss, in front of you!" The concern in his voice was evident, and I instantly went for the pulse pistol holstered at my side.

A panicked series of tweets and chirps carried to me from down the hall, and I put a hand up, letting the others behind me know to stop. "Suma?" I called, seeing a small form in a white EVA of her own. Her proboscis twitched behind her facemask. I flipped on my translator, using my arm console.

"What are you doing here?" I asked her, knowing she had her own built-in device that would allow her to understand me.

She stood proudly with a pack on her back and a rifle in her hand. "I'm here to help."

"Does your father know you're here?" I asked.

"Yes. He only hesitantly approved, but if there's one thing you've taught me, it's to go with your gut." Our translators worked much better now, and with their entire language in our catalog system, the clipped translations were a thing of the past with the Shimmali people.

"You have to go home, Suma." I walked up to her and started to lead her back to the portal room.

In our suits, the top of her head came to the middle of my chest, and even though she seemed the size of a ten-year-old human, she was technically an adult of her race. This was something she loved to remind me and her father of, any chance she got.

"I'm old enough to make my own decisions," Suma said, proving the point I'd made to myself.

"It's too dangerous. Let's get you back."

She stopped, feet planted firmly in the hall. "No. I'm coming with you. Mary is my friend too. I've brought some things to help as well. You know I'm resourceful. Slate, am I right?"

"Whoa, Suma, leave me out of this," Slate said before adding, "but she is right, boss. We could use her. That alien mind works in ways ours don't, and it might prove useful."

I shook my head in disbelief. Sarlun was going to kill me. "Okay, Suma. You're in but be careful. If anything happens to you, I won't be able to live with myself." I turned to my three counterparts. "Everyone watch and protect her. Got it?"

Magnus grunted. "As if we'd do anything but. Stop worrying so much, Dean. We got this. Let's go." He pushed past me and led us to the portal room.

I found myself perched before the table with the icons. The stone glowed brightly beneath it, and the symbols on the walls danced in light as we'd entered the room. My hands shook slightly as I scrolled down before entering the pattern I needed to unlock the hidden symbols. The screen changed, showing me the concealed worlds in muted gray.

I knew the icon was here, but where? I flipped through the pages until I found it, the symbol I'd initially been looking at the wrong way. This was the way to the portal on the water world, where we'd resurrected a space station in the likeness of what we thought was a Theos symbol. Now we knew it for what it was: a test by the Iskios to find a worthy flesh-and-blood vessel.

The symbol stared back at me, and I glanced at my crew. Magnus gave me a wink, and I pressed the icon. Everything went white.

We appeared inside the metallic-floored portal room, tucked away on the island in the water world. The symbol, Mary had instinctively known, would lead us to the small world where we'd loaded up on fruit and nuts and found the ship that led us to the crystal world.

I scrolled through the floating icons, knowing the symbol wasn't on any other table I'd seen. The Iskios had somehow ensured that. I stopped at the right one, ready to press it. Before I did, I turned and looked across the room. Stone walls were wide apart, opening into the place with three chairs, the very same ones where Mary and I had traveled to the day of the Event in our minds together.

No one bothered me as I crossed the space, resting a hand on the chair Mary had been lying on only a couple of weeks prior.

"Dean, let's go." Slate was beside me, hand on my shoulder.

I nodded and went back to the portal table. Everyone stood quietly, and I pressed the icon.

The room we appeared in wasn't the same one we'd entered only a few weeks ago. "Wait, this isn't it!" I couldn't believe it. It had to be right.

"Boss, it is. Look at the doorway, the design of the walls. It just looks more...aged," Slate said. He'd been there with us, and he was correct.

I ran a gloved hand along the wooden support beam along the wall, and a few rotten pieces of it fell to the floor. "How is this possible?"

"I have no idea. Let's get out of here." Slate led the way, with me bringing up the rear.

We ran through the semi-familiar corridors, but something was off about them now. The shiny metal was dulled, as if it needed a polish.

"Hangar's ahead." Slate's voice entered my earpiece. He stopped so abruptly, I saw Suma run into his back.

"What is it, Slate?" I asked, pushing past Magnus and Leonard.

"The ships..."

I finally saw what he was talking about. The previously colorful hangar was now covered in shrubbery; a large tree grew in the center of the space, thick brown branches stretching the width of the building.

"We were just here," I said quietly as I walked toward the tree trunk. I looked for signs of the ships we'd left behind.

"Are you telling me this place wasn't full of foliage a couple weeks ago?" Magnus asked.

Leonard walked around the room, eyes wide. Only Suma seemed to be on a mission. I spotted the top of her helmet over some weeds twenty yards away. "Dean, over here," her tweets translated.

I caught up to the small Shimmali girl and spotted the ship. It was larger than the tiny one the three of us had cramped onto, and I recognized it from before. Suma was already at the rear underside, trying to access it.

"Even if you can get in, this hunk of junk looks like it'll never see the light of day again." Magnus kicked the landing gear with a thud. Something fell off the side of the ship.

A huge branch hung overhead, threatening to crush the idle vessel at any moment. "Let's see if we can find one of the others. We left a couple behind."

We each started in a corner of the hangar, looking for the other vessels in the thick brush. Nature had taken over the whole area, making it seem like decades had passed since we'd last been there. It didn't make sense.

"Here." Leonard's arm could be seen waving from near the room's left corner. "I doubt this thing is getting off the ground, though."

"Anyone have a hedge trimmer?" Slate asked. "There's another one of the ships like the one we were on, Dean, but same thing. It's pretty beat up."

Here we were, finally on the right track to get to the crystal world, and we were sidelined again. My heart rate sped up; the monitor on my suit began softly beeping an alert. The room felt like it was caving in on me. The looming tree surrounded by the dense plants was enough to throw me into a panic attack if I wasn't careful, so I did the only thing I could think of. I left the hangar.

The doors were broken off from the wall, and I stepped through the opening onto the long grass outside, into a morning on this world. The ground was dewy, and the buildings that had stood the last time we'd visited were nothing more than piles of rubble, crumbled from years of disuse.

"How is this possible?" I asked, not intending for anyone to answer.

Leonard appeared behind me, gawking at the scene before him. "This is the same place you were at? The one with the fruit?"

"The one and the same, only it wasn't like this. Not quite." I started forward, following the path we'd taken before. Leonard came along, matching my pace with long strides as we roamed down an old road past the beaten buildings and into the copse of fruit-bearing trees.

"Is the air okay?" I asked him, not wanting to spend time checking our sensors. I was looking for signs, any indication we weren't at the right place.

"Should be compatible," he suggested.

A lot could happen to a planet's atmosphere in a century, or however long had apparently passed in the span of a few weeks. I hit the helmet release and lifted my mask, letting the warm breeze brush against my face. This was the spot where I'd kissed Mary, the taste of overripe fruit lingering on our lips.

I grabbed a piece of the hanging food and took a bite, and was rewarded with its pleasant flavors.

"Want one?" I asked, tossing one of them to Leonard. He caught the yellow fruit and released his helmet, raising his mask.

"Thanks." He bit into it and smiled, yellow pulp stuck in his teeth. "It's good. Dean?"

"Yeah?" I asked, still looking around the alien orchard.

"What do we do if we can't get one of the ships to work?"

I didn't know. "That's not an option."

"Dean, you better get back here," Magnus said through my earpiece.

"Come on, Leonard. Grab some for the others. Let's get going." I picked as many as I could hold, and we wound our way back as the heat of the morning grew stronger.

Slate was outside, peeling off his EVA when we arrived. "Look what I found!" He had four machete-type knives leaned against the hangar's exterior wall.

"Perfect. Time to get to work." I began removing my EVA and piled it beside Slate's.

We began hacking away pieces of the dense leaves, branches, and plants away from the largest of the three vessels. By the time we had it all cleared, we were drenched in sweat and panting. My palms were thankful I had on the thin gloves that I wore under the EVA suit; otherwise, they'd be covered in blisters.

Suma and Leonard were piling the debris to the side, and we were ready to board this ship and see what kind of condition it was really in.

I tried to get the ramp open from the exterior, but the computer screen wouldn't even boot for me. This was a problem.

"Let me try." Suma grabbed something from her backpack, sticking it magnetically to the side of the vessel. It turned on, and she tapped a small screen, typing away on a clear keypad. The blank comp-screen on the ship blinked on before flashing off again. "Almost there," she said, her proboscis bending to the side in concentration. She keyed more commands into it, and before we knew it, the comp-screen was activated.

With a last flurry of typing with her short fingers, the ramp lowered with a hiss. "We're in!" her tweet translated.

I was so happy I could have cheered and carried her on my shoulders, but the enthusiasm was short-lived when I saw the interior of the ship. Junk was piled high in the rear cargo area, and a pitiful light flickered on and off, setting a series of shadows against the walls.

Magnus was beside me, hands on hips. "Think she can fly?"

I blew out a deep breath of air. "I don't know. Let's hope so."

Suma went with Magnus to the engineering room, and Slate and Leonard continued to help me in the clean-up effort. We pushed ourselves, unloading crates of rotten food, spoiled supplies labeled in strange languages, and what looked like a bunch of junk. It reminded me a bit of the robo-pirates we'd encountered, and I made sure we checked every crevice of the ship for hidden deathbots before we could relax and set our weapons down.

The ship was a different layout from the ones we used. The cockpit, or compact bridge, was above the rest of the space in the center of the ship. It was only large enough for three people to be on it at a time and had two consoles. It appeared one was for piloting, and the other for manning the weapons, which Suma warned me were plentiful, even on the small craft.

The cargo area was in the rear, with bunks at the front left side, and an open room for eating and maybe socializing on the opposite end of the corridor. The whole ship had a stale scent to it, and we left the ramp down, hoping some fresh air would filter through it. Once we could power it on, the filtration system could clear that up for us, if we got it running.

I tried not to think what it would mean if we were stuck there. We'd have to go back. It meant I either boycotted the trip to the crystal planet entirely, assuming Mary was gone already, or I went back, this time alone. I already started to think of worlds I could reach with the portals that wouldn't make the trip by hyperspeed so long.

I even considered going back to Volim to ask them for help. If they used a wormhole, I could do the same, because I didn't care if I lost years back at New Spero. Only getting Mary back mattered.

"Dean, you're going to want to see this." Slate's voice was calm but urgent. "Bring your pulse rifle."

The cargo area was mostly cleared, with a few crates of unknown goods still stacked neatly on the far edge. Slate stood looking at the wall, Leonard was close beside him, and they were blocking my line of sight.

"What is it?" I asked.

They parted from each other, giving me a view of the hidden panel that was now open. A figure stood inside the space in the wall.

THIRTEEN

"What do we do with it?" I asked them. No one spoke for a minute; we all just stared at the unmoving body.

"Turn it on?" Leonard offered.

"I'm not sure that's a good idea. The last time I came face to face with a robot, I was almost killed." This didn't look the same as the pirate robots, though. This was thinner, sleeker, its gray metallic material scuffed and worn, making me wonder if it was ever shiny and new.

I tapped my earpiece. "Magnus, where are we with the engines?"

The pause told me the news wasn't going to be good. "You don't want to hear it." Magnus sounded stressed. "Give us a while longer."

"We found something. You might want to take a break. Suma may have a better idea what to do with it than us," I said.

"What is it?" Magnus asked.

"A robot, an android, I don't really know. It's metal and powered down," I answered.

"We'll be right there," Magnus said.

We stood there watching it for another minute before Magnus and Suma found us. Suma made her way to the front and let out a series of excited noises. "This could be just what we need."

"How so?" I asked her.

"The engines are damaged beyond my ability. But this"

— she pointed at the slender android — "this could help us. Many races have onboard androids to assist with engineering or repairs. This looks like one of those races."

Hope welled up in my chest but didn't last long when I remembered the android wasn't on either. "How do we fire it up?"

"Give me a hand," she said, and we made room for the largest of us, Magnus and Slate, to slide it free from the hiding space.

They grunted as its heavy feet dragged behind it on the metal floor, leaving scratches. We all pitched in and got it lowered to the ground, face up. It was shaped like a humanoid, which I found made sense, since most of the creatures we'd encountered had been bipedal. It had two eyes and a slit for a voice to carry through. The joints were smooth, like the creator had attempted to hide the fact the body was robotic. Its legs were proportionately thinner than the torso, the arms a little too short to be human.

I also noticed it had seven mechanical fingers and a thumb on each hand. Did the creators make it after their image, or was there a superior functionality to this many digits?

Suma looked around, trying to find something. "What do you need?" Leonard asked her.

"Power cord," she said, scouring.

"I think I remember seeing one." Leonard ran down the ramp and into the hangar.

"Even if you find a power cord, how are you going to juice him up when the ship's dead?" Magnus asked.

She tapped her head with a short digit. "I told you I'd be valuable." Her utilitarian backpack was in the corner of the room, and she went to it, rifling through what looked like a never-ending pile of devices. She pulled something compact from the bag and began unfolding it.

Leonard stumbled back in a rush. Sweat dripped down his brow. "I found the cord!"

Suma took the cord and attached one end to the still android. It plugged in near the base of its heel.

"Now what?" I asked, and Suma's snout twitched.

"Now I hook up this adapter." She fumbled around her pack, trying a few pieces until she found one that fit. "Then I take this solar panel, bring it outside, charge it, and bring it back inside, thus powering up the android."

She made it sound like this was an everyday occurrence. Simple.

"Well, I'll be. You're quite the Shimmali!" Slate put his large arm around her shoulder and she beamed up at him.

"Do you want the honor?" She passed Slate the unfolded solar panel. It was only a couple of feet in length and a handspan tall.

"Where does the energy store?" I asked her.

She tapped the bottom of the panel, where a small box attached to it. "In here."

Slate took the panel and said he'd find an extra-sunny spot for it.

"What now?" Magnus asked.

I pulled over a couple of crates and sat on one. "We wait."

---

*T*wo hours passed, and we cleaned every inch of the ship we could. It was in surprisingly good shape once we cleared the debris from inside, but we still wouldn't know if it was spaceworthy until we got the system up and running.

"It's charged." Suma walked up the ramp. "Good thing too, because night is falling out there."

She attached the power source to the adapter on the cord plugging into the android and hit a few icons on the panel's screen.

I held my breath as it started to charge. We now had to wait for the android to power up, if it still worked. I couldn't help feeling like we were wasting time, but we had no choice.

We talked about anything but the trip ahead while we sat there. Dust and dirt covered my sweaty body, sticking to me in any place my jumpsuit didn't cover, and even some where it did. Slate told us about Denise, but only after Magnus poked and prodded it out of him. It was nice to see Slate's eyes sparkle as he spoke about a woman. He'd been through so much, and I was thrilled he'd finally met someone.

It only brought my own excruciatingly painful emotions to the surface, but I pushed it down. There was only the mission now. No matter what small talk we made, I had one objective: to find Mary at any cost.

"Dean, look," Suma said. She'd been perched over the metal man since she'd plugged it in.

Its eyes began burning a hot yellow. "It's working," I whispered, trying not to jinx it. I ran my hands along my bearded face to help mitigate the stress I was feeling.

We all leaned in over the android, watching it power up. With a sudden jerk, it hinged upward into a sitting position, nearly head-butting Magnus. He moved out of the way just in time, and for a second, I thought he was going to shoot the android in reflex.

A monotone voice box transmitted a series of nonsensical phrases as its head turned left to right, looking at each of us: evaluating.

Suma opened a panel on its right forearm, and it didn't fight her. She grabbed a datastick from her pack and plugged it into a receptacle. Its eyes turned light blue for a moment before going orange and staying there.

She closed the panel and looked at us smugly. "What did that do?" I asked, unsure why she looked so happy.

"Hello. I am W88473587369. Excuse me while I check my condition," it said in a low monotone voice. Its eyes dimmed, then went black.

"Is it...?" Magnus asked.

"It's just doing a diagnostic check. It should be back online soon," Suma said.

"This is so cool." Leonard was using his suit's camera to take images of the android, likely for later issues of his Survivors comic. Every comic needed a robot.

Soon it was back, orange eyes looking around once again. "I seem to be fully operational." It stood up, forcing us to jump back. It was quick when it wanted to be.

"Hello, W884... how about I call you W?" I asked.

"W is acceptable. Where is my crew?" it asked, peering past us toward the corridor that led to the bunks and the stairs to the bridge.

"I'm sorry, W, but they aren't here," I said.

"Were we attacked?" it asked.

"That much isn't clear either. We need to get this ship operational so we can take it into space. Can you assist with that?" I leaned forward. The android was a couple of inches shorter than I was, and I looked down into its glowing orange eyes. Its voice was low, and I instantly thought of it as male, though that wasn't necessarily true. Humans, always trying to put things into categories. It must make us feel better somehow.

"I will get it running. Then I can access the records and identify what occurred." It turned and began walking away from us with no further comments.

"Suma, do you mind watching it? Maybe you can learn

something important about the ship." Before I finished speaking, Suma was already trailing W down the corridor toward the engine room.

"We may as well get some rest," Magnus said.

Leonard was yawning, and Slate was slouched on a crate, gazing after the android and Suma. "I sure hope this bucket of bolts can get us up there."

"Me too, Slate. Me too."

"*T*ry again," W instructed Slate, who turned the tool as hard as he could. Veins stuck out of his thick arms as he pulled with all his strength.

W tapped the blank screen, and it whirred to life. The engineering room filled with banging and rough-sounding noises but calmed as W typed codes into the screen with all fourteen fingers in a blur. Soon there was nothing more than the constant hum of the drive powering up.

"We did it!" Suma called, hugging the android.

He patted her on the back. "It appears we did."

"W, run a full system check on this vessel. Find out what else needs to be repaired. It's all well and good to get the drive working, but if we get to space only to be torn apart because of a hole in the hull, we've succeeded at nothing." I wondered how the android would accept taking orders from me.

"Already begun. We should have a readout in four point oh eight seconds. There it is." W scrolled through the data on the screen, and I glanced at it, seeing nothing but gibberish.

"Nothing serious, Captain." W had begun calling me that, and no one had corrected it. "A few minor welds to the exterior, a filtration change, a septic flush, and a thorough blow to the thrusters. Then we should be operational."

The list wasn't tiny, but it sounded better than I'd expected. "Tell us what we can do to help." Magnus looked rested, but Slate's eyes were dark and puffy as if he'd stayed awake all night, his nightmares coming back to haunt his dreams.

"You two can do the septic flush. It does not require my particular skill set." W's voice stayed steady, but it felt like he was trying to make a joke.

"I knew it," Slate said, punching Magnus in the arm. "If you'd have kept your trap shut, we could be changing filters or pressure-washing the exterior."

I left them to bicker and found Suma at the computer screen on the side of the engineering room.

"Thanks for doing all of this," I said. "We couldn't have done it without you."

She smiled like only a Shimmali could. "It's my pleasure. Anything for you or Mary. But we haven't got it off the ground yet."

I settled my arm over her shoulders. "We will."

We had to.

FOURTEEN

*I*f there was one thing I knew from my previous life in the business world, it was that things often happened when you least wanted them to. After repairing the list W had given us, three more issues popped up. It was like renovating. If you tear open the wall behind that shower, be prepared to find something you didn't expect.

Once the ship was able to pressurize, we found the filtration system couldn't handle the load, so we had to unwind part of each cartridge in order to allow the right amount of airflow through. Then we blew the lights in the bunks while cleaning the thrusters, which wasn't the end of the world, but I'd stubbed my toe on a bed post and was now hobbling around the ship.

Two days. Another two lost days. That morning as I'd slept, I dreamt I'd found Mary on the crystal world, the Iskios gone from her eyes. She embraced me, kissing me deeply as we celebrated her pregnancy. I promised her we were done with everything, that we'd live our lives in peace. She smiled at me, eyes turning misty and black, and said it wasn't possible. The Unwinding was too far gone.

I'd awoken in a sweat and knew it was just my psychosomatic mind creating illusions, but... it felt real. It felt like her lips lingered on mine even as I lay there.

"Dean?" Leonard called my name, and judging by the look on his face, it hadn't been the first time he'd tried for my attention.

I looked down at the table where I sat; my food sat untouched. "Sorry. Just a lot on my mind. Any news?"

"According to W, all systems are go." Leonard smiled before grabbing himself a meal pack. With the pull of a tab, the breakfast meal heated itself. His overcooked scrambled eggs and sausage were ready in under a minute.

We were ready to leave this world. Magnus and I had done a hike the day before, after the android told us he needed a few hours, and that there was nothing us humans could help him with. The planet was peaceful. It was a classic case of nature taking over what had once belonged to it. Signs of an ancient civilization were everywhere, even miles in the distance, but the only life we saw were some bird-like creatures and small multi-limbed furry animals scurrying around the tall grass.

I made a note to ask W again about the crew that belonged to the ship. When I first broached the subject, he was tight-lipped. W told me he hadn't had time to access the data yet, but something about the conversation made me think the android knew more than he was letting on.

I wolfed some of the cold eggs down and tossed the container in the trash. My heart sped up, and I moved faster through the ship, working my way toward the compact cockpit that acted as the bridge. Slate stood at the base of the steps and stuck a fist out. I tapped it with mine.

"Let's go find Mary, boss."

I pumped my legs up the steps, my stubbed toe a distant memory. Magnus turned to me as I arrived, and Suma said hello without looking behind her.

A viewscreen flickered on, and I laughed at the size of it. I used to watch Yankee games on a bigger screen at home.

"Engines ready. Drive charged. Pressure accurate." W listed off more necessary functions, and I watched as he handled the controls. He'd told us he could pilot the vessel, getting us to the coordinates we'd provided him. He didn't need to sleep or eat, so he made the best pilot we could hope for.

The ceiling was still open from the last time we were here, and we didn't have to contend with exiting the hangar. The thrusters kicked into life, and the whole ship rumbled with power. I stood there, anxiously anticipating the liftoff.

"Hold on, Mary. We're coming," I said quietly enough for no one else to hear. W lifted his head from his task and turned to look at me briefly before getting back to the controls.

With a slight lurch, the vessel rose from the ground. Magnus' jaw was clenched, his eyes staring at the viewscreen with intensity. I found myself watching the others on the bridge rather than the screen. We left the hangar and were over the dilapidated city when I looked out the viewscreen. I realized I was holding my breath when Magnus let out a whooping cheer.

"Dubs, you are a master in class, my friend," Magnus told the android, using the nickname he'd started for the bot.

"Er, thank you, friend." W brought us up higher, past the ancient ruins of the locals, into the sky. The android increased the propulsion, and we broke through the atmosphere and into the darkness of space. "Is everyone alive?" it asked. When we all stayed silent, it spoke again. "That's a joke," it said mechanically.

"Don't quit your day job, Dubs. Let's see what these engines can do," Magnus suggested.

W tapped instructions into the console. "Inertia field is live. Drive is charged. Activating."

The hum of the ship picked up speed, and the whole

vessel shook enough to feel it carry through my feet and into my knees.

We all stared out the viewscreen as the ship raced away from the world, and when W made one final tap on the console computer, I felt my gut heave. Stars stretched on the screen, and we were off.

After far too long, I'd made it. We were only a few days from getting to the crystal world, where the Iskios had lain in wait after leaving a trail of bread crumbs for us to follow.

---

*T*he lights were dim on the bridge. W was propped in the pilot's seat, unmoving. For a moment, I thought he might be deactivated, but when he heard my footsteps, he turned his head toward me.

"Hello, Captain." His robotic voice was low, as if he was concerned with waking someone.

"Hey, W. I just wanted to say thank you again."

"You do know I am an android, correct?" he asked.

"Of course I do."

"Then why do you acknowledge me as if I am one of your own?"

This conversation was getting strange. "Because you helped us, and I do see you one of us, as far as I'm concerned. Where I come from, someone helps you, you say thank you."

"Intriguing. Then you are different from my crew." He turned back, silently looking out the viewscreen. I knew he didn't need to see the streaming stars beyond to know where he was, but it added to my humanizing of the android.

"Tell me about them," I urged.

"They bought me on Treznar Eight. I worked for an ice mining crew for forty years: a family business. They were killed in a border skirmish that was so common for the region. When things got serious, they conscripted all vessels into battle. They didn't stand a chance. The AX-3694 vessel was good for one thing only: hauling ice."

I was surprised by his response. I hadn't expected this real discussion. The android we called W continued to amaze me.

"That must have been hard," I said.

"How so?" he asked.

"They were basically your family. You worked with them for forty years, then one day they were gone."

"I do not understand. I am an android."

It was easy to forget he didn't have feelings as we did. "I'm sorry. Go on."

"The winning government took all debris, and they found me among the wreckage. I was rebuilt, memory intact, and I was sold to a new crew. Of this vessel."

He stopped, but I didn't think his story was over. "What did they do? Who were they?"

"They were traders. They went from planet to planet exchanging goods, and transporting people when necessary."

"Where did they come from?" I asked.

"They were from Mawitakos." He brought up data on the console and showed me a map. It wasn't anywhere I'd ever heard of before, but the images were depressing: the planet was gray, with two dim stars in-system, looking on the verge of being snuffed out.

"No wonder they left," I muttered.

"Yes. They often claimed to be glad to be gone from Mawitakos, but occasionally, Yeloik would regale the others with songs about home. The captain would allow it if he was feeling homesick," W said.

I was genuinely curious. "How did you come to arrive on the world where we found you?"

"Larsk Two. Much nicer than Larsk One. They have insects there the size of your friend Slate," W said, and I shuddered. I'd seen enough insectoids and giant moths to know I didn't want to deal with life-sized black widows, with or without guns. "We were bringing some antiquity or another to Larsk One when we were sidelined with a ship malfunction. I had to land before we ran out of oxygen."

"Why did you never leave?" I asked, resting on the second seat.

"I don't recall," W said. "We fixed the ship, and the captain and the others went looking for treasure, they said. The world was empty, buildings everywhere, only they were still standing back then."

"How long ago was this? Give or take."

He paused, as if calculating. "From the data Suma provided me, it would equal one thousand four hundred and eleven years and twenty-five days of your Earth time. Give or take."

My jaw dropped. "You were sitting there for fifteen hundred years? Why didn't you leave?"

"They never came back from their search of the city. The captain told me to wait, so I did. Eventually, I could not charge any longer. I closed myself into the wall and shut it before powering down."

My hands went to my face, and I took a deep breath. "Wow. You were there when we came a few weeks ago."

"I suppose I was."

"Well, if we ever get into a situation like that, feel free to find a new life. Just come looking for us first if we disappear." I tapped the console with my index finger. "How long?"

"Fourteen hours, Captain," he answered.
We were almost there.

FIFTEEN

My hands shook as W cut the FTL drive. The image I saw on the viewscreen didn't compute.

"W, this isn't the right place," I said, my voice betraying my nerves.

"These are the coordinates you provided me with." The android brought them up on the screen to show me. They indeed matched.

Had Sergo sent me on a damned wild goose chase? I pictured wrapping my hands around his neck, crushing his windpipe with the crunch akin to stepping on a beetle.

"Dubs, zoom in." Slate had taken to calling the android Magnus' nickname for him.

"Zooming." The planet was clear. It sat between us and the system's star, and I could see dim light through the core of the world. With each percentage of zoom increase, the surface grew more focused.

"Just as I thought. It *is* the right world," Slate said, walking forward toward the viewscreen. "Look. Those are crystals. They've just lost their pigment."

I had no idea what this meant. "Let's go in." I told W what I knew about the quadrant we'd been in, the one with the blue crystal pyramid. Only now it wouldn't be blue, apparently. How could the color have been sucked out of the gemstones? I had far too many questions, and no one to answer them.

As the ship lowered into the atmosphere, my breaths

came faster and shallower. The bridge suddenly felt too small for us to all be on, as if the walls were closing in on me.

"I'm going to get my suit on," I mumbled and left.

"Wait up," Magnus was behind me. "I know it doesn't look promising, but she might still be here."

"Maybe. Something feels very off about this. I know it makes no sense, but I somehow feel like I'd know if she were here. My gut's telling me she isn't." I talked as I walked, not trusting my legs to work if I stopped. We were there, and in a short time, I'd possibly find out if Mary was alive.

I opened a storage closet in the cargo bay and started to put my EVA on.

"Dean." Magnus grabbed me by the shoulders.

I fought the urge to push him off. "What?" I yelled.

"We're in this together. I know you feel alone without her, but we're here. Slate, Leonard, Suma, me…"

I held my helmet under my arm and looked up at Magnus. He was right. I needed their help. "I'm sorry. Let's get suited up and see what we can find." I stuck my hand out, and he shook it firmly.

"Good."

The others emerged into the back, as if they were waiting to see how I was going to react.

"Come on in, guys. Slate, did you direct W to the right spot?" I asked.

"I described it as best as I could, and he used the ship's scanners to lock in on the region. Pretty cool technology." Slate began to throw his EVA on, as did the others.

"More than cool," Suma tweeted. "We can use that on Shimmali vessels, moving forward."

W's voice carried through in-ship speakers. "Approaching landing location. Set down in eight point oh…"

I cut the feed on the wall. "Everyone ready to go?"

Magnus walked from person to person to alien and made sure their suits were locked and pressurized properly before we turned on the containment field and opened the ramp.

The ship landed on the crystal world and it all became real. Sweat beaded beneath my suit and drops rolled down my spine. What was I going to find when I stepped off this ship and onto the colorless ground?

I stood at the top of the ramp and took a deep breath of recycled air. It was time to find out. Moving one foot before the other, I walked through the containment field, down the steps, and to the hard, clear surface.

My team followed, Magnus and Slate ready with pulse rifles in their grip. Leonard carried Suma's pack on his back. I left my gun in its holster, as the only person I expected I might cross paths with was my wife. I wouldn't be shooting her.

The landscape was familiar. Even though it had only been a few weeks since I'd set foot on the same rock, it felt like a lifetime had passed. Slate came to stand beside me as we peered down the ledge of the cliff and toward the now-clear crystal pyramid.

"Boss, wasn't there a moon in the sky last time?" he asked, a note of concern carrying through.

I looked up to the bright sky. "Maybe it's on the other side of the planet right now."

He shook his head. "It wasn't there. I wasn't even thinking about it then, but there was no moon out." He pointed up.

What did that mean? Were we even at the right place?

"God knows what the Iskios have done. We just came from a planet that appeared to have aged a century in a few weeks, and now this…" I didn't even know how to describe the changes.

"Something serious has gone down. Come on, we're not going to get answers up here, boss." Slate started the descent down the smooth angled surface, and the others followed. I waited for a moment, staring out toward the looming fortress. *Grave*. That was what the Iskios had called it. I'd thought it was a throne room, but he'd called it a grave. They'd been dead, according to Sarlun's information: second-hand details, passed down over generations and through races across the galaxy. Who knew what was true and what was just a bedtime story?

The symbol was still cut into the ground, visible from here only by the now-murky water sitting in it. Before, it had been a vibrant blue; now it looked dirty on the otherwise pristine, crystal-clear scenery.

"Dean, you coming?" Magnus' voice asked through my earpiece.

"On my way," I said and saw them down a half mile away. I hadn't realized just how long I'd been staring into the empty distance. I caught up with them in a few minutes after jogging, careful to not twist my ankle on the protruding crystal ends.

We reached the symbol, the one we'd thought was to indicate the Theos. I didn't even know if that symbol was for the real Theos, and the Iskios had just used it to trick us, or if it really meant anything at all. It might have been made up by them, purely for the purpose of finding this worthy vessel. Mary.

Suma captured images of it, but I kept walking ever forward, toward the magnificent pyramid I was nearing. It had started raining last time we'd walked this path, and among the lightning, we'd seen the Padlog ship coming down. This time, the sky was empty of both ships and clouds.

The world felt cold now, sterile.

No one spoke as we solemnly approached the entrance we'd used last time. The large-eyed tiny creature had guided us then. Now we saw no sign of the little guy. Was it still lingering on the world? Was it placed there only to act as a guide, should a potential vessel finally arrive?

"Leonard, Suma, stay outside," I commanded, and before I got an argument from the Shimmali girl, Slate shook his head at her, telling her it wasn't the time. "If something happens to us, get out of here. Get W to bring you back to Larsk Two. Go home from there. Use the portal. Got it?" I asked forcefully.

Leonard nodded, but Suma stayed still, withholding a reply.

I walked over to her. "Suma, whatever you're thinking, forget it. I don't like the look in your eye. Your father needs you to come home to him, so no heroic stuff today, okay?"

This time, she did answer. "I can't promise anything."

It was as good a response as I was going to get. "Leonard, you understand, right?"

"Yes, Dean. I do." He stood straight-backed and looked like he was about to salute me. He caught himself and relaxed his arm.

"Good. Let's go, gentlemen." I stuck my leg through the opening, and before I knew it, I was back inside the pyramid where Mary had been possessed.

The halls once again lit with the LEDs shining forward off of my suit, but this time, there was no blue tinge to it. The crystals were all clear, the pigment sucked from every ounce of the stone. What could do that?

"Which way?" Magnus asked, and Slate pushed past me, leading the charge.

"Follow me." Slate took us down the corridors, toward the throne room. In a few fuzzy minutes, we were approaching the large open cavern. I didn't recall walking to the room, so distracted were my thoughts. I ran the last remaining steps and into the room with its immense vaulted ceiling. It was dark inside, save for the light beams tracing our movements. Gone were the glowing blue stones, as was Mary.

"Mary!" I yelled. I clicked my suit's exterior speaker on and continued to call her name as I rushed to the empty crystal seat in the center of the room. Piles of broken crystal stalactites lay nearby, where Mary had been covered by them after the Padlog had shot the ceiling. The only color remaining was a few blotches of red. Mary's blood.

I fell to my knees, moving chunks of rock, hoping she was there, that we could save her, but Slate and I had both seen her rise. We'd seen her use her new gifts to send us home before the startled mist took over once again.

"Boss, you're okay. We knew this might happen. We'll find her." Slate was beside me, crouched low to the ground.

I'd wasted so much time coming here. To what end? She was long gone, the world free of the Iskios once and for all. Had the Unwinding already started? That might explain the missing moon.

Not only did I need to find my wife, I needed to stop what she was wielding – carrying. I'd have plenty of time to feel sorry for myself, but now, Mary needed me. Everyone needed me.

I choked back the sorrow and felt resolve firm in my gut. The Iskios would pay. They didn't stand a chance, not against me. Not when I found the Theos and brought justice back to them.

I noticed the floor; the whole pyramid, in its entirety, had lost the vibration effect from before. The energy stored there had dissipated, or had left with the Iskios and Mary.

My earpiece chimed. "Captain," W's robotic voice said.

"Go ahead," I said, clearing my tight throat first.

"I've found an anomaly. It's four hundred twenty-seven point eight kilometers from our position."

Magnus looked at me, right eyebrow raised. "What kind of anomaly, Dubs?" he asked the android.

"Pigment. There is a section of crystalline material that is still amber in hue." Even for an android, he seemed specific about things.

"Are you sure?" It might be a clue to Mary. Maybe she was still here after all.

"I released the probes upon entry, and the images sent back are free of tampering. I am sure," W said.

"I never doubt a robot," Slate said. "Come on, let's go."

Slate and Magnus ran for the corridor we'd entered from, and I took a final look at the room I'd last seen Mary in.

"Until we meet again," I whispered.

SIXTEEN

"There it is," Suma tweeted, her snout wagging side to side. She was more excited than I was about seeing what this could mean for us. A section of orange crystals could mean nothing on an entire world, or it could mean everything.

W set the ship down on a flat piece of land just outside the still-amber region. It was much a smaller section than I'd expected, maybe five thousand square feet.

In a couple minutes, we all found ourselves standing at the bottom of the ramp, three feet from the border between clear and orange crystal ground.

"I'll go first," I said, stepping down on the colored rock. Nothing happened. "Mary!" I called, wondering if she could be there, hiding among the protruding stones.

No response came back.

"What the hell are those?" Magnus asked, and I spun around to see dozens of the little gecko-cats with saucer-shaped eyes staring at us from the center of the area.

"Those are like the creature that led us to the throne room." I had the urge to shoot them all, blast them each into nothing with my pulse rifle. They'd led us directly into danger, and seeing so many of them here now was like an alarm bell in the back of my mind.

Slate must have been thinking the same thing, because his gun came swinging into his gloved hand in an instant. "This can't be good," he said.

"Why not?" Leonard asked, eyes almost as wide as the small animals'.

"Because they led us into a trap last time." I took a step toward them, and they didn't flinch. "If they're all here…"

Slate finished my thought. "Then one of the Iskios has been left behind."

"It all makes sense now," Suma said. "They were placed here by the Theos, their bodies sealed away in the stones. Their essence colored them, but when Mary…" She paused, looking at me before continuing. "When *they* left, they must have had the power to vacate the world."

"They all went into Mary?" I asked.

Suma shook her head. "I don't think so. That much energy… it would destroy any living creature. They had to have left in a different form. Something so full of energy…"

"That it could destroy a moon?" Magnus finished.

Suma softly chirped; the translator replied with a single word. "Yes."

I was flabbergasted but glad to think Mary hadn't been bombarded with the souls of millions of dead Iskios. "The Unwinding. They have to make up this energy source they were hinting at. They're going to try to Unwind the universe, with nothing but the force of their own energy that had been trapped inside this crystal world."

"That's some serious stuff." Magnus took a deep breath. He pointed to the standing orange crystals. "What about this?"

"I don't know. It appears one of them was left behind." I glanced over and spotted Leonard walking over to the small creatures, who didn't seem afraid of the incoming guest.

"So those guys are here to lead someone to the Iskios, should they arrive. They must have been trained to do this.

When we arrived near the blue crystal pyramid, it wasn't long before one found us and gave chase," I said.

"And now that the others are gone, they're coming from around the planet to the last remaining spot with one of their owners. Poor little guys," Slate said, looking over at them now too.

"They're really quite harmless," Leonard said, crouching down to pet one of them.

"Be careful, Leonard," I urged, but it was too late. I saw the mist before he did. It rose quickly from the stone, the color lightening from the entire area as it lifted from the hard surface and into Leonard's mouth.

"Help!" he called, stumbling forward. He groped at his helmet and tripped on a crystal end jutting from the ground. He tumbled to the ground, and I was at his side in a few seconds, rolling him onto his back.

"You're going to be okay!" I shouted, but his eyes were already turning black.

"Dean… help…" He stopped talking, and his body went rigid. The small animals scurried away from us.

"Get back, Dean!" Slate shouted. He held his pulse rifle up, aimed at our young friend.

"You won't shoot him," I said to Slate, trying to sound as calm as I could. I couldn't help but picture Slate's large frame towering over Mae's small body as she lay crumpled on the floor of the Bhlat base so long ago. "We don't know what that would even do. It might just fly into me, or you."

Slate lowered his gun.

I looked back to make sure everyone else was okay, and saw W standing on the ramp, watching us blankly. Suma was nowhere in sight.

Leonard got up, black mist covering his eyes. He smiled. It was grim, alien on his boyish face. It faltered as he heard a noise behind him, and then I saw Suma, raised above Leonard on a crystal mound. She dropped something over him, and four objects hit the ground before power shot out of them, surrounding Leonard.

The mist poured from him in the blink of an eye, and the black smoke rushed for the highest corner it could, trying to evade the blue energy surrounding it. It hit the invisible wall a split second later, the section buzzing blue. It scampered away, shooting toward the bottom right side. It met the same fate.

It was trapped.

"Get me out of here!" Leonard called, tears falling down his red cheeks. His fear dripped on each word, and I went for the wall, standing close.

"We'll keep you safe. I'm sorry," I said as the mist realized it was trapped and had no exit.

As Leonard opened a confused mouth to make a reply to my statement, the mist shot right back into him. If we were going to trap it, it was going to trap our friend. The Iskios had made its point.

"Suma, where did you get that?" I asked her as she clambered down from the crystal perch.

"I told you I was a valuable asset." I knew she would have smiled if her new friend hadn't been trapped because of her.

"Good work." I stood at the edge of the shield. It acted like a containment field, but it was some sort of portable shield. "It can't get out?"

"Nothing gets out, or in." Suma was now down and beside me, looking at Leonard, who was only a couple feet away. His smile had turned to a scowl upon the Iskios' sudden return.

"How will he breathe?" Magnus asked.

"He's in an EVA with a recycled air processor. He should be fine for the time being," Suma said.

"*Dathhe ablioni tremlle.*" The words were uttered from Leonard's mouth but weren't his voice. "How dare you?" it then said in English.

I scoffed back a laugh. "How dare we? How dare *we!* You shoot yourself into our friend and have the nerve to ask us that?"

"Pitiful humans. I can feel his weakness even as I invade his body. He only uses a small part of his mind. How do you go on like this?" it asked with a thick, deep voice.

"You know of us?" I asked it.

"This low-functioning mind gives me some answers."

"You might want to stop insulting us while we have you trapped," Magnus suggested.

"Now this one." Leonard shifted his gaze to Magnus. "I should have taken this formidable vessel."

"Stop leering at me," Magnus yelled.

I was getting tired of the Iskios already, but he had valuable information we needed. "So they left you behind, did they? Didn't make the team? Riding the pines all season while your friends attempt to destroy the universe? Must be difficult on you."

Leonard's head snapped back to stare at me. "I know what you're attempting, but it will not work. It was merely a coincidence that I was left behind."

"Or maybe, just maybe, they knew you'd just mess it all up, like you always have." I threw more fuel on the fire, hoping it would catch. "You're probably better off, because I hear this Unwinding has already sputtered out. Took down a few moons, a couple empty worlds, and poof" – I stretched my fingers out into the air – "nothing."

"You speak lies. I can feel it. The energy is powerful. The Unwinding has just begun." Already more information than we'd had. The Unwinding was real, and this one could sense it. Maybe we could get the location from it, use it as a homing beacon to Mary.

"I don't believe you. Tell me what worlds it's destroyed, and I'll confirm you are the liar," I said, mentally crossing my fingers.

"Do you think we are that foolish? Do you think I would betray my kind? We are Iskios, bringers of destruction, the balance of the universe."

My heart raced in my chest. I'd been missing something this whole time. The balance. Good versus evil, the light against darkness. "The balance is off," I said softly, feeling veins throb beneath my jumpsuit.

It stopped smiling now. I saw something new in Leonard's black eyes: fear. "Yes, the balance is off. If you're out there destroying things with the Unwinding, there's been a shift in the galaxy. The Theos come. There is no other way." I said the words as lies but felt them as truth.

Its deep voice got lower in pitch. "They are gone."

"You're wrong. They were like you. Lying dormant." It all snapped into place, then and there. It was as if the skies had opened wide, shining a beam of light into my very essence.

"How do you know? We erased all knowledge of it. We spent centuries making sure it was gone from all records. You can't know!" It screamed the last three words, spittle flying from Leonard's mouth onto his helmet's facemask.

"But I do know."

It screamed again, this time the anguished cry of a trapped animal.

The others were looking at me with questions in their eyes.

We hadn't found Mary, but I'd learned something perhaps even more important to the overall cause.

I knew where the Theos were hiding.

SEVENTEEN

"$\mathcal{A}$re you going to tell us your theory?" Magnus came into the bunk, where I was tucked away, sitting on a bed with my back against the room's far wall.

"Not yet," I said, breaking my gaze with the tablet to look him in the eyes.

His posture changed, as if all the air pushed out of his body and he was deflated. "Fine. I trust your caution." The room had four bunks, and he took the one beside me and sat on it, his weight causing the frame to groan in protest.

"Thanks for understanding. I don't want the Iskios to catch wind of my findings. I don't know if they have supersonic hearing, or if they have other ways of digging information from our minds. It's still contained?" I asked.

"Yep. Still in the closet Dubs had been hiding inside. Suma turned on the noise cancelation feature so we don't have to hear its non-stop calls for freedom. That thing has a salty tongue. You should hear some of the things it's going to do to us when it gets free." Magnus made it sound like a joke, but his face was hard and stoic when he spoke.

"I imagine none of them involve dinner and a movie," I said, getting a forced smile in return. Crows' feet lined his eyes, and I noticed just how much older Magnus looked. He'd aged seven years while we'd chased the hybrids around through wormholes, and his duties as a general and father had taken their toll on the once-youthful face I remembered meeting all that time ago on a dirt road in South

125

America.

"Still making jokes when you're uncomfortable, I see."

I set the tablet down on my lap. "What can I say, it's a character flaw."

"I don't think so. It's a good thing. It's when you stop joking that I get worried. Like the last month."

He was right. "A weight's been lifted. I didn't think she was going to be here, but I had to have the closure. At least we know she left with them. She's their vessel, and they won't let her get harmed. I just need to find a way to break her out of their possession."

"That's the tricky part. You really think we can get that misty bastard to lead us to them?" he asked.

"Here's what I do know. There has to be a balance. You want to know part of my theory on these ancient races?"

Magnus leaned forward, nodding.

"The Iskios were a bunch of sickos. Sarlun told us that much. They were into pain. Killing things. They thought they were gods themselves, and when the Theos threatened them, they didn't think the other race had the balls to do anything about it. When they started to get picked off by the Theos, they set this elaborate ruse to trick a worthy vessel into finding them.

"Only the Theos hadn't thought it through. They were the first. The oldest. The ancient beings of the universe. When they packed the Iskios away on the crystal world, they unbalanced the universe. In order to right the path, they had to banish themselves away." I was sure I was on the right track. Everything I read about them kept pointing back to the fact they were honorable, strong, but fair.

"Dean, that's it. So where are they?" He looked into my eyes and smiled, genuinely this time. "Never mind. I don't want to know, not yet. How about some dinner?"

"I'll be along in a minute."

He stood in the doorway a moment, a large shadow looming on my bed before he walked away. I went back to my tablet.

There isn't much to know about the physical appearance of the Theos. Some texts say they are eight feet tall, thick as a glargon truck. Others say they appear different to different races; that they become what someone wants them to look like, to ease the minds of those around them.

Did this change anything? I didn't think so. The Iskios said they'd ensured their history was wiped from the records. The same must be true of the Theos. The old saying about history being written by the victors sprang to mind.

I powered down the tablet and decided to take my growling stomach's advice.

———————

"Captain, are you sure I can transport through the portal?" W asked, looking inside the portal room back on Larsk Two.

"There's no reason you can't. We bring through equipment all the time. No offense," I said, cringing at my comment.

"None taken. I am, after all, machinery."

"Dubs has broad shoulders, Dean." Magnus hefted the last bag from the ship and tossed it into the center of the portal room beside the others.

I looked toward the containment shield, where Leonard was still invaded by the entity. It was being dragged along by Slate, and it was obviously fighting him the whole way.

"Everyone present and accounted for?" I asked. The

rundown walls of the portal room were glowing from the main portal stone. The second the Iskios entered the room, the stone dimmed and began to flash.

"That can't be good," Slate said, sweat pouring down his face from exertion.

Excitement ran through me. This reiterated my assumption.

"Come on, let's get out of here," I suggested.

Leonard's face was twisted in a look of abject terror, so much so that I worried for the man. Would this work?

"Bring him closer," I said and scrolled through the table of symbols until I found the one for home: New Spero.

Magnus helped Slate as they dragged the corners of the shield toward us. Suma looked at the glowing portal stone with concern.

"Dean, I've never heard of this happening before," she said. She would know, having grown up as the daughter of an important Gatekeeper. I suddenly wished Sarlun was with us. I could use his mastery of the portals.

As everyone stood there, waiting for me to hit the icon that would take us home, my hand shook as it hovered over the symbol. What if this didn't work? What if it killed Leonard? I had to know if I was right about the Theos. Was it worth the risk? I closed my eyes, the flashing light burning red behind my tight eyelids.

I had to know. I pressed the symbol.

I was stuck. Usually, I blinked and I was at my chosen destination. This time was different. I felt a struggle around me. I opened my eyes, but there was nothing to see. Not light, not darkness. Nothing. Panic raced through me, but it lasted only seconds.

One more breath, and I woke on the floor.

"Dean!" Slate stood over me, shaking my shoulders.

I tried to get up, but my head pounded so much I almost blacked out. "Enough, I'm fine."

"What did you see?" Slate asked me.

"Nothing. Absolutely nothing." The feeling of nothing around me sent a shiver down my spine. "Help me up."

We were in the portal room outside Terran Five.

"Captain, I made it," W said matter-of-factly.

I was leaning on Slate, my head still spinning when I heard Leonard's voice. "Guys, what happened?"

Suma ran to the containment shield, which had stayed active through the portal. "Is it you, Leonard?" she squawked, translating to English.

"I hope so. I don't remember... we were at the crystals...funny little animals." His eyes went wide, and his hands raced to his mouth. "Then it came at me. Is it gone?" He scrambled to the back corner of the shield and frantically looked around for the black mist.

It worked. "I think it's gone, Leonard."

"Wait, how do you know?" Magnus looked at me skeptically.

"Because I know how the portal stones are powered."

"You do?" Suma asked.

"Get him out of there. I'm sorry, Leonard, but I had to be sure."

Suma turned off the containment shield and went in, giving Leonard a big hug. "I'm glad you're okay."

He returned the hug. "I don't understand."

Every pair of eyes in the room was on me now. "The Theos. They're inside the stones. Part of them anyways. Their essence. It's the only explanation. We all know they created the portals, but no one really knows how or why they work."

I waited for someone to comment, and when no one did, I continued. "The Iskios were once flesh and blood, but they were contained on the crystal world as another state of matter. Even now I imagine their energy has created the Unwinding, which we can only make assumptions about.

"The Theos destroyed their counterpart and quickly realized they'd upset the balance. They created the portals and sacrificed themselves into them as a last gift to the galaxies."

"How did you know the Iskios wouldn't come with Leonard?" Suma asked.

I shrugged. "I didn't. It was all a hypothesis. When the stone began its alarm, I hoped it would work. I felt the fight before I came to. The Theos couldn't let the Iskios go."

"Look, the Larsk Two symbol is here now," Suma said. I went to her side, where the once-hidden symbol appeared, but in a muted gray color. Suma stood at the portal table, eyes wide. "And now it's gone."

I glanced back, only to see nothing where the symbol had been. My head still swam as I moved, but it was getting better by the minute.

"The symbol for Larsk Two. It's vanished," Suma said.

EIGHTEEN

Maggie licked my face, and I glanced out the window to see how high the red star was in the sky. It had to be afternoon, judging by the heat in my room and the angle of the light.

"Hey, girl. Aren't you a good puppy? I'm sorry I've been away so much. This will get better, I promise."

Maggie rolled around the bedding, her fuzzy ears dancing as she flopped from side to side. "I'm going to bring Mommy home, then we can finally be a family together." I thought of Mary and the child she was carrying, and felt the darkness threaten to cloud over my mind again. Instead of letting it, I trundled out of the blankets and hopped beside Maggie, giving her a ferocious belly rub, and kissed her on the top of the head.

She sneezed, shook, and jumped off the bed. She had me trained. I let her outside, and after my own bathroom pit stop, I made a pot of coffee. The tablet on the Theos sat on the table, and I fumbled through it, getting no more information than I had the first four times I'd sifted through it. It was garbage, nothing more than a pathetic distraction from the Supreme.

If I was going to get help from the Theos, I needed more than a child's guide to an ancient race. I needed to get to Bazarn Five. Maggie ate her kibble loudly beside me, and I pecked away at an overcooked fried egg, wishing Mary was there.

I caught a look of myself in a mirror on the adjacent wall as I got up to clean my dishes. My hand instantly went to my face, where a full beard had grown. It made me look older: angrier, somehow. I considered shaving it then but decided to keep the facial hair. I'd shave it when I found Mary, if she wanted me to.

The sides and chin were specked with gray hairs, some white, betraying my true age. When had my youth disappeared? I'd started this all in my mid-thirties, and I honestly wasn't even sure of my real age any longer. Somewhere around forty, I guessed. I could do the math, but my mind wasn't willing at the moment. I had too much else to do.

"Come on, Maggie; let's go for a walk." The cocker sprang to her feet and ran to me, jumping on my legs. "I know, I know. It's been a while. I'm sorry."

I tossed some pants on, and a standard-issue blue t-shirt made with pride at Terran Three, before slipping my runners onto my feet. I laughed to myself when I recalled all the times on our false journey to the Theos that I'd ended up with no shoes or boots on. "That must be how you feel every day, hey, Maggie?" She tilted her head at me, probably trying to decipher if I'd said anything about food.

"Come on." I opened the door for the dog, and she ran out to the front yard ahead of me. I didn't bother with a leash out here. The only time I did was when we brought her into town.

Our garden was overgrown with weeds, and I decided to hire someone to clean it up for us. Mary and I had built that together our first summer here, and I couldn't let it go. Large tomatoes grew on the left edge, and I stopped to peer into the thick plant to see heavy green ovals weighing it down. The smell of summer, dirt, and tomatoes threatened to overwhelm me with sorrow.

"I'm going to find you, Mary." I looked to the blue sky,

where thin wispy white clouds rolled by. "I'm going to bring you home."

Maggie barked, and I looked across the yard to see her urging me to join her. She had important things to smell, and I was keeping her from it. "I'm coming, I'm coming," I called, and she ran a circle around me, herding me.

The heat of the day made me sweat after less than half a mile, and I wished I'd brought some water with me. As Maggie sniffed around, I thought about the problem at hand. We needed the Theos. They had to be awoken to counter this Unwinding we knew so little about.

I was confident I was right. The Theos were inside the portal stones. But how many? Did each house one of the ancient race, or was there a collection of their energy powering each stone? How could I harness them from inside? When we'd tried to travel from Larsk Two with an Iskios inside Leonard, there had been a battle. If I was a gambling man, I had to say the Theos countered the Iskios, leaving the portal immobile, and that was why the symbol had disappeared.

Bazarn Five might contain the answers I needed. That was another large problem. I knew how to get there, but would I find roadblocks there too? I had no idea how far my title of Gatekeeper would get me.

I really didn't even know the best route. Even if I could somehow talk to a Theos hiding inside the portal stones, would they heed my call for help? I ran my hands through my hair in frustration. Getting angry now wasn't going to help me.

I pulled an earpiece from my pocket and pushed it into my ear. "Magnus, you there?" I asked, knowing his integrated comp-system would alert him that someone was trying to contact him.

I turned around, and Maggie ran ahead, heading back

home. Her tongue lolled to the side, and she looked back, a dog smile on her face.

Magnus' voice cut in. "Go ahead, Dean."

"Is the team ready?" I asked.

"The team's a go. We're ready when you are."

"Tonight we travel to Bazarn Five."

"Leonard, are you sure you're up for this?" I asked the young man.

"I think so. I want to help." He fidgeted with his glasses; his thick black hair bounced as he threw a pack on his shoulder.

"You've been through a lot. I don't want to ask any more of you."

"Dean, I'm fine. I'm just glad I could be of assistance."

"Assistance? Without you, we wouldn't have known about the portal stones," I suggested.

"You knew already," Leonard said.

I grabbed my pack, slinging it on my shoulder. "I had an inkling, a theory. You helped solve it. Either way, thanks."

Clare passed me the device. "I know I said it works, but its range is still limited, and I didn't have the real Mary around to test it with."

"You think I'll be able to find her with this?" I hefted the handheld cellphone-sized electronic piece in my right hand.

"Yes, but only when you're within range. It's set to constantly search her out, and it'll alert you when her DNA is nearby." Clare was staring straight into my eyes.

"How far is that?" I asked.

"It's hard to tell. I've only tested things on New Spero."

I didn't like her answer, but it was better than nothing. Worst case, it didn't work at all. No harm, no foul. "Thanks." I kissed her on the cheek, and she squeezed my arm.

"Bring her home, Dean," Clare said softly.

"I will." I made the promise, and I was going to keep it. "You going to be okay with W staying with you for a while?"

"Of course. He's quite the discovery. He's a very old model, apparently, but as the old saying goes, 'they don't build 'em like they used to.' We can learn from him."

I cringed. "Just take it easy on him. He's been through the wringer."

Clare gave me a surprised look that turned into a small smile. "He's in the best hands. Take care of yourself, Dean."

"I will," I said quietly before bellowing, "Everyone ready?"

A lander flew in the sky, lowering toward our position. "Who the hell is that?" Magnus asked, using his hand as a visor as he stared at the incoming vessel.

It set down on the gravel near the portal caverns outside Terran Five, and a familiar figure stepped down as the door hissed open.

Magnus rushed over to her. "Natalia, is everything okay?"

Slate came and stood beside me as we watched the married couple.

They spoke in hushed tones, their body language saying they were knee deep in an argument. This went on for a couple of minutes, and we did our best to mind our business. At the end of it, Nat and Magnus were walking toward us, a resigned look covering Magnus' normally neutral face.

"Guess who's coming with us?" he asked, stating the obvious.

"Glad to have you, Nat." I knew she wouldn't leave her kids behind if she didn't feel this was necessary, so I didn't press the subject.

"She's my friend too. More than that. She's my sister. We were all reborn that day when we met, and we're family. All of us." Tears formed at her eyes, and I embraced her, getting a firm hug back from her. "We'll find her, Dean." She whispered the last in my ear, as if it was a secret between the two of us.

"You know we'll make it happen," I said, and Magnus glanced at me before giving me a wide smile.

A while later, we stood in the portal room. I took a head count. Leonard was there, nervously moving around the space; Magnus and Natalia stood next to each other, the ever-formidable pair. Slate finished off the crew, my ever-loyal buddy, like the younger brother I never had but knew I couldn't live without.

"Sarlun going to be ready?" Slate asked.

"He better be. It's time we finished this, once and for all." I scrolled through the tabletop screen; the portal stone glowed hot and bright. When I found the symbol for Shimmal, I took one last look at my friends. I was grateful for the support and help from each and every one of them. I hoped we made it out of this unscathed.

I tapped the icon, and white light enveloped us.

NINETEEN

Suma slumped in her white chair. "I'm sorry I can't come."

"It's okay," I told her. "I can't believe your father let you come last time."

"It's not fair. Did you tell him how much I helped last time?" she prodded.

I had, and I told her so.

"Then why? Why won't he let me come?" she asked.

"Suma, that's for him to know." The fact that Sarlun had let Suma join us on a mission to the crystal world but wouldn't let her come to Bazarn Five worried me. Just how dangerous was this "luxurious" world? There was so much about the universe I didn't know, and I couldn't help but feel I was about to walk barefoot into a snake pit.

"Take this." Suma looked around the room, seeing we were still alone. Her wide black eyes scanned the corners, checking if the cameras were on us. They were pointed away in their constantly rotating pattern.

I palmed the gift and slid it into a pocket, sensing she wanted me to keep it between us. "What is it?"

"It's a recorder. Set it on any physical book, and it will record everything inside digitally, allowing you to translate or decode whatever you need. I thought it might come in handy."

"Where did you get this?" I asked, thinking how valuable it might be on a world with the largest library and encyclopedia in the known universe.

"From Father's room." Her gaze cut through her quiet words. "Don't tell."

Sarlun had a room full of amazing artifacts from hundreds or thousands of worlds. It only made sense he'd have cataloged them, and that Suma would have access.

"Thank you, Suma." I didn't know what else to say. "I don't know what I'd do without you."

She beamed at that, and the door opened. Sarlun entered, wearing a pristine white suit with the Gatekeepers' logo on it: a portal stone with two spears crossing over it. I'd never seen any Gatekeeper with the actual weapon before, but the point was made.

"Let us depart. Suma, you'll enjoy your week at our second home."

Suma looked down at her feet. "Yes, Father."

"Chin up, Su." Slate put an arm around the small Shimmali girl, and she looked up at him begrudgingly. "We'll be back before you know it, and we'll have you over for a holiday. Right, Dean?"

"Of course," I said, and Suma rushed me, giving me a hug before leaving us in the portal room with her father.

Sarlun didn't comment that his daughter had avoided a hug with him. He passed me a bag. "Dean, it would be prudent for you to change as well."

I looked down at the same T-shirt and shorts I'd been wearing all day. The others were in New Spero jumpsuits, and I took the offered clothing from Sarlun, heading to the corner to change. When I was done, I caught a glimpse of myself in the shiny metal door. I didn't recognize myself with the graying beard and white suit.

"Looking spiffy, boss." Slate picked up our bags and hauled them to the portal table.

"Everyone ready?" Sarlun asked, tapping at the table.

"*Da*," Nat said, and we all agreed.

I didn't know a lot about Bazarn Five, except that the wealthiest of the wealthy went there to trade antiquities, shop, vacation, gamble, and to learn from the library. I'd seen opulence when I'd visited Europe after graduating school, but our lives had become simple on New Spero.

I wasn't prepared for the onslaught of beauty when I opened my eyes after being transported by the portal.

It was unlike any portal room I'd visited before. The ceilings were at least thirty feet tall; giant pillars carved from what looked like golden marble supported the ornate carved display above. My gaze lingered on the images of worlds on the ceiling, carved and painted with the most stunning color palette I'd even seen. I had to believe some of the tones had never been duplicated on Earth, and I was speechless at the exhibition.

"Wow," Slate said from behind me.

"Yeah, wow is right." I broke my stare to look forward at the armed guards approaching. There were four of them, encased in formidable golden armor. This world certainly had a specific feel to it.

The guards had four arms, each appearing powerful, but the more impressive thing was their height. I couldn't tell when they were across the room, but as they neared, I saw they had to be at least eight feet tall, towering over Magnus and Slate as if they were children. They wore helmets that left their faces open. Small eyes assessed us over short, thick noses. Their skin was dark, gold flecks either naturally present or painted on.

They all stopped a few yards from us, and one stepped forward. He spoke, revealing sparkling white teeth.

"Greetings, Sarlun of Shimmal," he said in the Shimmali tongue, and his welcome translated for us.

"Greetings be upon you." Sarlun handed the guard a

small disk.

The armored giant scanned it, handed it back, and then smiled a toothy grin. "Welcome to Bazarn Five," he said, this time in English, before eyeing us each suspiciously. He apparently took a special interest in seeing a human in a Gatekeeper uniform, and I wondered how he possibly could have spoken our language. But after a few moments of scrutiny, he smiled again and waved us in. "You can never be too careful. We're under high alert here."

Sarlun was walking ahead of us now. I grabbed my bag and hurried to hear their conversation.

"Why's that?" Sarlun asked.

"Someone sent pirates after one of Garo Alnod's vessels." The guard led us down the portal room, and as I listened, I observed. The carvings and paintings continued down the long room, impressing me to a new level with each passing frame. At the end of the room, a painting of a colorful wormhole lightly swirled as we walked toward it. The center appeared to be the exit.

"That's not surprising. I hear his ships are often a target."

"This time, his daughter and her paramour were on it," the guard said, pausing at the doorway.

"What happened?" Sarlun asked, his eyes wide.

"The ship was found destroyed, Rivo taken hostage."

It finally clued in. "Rivo?" I set a hand out palm down just over my hips. "About this tall? Blue?"

Sarlun and the guard turned slowly to me. "What do you know about it?" Sarlun asked.

"Remember I told you about getting boarded by pirates?"

Sarlun nodded slowly. Magnus moved behind me, a laugh building in his enormous chest.

"You're not saying it was you who freed her from the

confines of those pirates, are you?" the guard asked in perfect English. I realized then he must have a built-in translator. The things the wealthy could do.

I shifted uncomfortably under the huge alien's gaze. "Kind of."

"Kind of? She told her mother and father she was saved by a skinny pale being. That could be you," he said, and Magnus barked out a laugh.

"Guilty as charged." I waved a dismissive hand in the air, as if to put it behind us.

"She also said the being was offered riches, but all it wanted was for her to blow the pirate's power stealing units up. Is this true?" The other guards stood around us now, all intent on my words.

"That's right. We helped each other. Without her breaking us free from their energy drain, we couldn't have escaped. Look, can we get moving? I have some important business here, and every minute we're delayed could mean something bad happens." I stepped forward, hoping the guards would let me pass through. They didn't.

"Hold it. Was that a threat?" Two huge gloved hands pushed against my chest, stopping me in my tracks.

"Surely not. He's not familiar with the ways on Bazarn. Let us enter, and we'll keep to ourselves," Sarlun said. He slipped the disk out of his own pocket and placed it on his palm. The guard shrugged and scanned it again, this time with a smaller device.

"You may pass but be careful. There's something brewing in our midst. A rival house may be making a move against the Alnods. We're doing everything we can to ensure no harm comes to them, or to anyone else on Bazarn Five, but we're dealing with cunning and very wealthy beings here." They moved out of our way. "And leave your weapons in your bags, out of sight. It won't do you any good getting picked up by the Protectors."

I had a feeling my foot might get caught in my mouth a few times on Bazarn, so I had to ensure my safety. "How can I reach Rivo? Is she here?"

"She's here. Arrived by this very portal two cycles ago. Your Gatekeeper will know how to reach her parents." With that, we walked into the center of the wormhole painted on the wall. I passed through a containment field, sensing an energy buzz around me.

"They imprint everyone entering their world," Sarlun said after he passed through the barrier.

We might as well have traveled through a wormhole, because I felt like I had to be on another world. We were inside a gargantuan cavern. The portals were almost always found underground, and I thought about the Theos powering this portal. Did it know the luxury it was surrounded by, or was it no longer aware of anything at all? Was there more than one inside it?

The cavern was quiet, though there were a couple dozen various beings lingering about it.

Images of the world above shone on the flat walls of the cave to our left, showing videos of tourist destinations. In the span of two minutes, I saw a video stream of small ships racing over calm green waters, a hike up a tall thin mountain with clouds hung halfway up it, and a group of round orange beings played in a floating swimming pool above a lush rainforest.

I couldn't even register half of what I was seeing. It came in flashes and made my head spin.

"Where are we?" Natalia asked, her voice quiet and full of awe.

"We're not in New Spero anymore, hey, Auntie Em?" Magnus joked.

"I, for one, need to see those ship races. Now that's

something Mary would – " Slate cut himself off.

I was getting annoyed, but I told myself they had my back. Just because they were impressed with the traps of this rich world, that didn't mean they weren't here to do a job and leave.

Sarlun, sensing the tension, stepped forward. "Dean, let's go to the surface. We have rooms waiting."

I looked to his pocket. "Sarlun, what's on that disk?"

"Creds, of course."

"You paid to get here?"

He shook his head, his long snout waving back and forth slowly. "No. We got here by the portals. I paid to get past the guards. There's a difference."

"And the second time?" I asked, lifting an eyebrow in curiosity.

"That was for the guard's patience. He'll keep an eye out for us, and should we need protecting while we're here, he'll answer my call."

"How many times have you been here?" Natalia asked the Gatekeeper.

"A few. I can't afford it often, nor can I afford most activities here."

That surprised me. From everything I'd seen, Sarlun was as well off as a Shimmali could be. Just how many creds did someone need to vacation here?

We carried on, heading across the ornate stone floor to wide sweeping steps ahead. Statues rose from the end of each step, all taller than me, each portraying a different race.

As I was about to step on the first stair, a purple being appeared before me with a pop. Energy swirled around her before dissipating. Slate pushed me out of the way, ready to protect me from an assault. He fumbled for a pulse rifle that wasn't strapped to him, since it was inside his pack.

"Easy, young one," Sarlun said. "Greetings. We'll be staying at the Peaks. Thank you." He turned to us, frowning. "Set your bags down. They'll bring them to our rooms."

I thought of the device Suma had gifted me and was glad I'd left it in my pocket. I didn't want anyone going through my belongings and getting their hands on it. We placed our packs on the ground before the newcomer.

"Greetings, Gatekeeper." The purple being was stunning. Her long legs were casually hidden under a flowing pink dress, complementing her skin tone. Her six arms were thin, flowing before her like a harp player in midsong. Large blue eyes glinted in her oval-shaped face; wispy white hair hung past her narrow shoulders. "Your possessions shall be in your dwelling as specified. Enjoy your stay on Bazarn. May your trip fill you with incomparable dreams." With that, the air popped again, and she was gone, along with our bags.

"That's one hell of a busboy," Magnus said, getting an elbow from Natalia.

"Welcome to Bazarn Five, everyone," Sarlun said, urging Leonard forward up the stairs.

We walked up no more than five steps when I noticed the energy field ahead. Sarlun walked through it first, disappearing from our view.

Slate grabbed my arm and lifted a finger. "Let's go at the same time. I don't want an ambush."

"Honestly, who's going to ambush us here? No one even knows us." I strode up and through the field, stepping down on an unfamiliar pavilion near a busy street.

As if on cue, before I could get my bearings, someone slammed into me, knocking me hard to the ground.

TWENTY

I lay there, a body on top of me. It struggled to loosen itself from our entanglement, but I held on, not letting the perpetrator get away. Slate was there now, standing like an angry statue above us. He bent down, picking up the attacker with one hand.

"What do we have here?" he asked the wriggling alien.

A series of rushed words translated in our earpieces. "It accident. In the way."

I got a look at the wiry alien. It was thin, with the face of a rodent and a flickering tail to match that swung behind it, uneasy in Slate's firm grip.

Magnus walked up, giving me his hand, and I hopped back on my feet, wiping dust off my white suit. "Dean, you better check your pockets."

I patted them. "Why?"

"Because this is the oldest trick in the book. It seems some things translate universally. A pickpocket hangs out in the busy promenade, waiting for an unsuspecting rich tourist to pop out of the caverns below. When the prey appears, he knocks them over. 'Oops. Sorry. I'm just a clumsy kid.' And you're down five hundred bucks and an engraved lighter."

"It sounds like you know this from experience," Leonard said lightly.

"Could be. Natalia may or may not have witnessed it," Magnus said, looking sideways at Nat.

"But you didn't have a Slate around to catch the kid then," Nat said.

"It's gone," I whispered. The device Suma had given me wasn't in my pocket, where I'd left it for safekeeping.

"Hand it over," Slate said, lifting the rodent thief higher.

"I don't have," the rodent said.

I finally got a look around us and couldn't help but be reminded of a futuristic Times Square. Sky-high towers rose in every direction, reflecting stunning sunlight with a purple hue. The ground was golden even here, apparently a color the people running Bazarn couldn't get enough of. People of all kinds milled about, and now a few of them made way for two figures approaching us.

"What is the problem?" one asked. It spoke an unknown language to me, but my translator still allowed me to communicate.

"This thief took something from me. Knocked me down," I said. Slate lowered the perp to the ground but kept a firm grasp on its shirt.

The newcomers were dressed in black cloaks, their faces hidden from sight. I saw a badge of sorts on their left breast. These must be the Protectors the guards had mentioned.

"What did she take?"

"*She* took something of value to me. Small device. It has to be on her." I pointed at the rodent's pockets and the small pack on her back.

"Fine. Here," the attacker said, deftly flipping the gift from Suma between crooked clawed fingers.

"Come with us." Slate relinquished his hold on the rodent to the Protector, and they hauled her away, but not before offering a word of wisdom. "Watch your backs. There is always something looking to do wrong, even in paradise." He tossed the device in the air, and I caught it, quickly slipping it to another pocket.

His last words were said with a hint of sarcasm, and I wondered how safe this world was going to be. It reminded me of Volim, the Padlog home world. Above ground, everything seemed elegant and innocuous, but there was a seedy underbelly, like in every city, in every country, and now on every world.

There were others in the promenade, appearing from thin air and looking around with wonder. Beings of all shapes and sizes: some were corporeal, while others looked to spend only part of their existence on the same plane as us, as they vanished and appeared at will.

Lines of small ships formed at the end of the square, and Sarlun led us to one. Smells of every nature hit me as we crossed the way, and I was surprised to see food stations set up along the other side to the promenade.

"Food trucks? At Bazarn?" I asked Sarlun.

He shrugged. "They recently wanted to cater the experience to the well-off. Most of them won't travel to their own world's city centers, so they built a safe version filled with the sights and smells of over a dozen major shareholders' worlds."

I was about to remind him I'd been mugged two seconds into my trip but didn't bother. Maybe that was part of the experience. Leonard looked around, and I saw him making mental notes for his comic series. The kid was always thinking of his big cover shot, and it inspired me. He was still doing something he loved, even among the chaos of our new lives.

Nat and Magnus stayed ahead of us now, seeming to know our destination. Only Slate stuck close to me, his watchful eyes scanning every alien we walked by.

We neared the ships, and Sarlun went to speak to one

of them. We were then ushered into a shiny golden transport vessel, its gullwing doors opened on either side to let us in. It reminded me of a minivan with wings.

Sarlun tweeted something I didn't hear, and we were off. I sat at the window, curiously staring out at the square below. Smoke from the restaurants poured into the sky, hundreds of people moved from point to point like ants, and I saw it for what it was. The whole area was walled in. Within the walls of Bazarn's entrance was the city feel, but as we lifted above and away from it, I saw the real Bazarn.

Lush green landscape carried for as far as the eye could see to the left; widespread hotels ran along impressive bodies of water. Huge trees rose from the ground, so high we had to lift up in the transport vessel to avoid one. Nestled above the ground was an intricate city among the trees. Streets led from one tree to the next; lights were on inside round windows cut into the hollowed-out tops.

I knew I didn't have time to do sightseeing, but the young Dean inside me wanted to spend a night there, with nothing but three hundred feet of air between me and the ground. The ultimate tree fort. It would be a quiet paradise with Mary at my side. I shook the thoughts away and focused on the impending reality before me.

To my right, I peered over Natalia and Magnus, seeing a yellow-gold desert. Sand carried forever, its undulating dunes mesmerizing. The only respite from the sand was occasional resorts, their floating swimming pools showing rare water among the dry landscape. Just how many biomes did this world have?

"We're not far," Sarlun said.

"Quite the place," Magnus said from beside me.

"It is. I wonder where we're staying?" I asked. Sarlun hadn't told us much about our arrangements, just that he'd take care of it. We hadn't had a lot of time between getting home and coming here, so it was a whirlwind. I hadn't even told Sarlun about my Theos theory yet.

The transport started to lower as we passed the borders of both the desert and the lush tree city, and entered a rocky scene. White-tipped mountains rose from the ground before us, incrementally getting larger the deeper we flew into the region. They reminded me of shark teeth, and I had the feeling we could easily get eaten on Bazarn.

"This is it," Sarlun said from the front of the vessel.

"This?" Slate asked from the back.

We lowered toward the tip of a huge mountain. As we got closer, I saw the building hidden on the side of the peak. It was carved out of the curve of the mountains, and as the sun was lowering behind the far side of the crag, lights were turning on to highlight the natural beauty of the lodging.

The ship settled on a flat outcropping in front of the complex, and the doors opened simultaneously.

Without preamble, we exited and watched the ship rise into the sky, leaving us behind atop the mountain.

Two lumbering shapes headed toward us, and the ground shook slightly with each step.

"What are those?" Slate said under his breath. Only Sarlun didn't look concerned by them.

"They work here. The Peaks of Duup are legendary, and when their star threatened to die, they were transported here. The Duupa came with them," Sarlun said.

The Duupa arrived, and I looked up to their towering ten feet. They were half again as wide, and they looked to be cut from stone themselves.

When one spoke, it sounded like gravel rubbing against pebbles. "Greetings. Welcome to the Peaks at Bazarn. Can we assist with anything?"

The low grumbling speech translated for us, this time

from small speakers on their belts. I was still amazed they had our language in their system, or that their software could recognize us as human. Sarlun had explained that once he'd loaded it into his database, it was shared with countless other worlds.

The Duupas' heads seemed to melt into their shoulders, which gave the appearance of an absent neck. They wore thin gray outfits; the uniforms rested loosely but were unable to hide their tree-trunk legs and bulky chests.

"We're fine," Sarlun said. "Our things are inside already."

"Anything else before settling in?" they asked as another transport vessel sat down behind us.

"Can you send me details on the Eklack hours? We have some work to do this week." Sarlun stepped forward, and the two hosts separated, creating a path.

"Of course, sir. They will be in your rooms. Please don't hesitate to buzz, should you need it." The larger of the two passed Sarlun a tiny pen-shaped object. "Have a wonderful stay at the Peaks."

Four beings fell out of the vessel behind us, thick smoke following behind them. They were furry, with no faces or eyes in sight, and wore something akin to brown leather on their bodies. Each of them held a bottle of pink liquid, and judging by their inability to stand straight, they were here to party.

We turned and walked toward the hotel. It was amazing, and I forced myself to remember why we were here. I needed to find everything I could about the Theos, and more importantly, about the portal stones. They were the key I needed to solve our nightmare. Mary was out there, waiting for me to retrieve her. I knew it.

I walked behind our group, wondering how many suites must be in the place. It was at least a mile wide, but

I had no way of knowing how deep it went. The ground changed from black slate to patterned rocks, indicating a pathway to the hotel's lobby. Massive stone pillars were cut out of the rock face, the same symbol repeatedly carved into each pillar. It must have been the portal symbol for Duup. I wondered if it was still there, or if the star had destroyed the world after all. Had the Theos inhabiting the stone died with the world?

Wide terraces were cut into the front of each suite, and even from here, I could see unknown beings standing on them, admiring the view as a family.

Before we entered the Peaks, I spun around, catching the breathtaking vision. I'd been so hung up on the hotel that I hadn't taken the time to look in the other direction. With the sun behind the mountain we stood on, the valleys below were dusky. A large flowing river wound below, looking like a tiny garter snake from this vantage point. Other buildings were etched into the various mountains around us; some had lights on, smoke pouring from chimneys. I imagined the Duupa lived among them, a race without a home planet any longer.

We had something in common.

"Dean, you coming?" Slate urged from the doorway.

I ran to catch up and patted my young friend on the back as I passed him. The air was thin and cool up here, reminding me of the time I'd been up the crater on Maui.

Another giant Duupa greeted us and led us through the lobby, which was lit by torches on the walls, and down a hall wide and tall enough for their race to easily maneuver through. I looked at Slate and Magnus and thought how happy they must be to finally be somewhere with ample room for their large frames.

"Here you are." Gravel spilled out as words as the Duupa opened the door to the suite on the left and scanned each of our hands with a device. "You will each have room access now, and also to our amenities. May I recommend the hot stone meditation?" He glanced at Natalia, who did her best not to scowl at him.

I knew Nat just wanted to get the information we came for and get out of there. It was all over her face. She wore her emotions on her sleeve, and when it came to battle, it was all anger.

We all entered the double-wide doorway, and then the room. I'd expected it to resemble a cavern like the lobby, but inside, it was like something out of a palace. Polished gray stone floors led to an open room full of shelving stocked with art from around the universe. A circular fireplace sat in the center of the area, a low flame glowing hot already. There were chairs and cushioned seats atop pieces of carved rock.

"Everyone has their own room," Sarlun said. "Go refresh yourselves if needed, and we'll make a plan."

I grabbed my pack and picked the room farthest from the living space, and laughed at how universal our needs were. I threw the bag on the soft bed and spotted a shower capsule, as well as some sort of universal toilet. It appeared it would cater to any sanitary needs an alien might have. I hoped there was a manual on the thing, because it was already calling my name. I spent a couple minutes struggling with it before relieving myself.

The day had been long, and I was happy to have a home base on this elaborate world. I decided to change clothing for the evening and shut the door.

I jumped back at the small blue form hiding behind it.

TWENTY-ONE

"What the hell are you trying to do, kill me?" I asked the short girl. It translated into her native Molariun.

"Dean, I need your help," Rivo said as her four clear-white eyes blinked at the same time.

I stepped back and took a seat on the pillowy bed. It was so soft, I sank backward into it. "How did you know I was here?"

She tapped the side of her hairless head, and though there was no visible ear, I assumed that was what she was pointing at. She meant she was listening.

"Okay, so you found out I was here. Why sneak into my room?"

"Something bad is happening. I have no one I can trust. You… when I heard you arrived, I knew I had to bring it to you. Everyone's always wanted something from me. Being the eldest daughter of Garo Alnod brings a lot of attention, and not always in a good way."

She still wasn't making sense, and she was testing my already frazzled patience. "Tell me what you need."

She looked shocked at my tone. "I hear rumors my father is going to be attacked at the Eklack."

"What's the Eklack?" I said the word and recognized it as the same place Sarlun had mentioned outside.

"Bazarn Five is home to the largest gathered secrets in the universe. That's the Eklack. Do you live under a rock?" she asked, her thin mouth twitching into a grin.

I couldn't have the library getting shot up just before I found what I needed from it. Once again, I felt like my timing was more than a fluke. I resolved to hear her out and get to this Eklack as soon as possible to start searching it.

"How do you know he's going to be attacked? Actually" – I went to the door and opened it, walking into the hall beyond – "come with me. Let's include everyone."

She looked admonished that I wanted to share her plight with anyone. "If you trust me, you can trust each and every one of them," I assured her.

"Who're you talking to?" Natalia asked. She was already back in the living room, sitting on the rock sofa, where she held a clear tablet.

"Guys, this is Rivo." I looked behind me, and she wasn't there. "Come on out."

The short blue girl hesitantly stepped into the hall. I recalled hearing her aboard the pirate ship before I saw her. Her song had been so lovely, so poignant and sad. I also remembered that her significant other had been killed by the pirates sent to find her father's riches. In that instant, the confidant woman she was becoming was hidden beneath a frail outer shell. She was really scared.

"Hi, Rivo. I'm Magnus, and just so you know, I had a hand in ending a couple of those pirates when they boarded us. Thanks for shooting us free of their grasp." He hulked over the girl and stuck his hand out. It was clearly an unfamiliar gesture. She grabbed his thumb and shook it.

"That's good to hear, and you're welcome. I would have done anything for my hero. I was going to die on that terrible ship." Rivo entered the living room and nervously looked around.

"What is it that has you so on edge?" I asked her.

Sarlun entered, and I introduced her to the Gatekeeper. "I've met your parents before," he said. "Curious. How did you find Dean Parker?"

"One of the guards is on my payroll. I like to know who comes and goes. Someone mentioned my name and said he was looking for me. When he described you, I knew there could be no other human searching for me." She fidgeted with a purple gemstone around her neck. I felt for my own pendant under my shirt. It was still there.

"What can we do to help you?" Slate asked from the edge of the couch. Leonard was beside him, sketching on a notepad.

"And who wants to do your father harm?" Sarlun added.

"Who doesn't? He's always being threatened. But after we were attacked, and Nico… killed, the rivalry is only getting stronger." Tears formed in her four glistening eyes.

"Who's the rival?" Sarlun was standing, his posture telling me he would know the enemy of her father.

"Lom of Pleva." The second it took the translation to pass to Sarlun's Shimmali language was enough to change Sarlun's face. His snout twitched in surprise and his black eyes widened.

"Lom of Pleva is dead!" he shouted, his voice sterner than I'd ever heard it.

"No, he's not. He's back. Father doesn't believe the rumors, though."

"Okay, okay. Who or what is a Lom of Pleva?" Magnus asked.

Sarlun stalked across the room and tapped a screen on the wall. Part of the partition slid open, revealing over twenty bottles of all shapes, sizes, and colors. He took a blue crystal glass and splashed in some orange liquor. He downed it in one fell swoop and poured another.

"Who is Lom, Sarlun?" I asked more forcefully than Magnus' playful tone.

Sarlun's back was still to us. "He's a ghost. If there's anyone wealthier than young Rivo's father, Lom is it."

"So does every rich guy out here have to be an evil genius or something?" Slate asked from the couch.

Sarlun ignored him. "Lom's had a hand in many bad things. Things that may even have affected you and your race," he said.

My pulse raced at his words. "How?" I asked slowly.

"Hybrids. He funded the technology. Call it a pet project." He shook his head side to side and downed his second drink. "I was one of the few to see the images of his early cross-DNA projects. The horror he created. Those poor creatures. Did you ever think to wonder how the Kraski got human DNA for their plan?"

I shook my head. Truth was, I hadn't given it much thought. There had always seemed to be something more pressing happening.

"Lom spent years stealing samples from most inhabited worlds." Sarlun poured another one.

"You're telling us some of those ramblings about flying saucers stealing drunks out of cornfields could have been true?" Slate asked.

Sarlun nodded now, confirming Slate's question.

"You're serious? He took unsuspecting victims from Earth?" I thought of the models they'd cloned. Janine had been made after the image of a woman this Lom had stolen from Earth. Who had she been?

"And many more worlds. Many." Sarlun finally turned to us, and I saw something I hadn't seen in Sarlun's dark eyes before.

Fear.

"You say he's dead?" I asked, pressing the subject.

"Supposedly," Rivo cut in. "The story goes, he was visiting a lorgonium mine, and there was an accident while he was there. Lorgonium isn't the most stable metal and can react unpredictably when around oxygen. Somehow a leak occurred, and the rest is history."

"And no one has seen him since?" Magnus asked.

Sarlun answered. "Unless Rivo knows something I don't, no."

"His fingerprints are all over this. That pirate ship was full of his old junk. I saw his logo plastered on half of the garbage lying around the place. The robots come from his manufacturing plant. It's him." Rivo went to the bar and poured herself a drink.

"Are you sure you should be doing that?" I asked.

"I've been of age for some time, junior," she said, and the room chuckled at her jab.

"Then I'll take one too." She passed me a green drink, and I sniffed it before throwing it down the hatch. It started off smooth, but soon a fire was growing in my stomach.

"Why target your father?" Natalia prompted.

"They've always been rivals, ever since they were children. Father outbid him on a tech company a long time ago, and the product turned out to have extremely valuable uses." Rivo sipped her drink.

"Like what?" Leonard chimed in.

"You know the hyperdrives that get everyone around the galaxy?" She paused. "They make up ninety-nine-point-nine percent of the population's interstellar transportation."

We all nodded. "There's a piece in there that kept burning up under the heat and made the drives burn out too fast, or made the engines implode and killed the ship's inhabitants. It only happened once in a while, but that was enough to make every fleet owner want the improvement."

I cringed. That wasn't good. "Your father bought the company that made them?"

"Only Lom didn't know at the time of bidding, and my father had some inside information. An executive liked the idea of a condo on Bazarn Five more than the agreement they had within the company. When it solved a major issue, my father became the wealthiest individual in the universe." Rivo didn't look pleased with him; she looked worried.

"That's a big target to have. How long ago was this?" I asked.

"Three hundred cycles of Bazarn," she said.

I assumed a cycle would account for far less than an Earth year. Otherwise, that would make him a very old man.

"Sarlun, how long is that?" I began.

"In your years? About two hundred and fifty."

I spat my drink out mid-sip. "You mean that?"

Sarlun smiled. "Yes. They live to be five hundred or so, give or take a few decades or years."

"Once again, I hate to ask, but what do you expect me to do about this?" I asked, wishing I hadn't downed the drink. My vision was blurring; my tongue felt too fat for my mouth.

"Meet with him. Tell him what you saw on the pirate ship. He'll believe you, especially since you're a Gatekeeper too," Rivo said.

"I don't have time for this. The Iskios are back. Do you know who they are?" I stood, my voice rising to a higher volume than I intended.

"Some evil name from bedtime stories, I suppose," she said.

"No. They're very real, and they have my wife. The

Unwinding is real, and I need to know what that means. I need to find her. I have to find the Theos." The last was said quietly, and all four of her eyes went wide.

"Help me, and I'll return the favor. If anyone knows about the ancient gods that roamed our universe, it's Regnig." Rivo handed me a small coin.

"Who's Regnig?" I asked her.

"The Eklack is for the general population, at least those wealthy enough to be admitted. Historians, scholars, or priests. I've heard most of the knowledge gathered there is accurate, but there are certain things no one should know about. At least, that's what Father says. Regnig runs a section of the library no one may see."

Sarlun perked up. His back went rail-straight, a cautioning hand reached out to Rivo.

"And you can get me access there?" I asked.

She nodded. "Speak with my father, and you will get access."

What choice did I have? "What's this?" I held my palm out, the small metal coin in the middle of my hand.

"Access to the gala tomorrow. Tell the transport you're to join the Alnods. They'll bring you to the gala. And Dean?" she prompted.

"Yes?"

"Wear the uniform and come alone." She turned and walked from the room, leaving us in the living space, bewildered at our next step.

TWENTY-TWO

"*I* hope this isn't a big waste of time." I looked in the mirror, and Natalia brushed a hair off my white uniform's sleeve.

"She seemed certain this Regnig was the sure bet to help you find what you're seeking," Nat said, doing her best to smile at me. "I wish we could help more."

It all felt contrived. This whole world was putting me on edge. I didn't want to spend my time dressing up for a gala; I wanted to get off the planet, find the Theos, and bring the battle to the Iskios. But I understood that sometimes we had to take small steps. Bit by bit, a little became a lot.

"I know. I'm just frustrated, but you're helping by being here. By going to find any clue that will help us. Mary would be glad you're here, Nat." I ran a hand over my beard, trying to straighten the hairs with a mind of their own.

"Thanks, Dean." Nat smiled in the mirror's reflection, and I gave her a smile back. Truth was, even though they didn't feel like it, I was eternally grateful for their support.

"We'll be at the library today. Don't worry, Dean." The ever-vigilant Leonard sat there, a tablet in his lap. "Anything about the Theos, the Iskios, the Unwinding…"

I cut him off. "And most importantly?"

"The portal stones. What they are, when they first started appearing, and where the stone originates," Slate said, finishing the answer. "Dean, we know all this. Don't worry about it. We'll get what we need. Your job is to talk to Rivo's dad, get on his good side, get a one-way ticket to the librarian dude, and learn anything else you can."

He was right. "Thanks, guys. I'd better get going."

The gala was starting at midday, and we'd already wasted enough time talking through our plan this morning. Everyone was dressed and ready to go.

"Sarlun, you're sure you can get them access, right?" Our plan hinged on this.

"Yes. It will be done." Sarlun reached out, his thick hand on my shoulder. "Be careful, son."

"I will."

"And keep your earpiece in. We want to be able to get in touch," Magnus reiterated.

I left the room but hated to separate from my friends on this strange world. Slate had argued with me for a good hour at breakfast about being foolish for going anywhere without him by my side. He wasn't wrong, but Rivo had told me to come alone, and I wasn't going to risk losing the chance at speaking with this Regnig character.

The coin sat in my folded hand, my firm grip making a circular indent on my palm. I walked through the halls, into the lobby, and outside, without so much as seeing anything around me. I was distracted, staring off at nothing until one of the Duupa asked me if I needed something.

"Transportation to Garo Alnod's gala," I said, and soon a small ship lowered before me. I finally paid attention to my surroundings. Bazarn's star was high in the sky, and a light layer of sweat covered my lip, even at this high altitude. I attributed some of it to nerves.

The door on the vessel opened, and I got in. The ship was empty, but the Duupa stuck its head in, letting the robotic pilot know I was joining the Alnods. The ship rose into the sky, zooming away. The windows on the ship were tinted, keeping glare out. A few other transport ships raced around us as we headed for our destination.

Something else caught my eye in the air. It started out as a speck in the distance, but soon I saw the being for what it was. Huge wings flapped effortlessly, pushing the bird-like creature on nearly as quickly as us. It had bright colorful feathers and a smooth pointy orange beak, and was three times the length of the transport I was inside.

When we were past the amazing flying bird, I looked down to see yet another type of landscape below. Thousands of small islands speckled a blue-green body of water. We lowered, but not all the way to the water level. Instead we stayed around half a mile above, heading for a floating island. Soft blue thrusters burned below it, and the ship landed on the left side of the area. From my current vantage point, the island had to be a few square miles in size.

Only a man with Garo Alnod's prosperity would have the ego or funds to have a floating island on Bazarn Five. I imagined the islands in the water below were filled with rich dignitaries from numerous worlds, but none at the level Garo would accept. He needed to float above them. This told me a lot about the man, and I wasn't even sure if I could fault him for it. Would I do any different in his shoes?

"Thank you," I told the robotic pilot, who didn't even have a body. Force of habit.

I stepped off and was in a parking lot. Dozens of personal ships were landed in clean lines. One lowered to my right, and a three-headed reptile being came out, allowing a short blue valet inside his ship. He barked an order or two my translator didn't quite catch and stalked off between the ships toward what could only be called a palace.

At least a dozen golden spires adorned the roof of the

structure. Parapets ran along the many balconies on the side of the palace, while people mingled outside, drinks in their hands, claws, or whatever else they had for appendages. I felt alone and out of my element as I followed Three-head down the path. He turned and looked at me with all six eyes before flicking a tongue from the left head and grunting something with the right.

Beings of every color and shape stood by the entrance, some chatting in their own languages. My translator was going into overdrive, trying to identify too many things at once, and I flipped it off, happier to just hear the noises for once. A robed Padlog walked in front of me and entered, handing the hulking guard his coin.

I followed suit, passing the armored guard my token of invitation, and he waved me inside. The ceiling was tall: three stories high, and floating escalators rose to the upper levels on either side of the room. Opaque-skinned creatures with no arms or legs hovered by, with drink trays somehow upright beside them. One stopped by me, and I noticed it had no eyes either. With a slight hesitation, I took something that resembled champagne and said thank you.

It kept moving, stopping at the next approaching guest. I felt hundreds of eyes on me as I stepped deeper into the room. Presumably most of them had never seen or heard of a human before, and I was making quite the spectacle. It was odd to think that *I* was the outsider in a room full of aliens.

I heard a familiar voice cut through the chatter and saw Rivo wave in greeting. She was wearing a coral orange dress, a striking contrast to her dark blue skin.

I turned my translator on and keyed it to her language only. "Hello, Rivo."

Rivo blinked nervously. "Dean. Come. Let's get out of this crowd."

"Gladly," I said, setting my full glass down on a table as we neared the left-hand escalator.

"Father doesn't have long. He needs to make an appearance." She led me to the third floor and we passed by another guard, who stepped out of the way for her while eyeing me with contempt.

"Why are they so on edge?" I asked.

"He should have canceled the gala."

"Why?" I asked as we kept moving down a plush carpeted hall. A railing carved from what looked like a solid piece of crystal ran the whole way down, clear and sparkling in perfection.

"A ship arrived last night."

"Don't ships arrive all the time?" I asked, dumbfounded. I knew very few had access to the portals, so almost anyone coming to Bazarn Five would have to arrive by a vessel.

"The planet has a barrier. You don't get inside without a code. You don't get a code unless you've paid and are authorized." Rivo kept walking, and I slowed my steps to match her short legs.

"And?"

"And there was a glitch. A section of the southern entrance was opened for a moment, just long enough for a ship to come through," Rivo said.

"You think someone bribed the tower, and now Lom's on Bazarn?" I asked.

Rivo stopped in her tracks and spun toward me. She grabbed my suit with small fists and pulled me toward her. "Hold your tongue." She looked around and let me go.

"Sorry. I'm just trying to get caught up." I smoothed an imaginary wrinkle on my suit, and we kept moving toward the doors at the end of the hall. Two more large guards stood there stoically as we approached.

"Get inside," Rivo urged, and we walked through the doors as they slid apart, revealing an office. It wasn't what I'd expected after seeing the rest of the palace so far. This room was compact, an intimate setting. It clicked in that this was the room where Garo met with visitors. It would put them at ease. Surprisingly, almost everything inside was made from wood, when everything out there was crystal, marble, or metal.

A man sat in a chair, turned away from us. His head was midnight blue, bald. Smoke lifted in front of his face toward the ceiling, drifting effortlessly toward a vent. As he turned in the chair, I was surprised to see his size in comparison to his petite daughter.

He was at least as tall as me, his shoulders wider, and his well-cut suit was subdued and elegant. It was a muted gray color, the opposite of most things on this world. The fashion had no collar, and the sleeves went to the middle of his strong forearms. He inhaled on a pen-sized object and blew thick smoke out before talking.

He spoke something in Molariun before he cleared his throat and spoke in English. "Greetings, Dean Parker. I have much to thank you for." He stood and spread his arms wide. I didn't know what he intended to do with them, since there was a dark wooden desk between us, but I copied his gesture and he smiled widely.

"You probably wonder how it is I speak your language," he said.

I nodded, but this wasn't the first time I'd come across an alien speaking my tongue.

"One of my companies has developed an integrated language system. I won't bore you with the specifics, but once installed, you have access to any language your vocal ability allows. There are still some biological barriers, of course."

"Of course," I said, not sure I wanted anything of the sort installed into me.

"So you're the hero who brought my daughter back to me. I thought you'd be bigger." He then laughed, sounding eerily human.

"Father!" Rivo shouted, and he chuckled all the more.

"Daughter, you're too serious."

"Nico was killed, an unmarked ship crossed Bazarn's barriers, and you're here laughing in another language!" Rivo was still speaking Molariun, so I was sure she hadn't undergone the surgery yet.

"We don't know that for sure. It could have just been a glitch," Garo said.

"You don't really believe that, do you, Father? Something's coming. I know Lom was behind the attack on our ship. He was trying to blame pirates, but he was after your money. And your *secret*." Rivo hissed the last bit.

So there had been more than just treasure aboard Rivo's destroyed vessel.

He spoke once again in his native language. "Watch how you speak to me, daughter."

She averted her eyes from her father, but I watched him. He was trying to look confident, but I saw fear beneath the façade.

"Rivo's right," I said. "I saw a symbol all over that ship, come to think of it. A triangle in a circle, and two squiggly symbols inside."

"Did she prompt you to say that?" Garo asked me, another puff of smoke lifting to the ceiling vent.

"No, she didn't. Let's think about this, sir." I added the last bit to give him a sense of superiority, though I was sure I didn't need to remind him of his own stature. "Your daughter just about died. Her love, Nico, *did* die, and you almost lost something dear to you. Now she's back, telling

166

you that something's wrong. If Rivo says that someone's coming for you, then I'd be hard-pressed not to believe her."

Rivo smiled at me, and her father glared before glancing at his desk.

"It's in there, isn't it?" I asked.

"What is?" Garo said, shrugging it off.

"Whatever your daughter almost died to transport."

Rivo's eyes went wide, probably surprised I was astute enough to catch it.

Before he said anything, I spoke again. "Wait. It isn't you Lom wants to attack. He wants this...whatever it is you're hiding."

The wind burst out of Garo's sails, and he almost folded over, his hands running to his face. "I don't know what to do with it. If it stays here, they'll find it."

I walked up to the desk, leaning over so I was only inches from his face. "What...is...it?" I asked slowly.

"It's dangerous. We thought we were onto something with it. Dimensional shifting. What if you could transport yourself to another dimension?"

"Why would you want to?" I asked.

"Think about it. We catalog the parallel universes, and you choose which you want to leave to. Neighboring planet threatening to destroy you? Why not reappear somewhere else? Only glitch was, we couldn't figure it out. All the creds we could ever wish for to research it, and we couldn't get it to work." He slunk back down in his chair.

"What happened?" I asked, knowing there was going to be a lot more to the story.

"It functioned, or so we thought. We tested it, but it was a one-way trip. Everything looked like it worked, from what we could tell, but there was no way of knowing for sure." Garo leaned back, looking out the wide window.

"You sent subjects to their doom?" Rivo asked, hearing this part for the first time.

"They were compensated for volunteering, or their families were. I don't do business like Lom of Pleva. In the end, we shut the program down, only Lom caught word of it. Unfortunately, we live in a universe where creds talk, and so do employees."

"So he got wind of the dimensional shifter, and then what?" I asked.

"He wanted the technology, but he planned to use it as a weapon. That's not what it was intended for. Look, I'm not a hero. I've done and funded some horrific things in my time, but that was the younger, power-hungry me. Now I have a family." He stopped speaking and looked at Rivo, who was giving him a hard stare. "I couldn't let it get in the hands of that monster. I don't know how much you know of him, but if I told you half the details, you'd beg me to stop."

"I've heard a bit." I stood, trying to think of a way to help. I couldn't get tied up in their politics and rivalry. What I really needed was inside the vault. I needed the Theos to help me stop the Iskios. That was it. End of game.

"Then you can't blame me for setting up that 'accident' at the lorgonium mine."

"That was you, Father?" Rivo asked, her rushed words translating through my earpiece.

He nodded and looked out the window again. "He died that day, or I thought he did. Now I'm not so sure."

"Rivo, you think he sent someone here for the Shifter?" I asked, wondering if my friends were safe at the Eklack, where they were researching as I stood here, dangerously talking about something I didn't want to be involved in.

"I do. I didn't even know what it was. Father hadn't

told me. This is what Nico died for? Why not destroy it?" Tears were forming in her lower eyes, and she blinked them away.

"It's too volatile. It's made to move planets. If I try to destroy it, it could be the end of everything in its proximity." Garo was stuck. If he kept the shifter, he was going to be targeted, and if he sold it, it would be used as a weapon. If he destroyed it, chaos would ensue.

"I don't want any part of this, but I have a proposition for you." I shifted from foot to foot, knowing I should just keep my mouth shut.

"Go on," Garo urged. Rivo paled, seeming to know what I was about to offer.

"Bring me to this Regnig, and I'll take the Shifter."

TWENTY-THREE

"Why would you do that?" Garo asked.

"I have more important things than getting involved with your rivalry, but I need information. Data I think I can only find on your planet. I want the real source, not the edited, dumbed-down details on the Theos and the portals. You get me this information and I'll pocket the Shifter, taking the heat off you for a while." I had other ideas for it as well but wasn't going to share those with them. That was between me and the Iskios.

"And you won't sell it? It would make you a very wealthy man," Garo said, testing me.

"Look, I don't give a rat's ass about money, or creds, or palaces in the sky." I waved my hand around the room in disgust. "I love my wife, and I want her back. Safe. With me. I didn't help save my race just so we can be destroyed by the Unwinding and have Mary wielding its insane power because of me. I put her in that situation, and I couldn't stop her. It should have been me, at the very least." My knees gave out, and I found myself suddenly sitting in a chair, the emotional damage from the last month finally taking its toll on me.

I leaned forward, my face buried into my hands as a means of subtle comfort.

"Did you say the Unwinding?" Garo asked, his dark blue face a lighter tone.

"Yes. That's what they called it."

"They?"

"The Iskios."

"Rivo, tell you mother we won't be attending the gala." He tapped a screen on his desk. "Casell, get my ship and wake up Regnig. We'll be there soon." He tapped it off and waved me over.

I came around to watch him stick a blue finger into the air under his desk. A small containment field buzzed, and a drawer appeared from nowhere. He hit a pattern on a screen, and it slid open, revealing a plain metallic box.

I'd had enough of surprise boxes on the Iskios quest and never wanted to see one again. Now here I was, waiting for another to open.

Rivo read her father's mind and hit a button on the wall, closing the blinds to the room just before he pulled it out and set it on the desk.

"I hesitate to give this to anyone, but if you're willing to make that trade, I'll do it. We'll give you whatever you need to find your Mary." I could see the excitement in his body language.

It reminded me of a time a friend was giving away a dog online. They'd gotten the puppy without realizing how much work it was going to be, and how big a Great Pyrenees would get. When it was done eating the baseboards in their condo and ripping through a seatbelt in the back seat of their car, they'd posted an ad. I'd met up with him the night someone came to take the dog away, and the sheer relief in his eyes had been similar to what I saw now.

The box opened on a thin piano hinge. The Shifter was round, the size of a compact disc.

"How does it work?" I asked, wondering if he would even tell me.

He described the process in activating it, choosing what you were transporting, and entering the destination. I went over it with him twice to ensure I understood, and he didn't once ask me why I needed to know. I don't think he really cared; he just wanted it gone.

"There's no way to activate it from a distance?" I asked.

"No, someone has to do it. Why does it matter?" he asked with a worried look across his face.

"It doesn't, just curious."

A knock rang against the closed doors.

He said something in his native language, and they slid open, revealing a guard. "Your ship's ready."

———————

"Where is it?" I asked from inside the luxury vessel. Garo was drinking a clear liquid from a short glass, but when he offered me one, I refused.

The seating was lined along the edges of the ship, with open space in the center, and I got up, moving to the other end in an attempt at some privacy.

I tapped my earpiece to the right channel and spoke softly. "Magnus, are you there?"

The line was quiet for a moment before my friend replied, "Loud and clear, Dean. Where you at?"

"With Rivo and her father, heading to see this Regnig. I think he'll be able to help me get what I need. How about you guys? Any luck?" I was just glad to hear they weren't in any trouble down there.

"We've got datasticks full of information, and we've started to sift through it already. The portal stones are made from a stone only found on one known planet."

My pulse raced. "What planet?" I asked, anxiously.

"It doesn't say." My heart sank as Magnus told me the bad news. "Sarlun thinks it may have been edited out."

"Keep up the good work. I'll touch base soon," I said.

"Good luck, buddy. Stay safe. If you need anyone to come kick some ass, let me know." Magnus barked a quick laugh, and the call ended. I forgot they could track me by the GPS in my earpiece. At least I could count on them to bail me out of any trouble I found myself in.

"Get ready, we're approaching." Garo sat. His drink was still full, or had he poured another one?

I walked to the front of the ship, where a blue Molari piloted us toward the desert dunes. Wind swept in from the north, shooting sand toward us, and I could hear it ting against the hull of the ship as we raced deeper into the desert.

The ship lurched, and for a second, the viewscreen showed blue sky before we swung around nose first, heading straight for the ground.

"Stop, you're going to kill us!" I yelled right before an impact that didn't come. We entered the surface through a field that had looked like sand.

"Calm down. I'm sorry I didn't mention that. This place is hidden. Few know it exists. Fewer have ever set foot down here." Garo smiled grimly and finally took a drink, gulping most of the clear liquid in one swallow.

We were moving ever downward, through a tunnel only three or four times as wide as our ship. I expected my GPS wasn't going to work down here, and I tested my communicator when no one was looking. It came up offline. Great.

The ship slowed, and Rivo came to stand beside me.

"Have you seen this before?" I asked the small female being.

"Once. You know you don't have to take that." She pointed to my pocket, where the Shifter sat tucked away. "We'll help you anyway."

I doubted her father would feel the same way. "It's okay. Better one ordinary man be a target than a world full of rich tourists, right?"

We followed the tunnel, lights from the ship shining against the dirt walls as we came to a stop, hovering above a platform, the vessel now horizontal.

I felt the walls caving in around me. "How far down are we?"

Garo typed something into a computer pad beside him. "In your distance, around four hundred kilometers."

We lowered to the platform, settling down with a light puff of dust kicking up to the viewscreen.

"And Regnig lives down here?" I couldn't imagine anyone being so far below the surface and not losing their mind.

No one answered me as the door opened. "Don't be startled by Regnig. He's a little… different," Garo said.

I let the comment go for the time being and stepped onto the dirt-covered landing pad. An arched doorway was cut into the rock of the upper mantle; a solid wooden door sat closed and windowless.

I walked toward it and glanced back to see if Rivo and her father were following. I hit an invisible energy field and was knocked to the ground. Dust puffed around me in a cloud, covering my white suit with brown particles.

"Thanks for the warning," I muttered as Garo tapped a holographic projected screen that appeared as he neared the hidden wall.

"Sorry. It's been a while since I've been down here." His hand shot in front of me, and I grabbed it, getting to my feet.

Even after brushing myself off, dirty streaks stuck to my clothing. Rivo walked past the barrier that was now closed and urged me to the door.

This was it. I was going to find the secret to the Theos. I would discover their world, then… then what? How did I expect to raise them? I'd been so focused on learning where their planet was that I didn't know what I'd do to speak to them.

A knock broke me from my reverie. The large dark wooden door opened, but no one was on the other side. A throat cleared, and I tilted my head down to the source of the sound. A tiny creature stood before us. It was bipedal, but there the similarities to us stopped. It had a beak the same color as its brown skin, and a single large eye, with red lines stretching to all edges from a pinprick-sized pupil.

Come. You're letting a draft in. The thoughts slammed into my mind so quickly that I stumbled back. *Sorry if I startled you. I don't get many visitors.*

"That's okay. I'm here to see Regnig." I crouched down, trying to get on an even playing field with the little being.

You seek Regnig, do you? What business do you have down here? The creature peered around me, its large eyelid blinking a couple times as it stared at Garo and Rivo behind me.

"The Iskios broke free and have my wife. They stole her as their vessel, and she's wielding something called the Unwinding. I need to stop them and get her back."

You speak lies! This cannot be. They are long buried.

"Yes, I know," I said. "The Theos tracked them down and subjected them to an eternity on a crystal world, but they aren't there any longer."

How do you know this with such certainty?

"Because I just returned from there, and we took the last remaining Iskios through a portal, where it died after fighting the Theos inside."

Get inside! Now! The urgency behind its thoughts jostled my mind, and I had to shake the cobwebs out after a moment. The being looked at Garo and must have passed some silent thoughts, because my host just nodded solemnly and turned to walk back to the ship with Rivo.

I followed it inside, and the door flew shut behind me. "Will I see Regnig now?"

You fool. You're talking to him. Come. You speak dangerous words. Words no other ears are meant to hear. He walked slowly on small crooked legs.

Of course this was Regnig. Garo had warned me he was different. He certainly was that: a petite cyclops bird who spoke telepathically and had telekinetic abilities. "I only wanted to find what I need. I'll do anything to get her back."

I see. Saving the universe from its ultimate destruction doesn't play into it? he asked.

It was truthfully second on my reasoning, but I didn't want to scare the holder of the information away. "That too."

Regnig led me down a corridor made for someone shorter than myself, and I ducked as we made our way through the cramped space. The hall was rounded at the top like the door had been, and the walls were packed dirt. It smelled stuffy: a musk you could only get somewhere with no ventilation.

It shortly opened up into a massive domed room. Glowing stones hung on ropes from the ceiling, softly lighting the area. Shelves were cut into the walls, and books filled every available crevice in the whole room. There was a seating area in the center, with worn leather chairs of all sizes. The smallest looked particularly used, and I knew this was where Regnig would perch himself, reading from the ancient tomes one page at a time for countless years.

"This is amazing." I spun in the middle of the room, getting the full appreciation of what I saw. These weren't computers, viewscreens with missing details, or videos explaining history. These were books written by the historians, or perhaps diaries from long ago forgotten worlds. I suddenly understood Regnig's choice for being the one to watch over them.

It is.

"Are you here alone?"

That I am.

What had it been like to live there in solitude for so long?

Sit. Tell me what you know.

I did just that and tried hard not to gloss over any important parts. I wanted nothing more than to learn what I needed and run, but I understood this as a barter. Important news from the outside world, to an isolated being, wasn't even a fair trade for what I asked.

He sat there unmoving, unblinking even, as I described the Kraski, the Deltra, the hybrids. He twitched when I mentioned the Bhlat, and finally passed an *Oh* into my mind when I told him of us handing Earth over to them in exchange for peace.

He listened and didn't speak as I went into our year as Gatekeepers, with the first piece of what we thought was a Theos artifact in Sarlun's possession. Only when I told him of the ice world and the symbol where we found the second piece, the cube, did he stop me.

The Iskios are conniving. I see why the Theos dealt with them as they did.

I described in detail each of the challenges we went through, and he was extremely interested in the one where we were mentally sent back to Earth during the invasion. *That would take a lot of energy and strength to make work, especially after being dormant for so long.*

"I don't know how they did it."

Stored the energy inside the rock the island was made out of, perhaps. I'll have to study on it. When I didn't reply, he told me to continue.

When I got to the Padlog being at the crystal world, he stopped me once again. *And you have questioned these Padlog?*

"Yes and no. I didn't want to implicate us in their people's deaths. The Supreme did give me some information on the Theos after I requested it, but we really went there to get the coordinates for the world where we'd left Mary." Regnig closed his eye as we spoke, and for a moment, I thought I might have lulled him into sleep.

Go on.

He heard about our entrance into the pyramid and finding the throne room where the mist took over Mary, deeming her the True. I left out the part about her being pregnant. It felt too personal, a piece of the story I should keep for myself.

And she sent you back with a wave of her hand before the Iskios took back control? he asked.

"That's how it seemed." I thought of her eyes at that moment. Her face had been so shocked and sad, tears filling her eyes at the same time as the black mist.

I can tell you speak truth. How do you presume to solve this?

Had I told him everything? I'd already told him I knew the Theos were inside the portals. What choice did I have? Every minute that passed by with Mary under their control, my guilt increased, and I wasn't going to be able to live with myself soon.

"I think the universe is about balance. It's an age-old theory, right?" I suspected Regnig's idea of "age-old" was different from that of a young race like humans. "I'm told the Theos and the Iskios were the first two races. Whether that's true or not isn't necessarily relevant. What I do think is, they were both powerful. You spoke of energy, and that's what it comes down to.

"The Theos thought they were doing a service to everyone when they chose to cast a judgment of death on the Iskios, but by doing this, they caused an imbalance. Unselfishly, they made portal stones around the universe, using their own life force to power them. The ultimate sacrifice. Their lives for the return of the balance."

I waited, and Regnig finally opened his eye. *You are wise for one so young. I've read many philosophical collections about this very topic. It's been of interest to many for hundreds, even thousands of years, but no one has come to the exact conclusions you have.*

I felt a "but" coming.

But you don't have the whole picture.

"What am I missing?" I asked, my heart beating so fast I could hardly hear the thoughts he was pushing into my mind.

They aren't all dead.

TWENTY-FOUR

*G*oosebumps rose on my arms. "What do you mean, they aren't all dead?"

They couldn't make the ultimate sacrifice you speak of, and that's why we don't life in a peaceful, united galaxy. We have love, compassion, and times of peace, but still war, famine, and torture. Balance is important, and that's why people like you are born. To change the universe. You are a Recaster.

His words sent chills up and down my body. Kareem's dying breath echoed inside my head. "What do you mean?"

You stopped the Kraski. You saved a planet.

"Only to give it away," I corrected.

That's not the important part. You saved your people from a destructive race. You gave them a new home, a new future.

"I also helped unleash a devastating power." My hands ran through my hair. He was giving me too much credit.

Balance. You did something positive, and then something negative. But what you do next will determine what it means for the ultimate equilibrium. Regnig's beak opened, and a small pink tongue stuck out momentarily.

"Are there others like me? Recasters?" I asked.

He nodded. *I've read tales of them from many worlds, over countless centuries. They aren't frequent, though, and don't always do things on such a grand scale.*

The idea that I was anything more than an accountant from New York who'd somehow helped save Earth from an invasion by a scared and violent race was too much. I thought Regnig might be reading too much into it all. He was caught up in the fanciful stories in the books around him. "I'm just a man."

I know. I'm just a Quontre, but it doesn't mean I didn't rise above my station and become guardian to the universe's hidden knowledge.

He had a point. "How do I find them? My friend said he found a text stating there was an origin planet for the portal stones, but the name of the world was missing."

It's here somewhere. I've read it, but you see, there are far too many books to remember, and my memory isn't what it used to be.

All my hopes dropped with my stomach. I didn't have time to search the hundreds of thousands of volumes around us.

Good thing I have a system.

---

*H*ours later, we were both covered in dust, and dozens of texts lay sprawled out on a large wooden table. Regnig used ladders to get up and down as he searched for the books.

This is it. His beak opened, and he blew on a thin dark leather-bound volume. He handed it to me, and I felt a rush of excitement.

I scanned through the pages carefully and realized I couldn't read the language. He must have known that. "Here, I don't understand it."

I know, but it's the picture you're going to want to see.

I flipped a few more handwritten pages and found a map, carefully drawn in black ink on the taupe paper. It showed five planets circling a star; dozens of small moons were labeled as well.

Third from the star. That's it. His small clawed finger scratched over the page, on a name. *Elnan.* The name of their world clicked into my head, and for a second, I could almost see it; then it was gone.

I looked for coordinates but found none. "How does this help?"

It helps if you have this. He climbed down the steps, his little legs carrying him faster than I'd seen him move yet. I followed him, the book carefully gripped in my hands.

We stopped at the edge of the room, and he tapped a button on a tablet. One of the bookshelves moved forward and slid to the side, revealing a room with a screen and a short chair. He sat down and began powering up the screen. I had to crouch to fit into the space and began kneeling beside the little desk.

I often have to refer to the star mapping for my research. This will allow us to scan the drawing, and it will determine if there are any matches in the system.

"But this is just a drawing."

It looks to scale.

"But still." I passed him the book, when his clawed hands shot out for it.

Just be patient. He opened the book to the right page and pressed it against the blank screen. A green light rolled over the glass material, and he passed the volume back to me.

A symbol rotated on the screen in the universal "please wait" notification.

Three matches, he said in my mind as the screen showed three detailed images of different systems. We looked through each of them, Regnig zooming in on one at a time.

From the text, I recall the star being a yellow giant. From that, we can determine the world is...this one. He zoomed toward a small planet on the middle screen. A moon rotated around it on the computer's program. *Xatrin U3. Interesting. No details on it. No lifeforms noted. A hunk of rock, by all accounts.*

I couldn't believe what I was seeing. The Theos home world. "Can you give me the coordinates now?"

Write this now. He passed something resembling a quill and ink, and I dipped it before taking the series of numbers down on the same page with the map. "I'm assuming I can take this?"

No books may leave here. He slid a piece of paper to me and got up, stretching his back until I heard a loud crack. He stretched his wings out and flapped them vigorously.

"Thank you for your help, Regnig, but I need one more thing. Do you have a book on the portal symbols?"

Of course I do. He turned, hobbling back to the large open library. He tapped a claw to the tip of his beak and waved me to the far side of the room. *Climb this ladder. I'm getting tired.*

I did as he requested, feeling the first rung groan under my weight. It hadn't been built for someone as large as me to step on. I glanced up, hoping I didn't need to climb the full twenty feet up to where the ceiling began to curve.

Halfway. My mind was sent an image of the book's spine.

"I thought your memory wasn't what it used to be," I commented.

It isn't. I used to remember far more. Now don't dawdle.

I kept climbing. Each step up was rewarded with a creak of protest from the wooden rungs.

To the right. Almost there.

I stretched my right arm out, spotting the book he wanted me to grab. I held on with my left and kicked my right foot out as I stepped lightly on a railing Regnig used as a platform to walk among the levels of books, only it was far too narrow and thin for me to put my weight on.

With a little luck, my fingers found the book. I brought

it back to the ladder and felt the rung snap in half, and I began to fall to the ground. I held the book tight, as if it mattered more than my own safety in that instant.

A gust of air slowed me, and I landed with no more than a minor bounce.

I glanced around, wondering what happened, and I saw Regnig standing beside me. He grabbed the book and sauntered off. Then I remembered the door closing on its own and wondered what his story really was. There was a lot more to the small birdman than I could even begin to guess.

He was already flipping through it. I got up and joined him at the table we'd been using earlier. *Here it is. Xatrin U3.* He slid the book toward me. *I've been here a long time, and in all my daydreaming, I never imagined I could actually make a difference. Good luck to you, Dean Parker.*

I was about to look at the book when a rapid knocking echoed to us from the entrance door. "Sounds urgent."

I ran for it, unsure what I was going to find. When I opened the door, a frantic Rivo blurted out something. I didn't have my earpiece on, and I tapped it active. "Say that again!"

"Something's happening above ground. We've being invaded!" She was shaking, and I tried to process what I was hearing.

Garo was behind her, and he nodded, confirming the information was true.

"Garo, you stay here with Regnig, if that's okay with you?" I turned to the little one-eyed birdman, who'd finally caught up.

He may stay, for a short time.

"I can't stay down here. We need to fend them off!" Garo said in English.

"Father, you're too important. We'll scout what's going

on and send for you when we can. You have the best defenses money can buy. Don't worry. They can handle
themselves," Rivo said.

If they were under attack, that meant the invaders had
broken through the defenses already, meaning it was likely
an inside job. I didn't have to tell Garo that; he would already know.

"Let's go. Thanks again, Regnig."

Go and find the balance again, Recaster. Leave the book.

"But I need the symbols. There's no other way to get
there." A thought occurred to me, and I cursed my stupid-
ity at not having remembered the device Suma had gifted
me. I fished it out of my pocket and set it on top of the
book. It hummed to life and began scanning. A red light
shone around the book as I held it, tiny slivers of beam
folding between each page, making the volume vibrate.
Soon the light stopped, and I slid the device into my
pocket. I flipped it open to the page with *Xatrin U3* on it
and tried to memorize the symbol, but it wouldn't stick in
my jumbled mind.

"Dean, we need to go!" Rivo was pulling my arm now,
and we left behind Regnig, who didn't for a second step
outside his cavern. He held the book in his small claws. His
voice entered my mind for the last time – *Good luck, Dean
Parker –* and we ran for the ship. Soon we were back inside,
heading for the surface.

I tried to connect with Magnus but got nothing back. I
went through to each different channel and still came up
empty-handed. I hoped they were safe. The Eklack might
be a primary target for the invaders. Was it Lom of Pleva?
Had he come to get the device I now held in my pocket, or
was it just payback to Garo, his nemesis, for trying to kill
him?

We emerged from the sand to chaos. Ships were

everywhere, laser beams flew through the air, and bombs concussed all around us.

TWENTY-FIVE

I tried my earpiece again. "Magnus! Come in!"

"Dean, where the hell are you?" he asked.

"I just got back to the surface from underground. Are you safe?" Images of a crumbling building around my friends flashed into my mind.

"We made it back to the promenade. Everyone's hiding out here, but we're getting back to the stones. We were going to wait until we heard from you," Magnus said, concern evident in his tone.

"Just go! Get out of here. I'll find a way to get off this world."

He relayed my wishes to the others, and I could hear Slate in my ear now.

"Boss, not a good idea. Get over here, and we can leave together." Slate's voice was calmer than I'd expected.

"Go home. That's an order, Slate. Get them safely to New Spero. I'll be there shortly."

I wouldn't be, but he didn't need to know that. I had something to do and wanted to do it alone.

"Rivo, I need to get to the portal."

"Don't you see we're in the middle of something here?" Rivo stared at the battle going on around us. The pilot veered lower and raced across the dunes.

"I'm going to leave. I have somewhere to get to."

She looked about to lose it on me, but she held back, going to talk quietly to the pilot. He veered the ship right, and I hoped that meant he was going back to the promenade where I could access the portal and leave the invaded planet behind.

Fires burned in luxury hotels as we flew by, lives were being lost with each breath, and I knew I should do something to help. But I couldn't, and even if I were able, I had to find Mary. I was so close to discovering a way to end this all. I needed to balance things, and staying here wasn't going to accomplish that.

Eventually, we entered a quiet area where no fighting was taking place. The pilot sped over the landscape toward the promenade near the entrance to the portals. Enough time had passed I knew my friends would be back home, to the caves by Terran Five. I wasn't following.

"Rivo, I need an EVA." Mine was stowed away in my pack at the hotel at the Peaks. It wouldn't do me any good there.

Rivo crossed the ship to the rear, where she opened a closet. "You and my father are near the same size, even if you're a little skinnier. Try this on."

The suit was lightweight, top-of-the-line by all accounts, but what else could I expect from one so rich?

I hastily put it on, and Rivo cinched it at the waist for me. The boots were raised, making me six inches taller than I was.

"You can adjust the air levels here." She showed me, and I changed them to match my own suit's readouts.

The helmet was shaped differently from ours, but it was lighter, sleeker in design, and it connected with an energy seal. That was new. "Anything else I should know?"

"It has built-in thrusters on the back, and in the soles of the boots. The controls are here." She pointed to them in the fingers, and it reminded me of the controls from the Kraski suits, when Mae and I had raced to tether the vessels together. The gloves stretched out a little longer than custom ones would on me, but overall, the suit fit well.

"Show me the translator," I said, and she ran through it quickly. I connected my own earpiece to it wirelessly, since they didn't have ears like ours.

Not many Bazarn residents or tourists would have access to the Shandra, and the promenade was nearly empty. All the normal vendors would be tucked away, seeking protection from the surrounding war zone. The pilot lowered us to the ground, where we'd come out from below ground in a transportation field.

"I want to come with you," Rivo said urgently. She was already starting to put on an EVA.

"You can't. I have to do this alone." I was so close now. The pieces to the puzzle were finally falling into place, and soon I'd be able to see the big picture.

"But I can help. If you need someone to watch your back or fly a ship, I can do those things."

She made a good point. Maybe I could use the help. "But what about your planet? Your father?"

"We'll drive the invaders off. This isn't the first time someone has made a play for the world." Rivo sounded confident, but her posture belied her words. "And my father is underground with Regnig. He'll be safe."

I'd already sent my own friends back home to safety and suddenly wished I had one of them with me. Slate, preferably, but I'd put him through enough. As much as I appreciated everyone's sentiments, part of me wished they'd stop volunteering for these risky missions.

"I'm sorry, Rivo. I can't bring you where I'm going." I felt the circular disk her father had given me, confirming it was still there.

She looked reprimanded, but she could tell I was serious. "Fine, but take this." She ran across the space again and unlocked a compartment with a scan of her hand. She handed me a weapon – a thin gray gun – and a box, which she set into a backpack.

"The suit has stim injections if you're hurt, as well as intravenous food. Just to be safe, take this too." She threw in some packages from a cupboard, and some water bottles.

I'd been so tied up in getting the information and finding the Theos, I hadn't planned on what I'd do about food. Maybe I should be taking someone like Rivo with me. Apparently, I needed to be looked after. I thanked her before I could change my mind.

The door opened, and I jumped off, my new weapon slung around my arm, my pack light on my back. "Thanks, Rivo. For everything. For getting me in with Regnig."

"Dean, I'd either be dead on a pirate ship, or worse, still alive on a pirate ship. Anything you ever need, come to me. Good luck." She smiled, and I found myself hoping I did see her again someday.

"Go help your planet," I said, and she blew out a deep breath.

"I will."

The ship's door closed, and it lifted off, heading in the opposite direction to the one we'd come in from. There were fewer explosions in the air. Maybe an end was coming to the conflict. I hoped so, for everyone's sake. If Lom was the one responsible for this attack, and he really was after the Shifter in my pocket, I could be in a lot of danger.

The whole promenade looked much different from when we'd first arrived. Only a couple of ships hung at the far end, likely empty. No smoke rose from the food vendors' establishments as I raced across the grounds toward the invisible energy field. I walked toward the pillars and felt the familiar change of vibration.

I appeared on the stairs beneath the boardwalk and ran toward the portal doors. I hardly noticed the amazing surroundings as I passed a few bewildered beings, hiding out below for the battle to end. The guards were still stationed at the portal doorway, two on this side.

"Stop where you are!" one of them ordered, sticking a meaty hand out to push against my chest.

I didn't have time or energy to argue with the guards. "I'm Dean Parker. Did Sarlun and the others travel through here?"

"Oh yes, the other Gatekeeper. I didn't recognize you in…" His eyes widened. "In an Alton's personal house suit. Where did you come by this?" He pushed me in the chest this time, knocking me off-balance, and I stumbled to the ground. The other guard lifted a rod in his hand, blue energy coursing through it.

Rage filled my veins. Mary needed me. The whole damned universe needed me to stop the Unwinding, and here I was being bullied by two ugly overgrown four-armed brutes. I felt my finger on the trigger before the action registered with my brain. Only at the last second did I realize what I was about to do, and I jerked my arm up, hitting the ceiling above them instead of pegging one in the head.

The gun was different from our pulse rifles. Instead of a beam cutting a hole above, a detonation blasted where it struck, and a hole five feet wide ripped open the ceiling.

Before they could react, I was up on my feet, pointing the gun between them, daring one of them to move so I could pick the other one off. "Listen to me. Garo gave this to me. He also has trusted me with something pivotal to stop the war going on out there. If you really want to piss me off, I'll shoot you both, and tonight when I go to sleep, I'll dream of nothing. No regrets, no blood, no violence; nothing."

The one who'd pushed me stepped out of the way. "Why didn't you just say so?" he asked, and the door opened beyond. Two guards inside looked ready to walk toward me, but the ones on this side waved them off.

I walked past the group of hulking guards and slid the gun back onto my shoulder. My hands shook as I lowered them to my sides, trusting I wasn't about to get shot in the head as I made my way through the opulent room. Now that I saw it as I left, the etchings, the gold, the carvings and paintings felt nothing more than ridiculous and pretentious.

The portal table stood at the far end of the cavernous room. My boots clanked with each step against the hard stone ground. I tried to recall the symbol for Xatrin U3. The symbols on the walls lit up as I approached, glowing in multiple colors. The clear table screen shone softly, and I entered the secret code Kareem had given me when we'd returned the hybrids from the prison on Earth.

How far I'd come. Just over a month ago, my life had been great. I was married, and Mary and I were on adventures as Gatekeepers, visiting barren worlds and gathering data on them. That damned artifact. How had we even stumbled across that symbol on the ice world? It seemed too farfetched to be a coincidence. Were these two opposing races really gods of some kind? Could they pull and push others' actions to suit their own needs?

The hidden symbols appeared, but not fully there like the others. They always stayed a little dimmer, like they were in the background of the otherwise clear screen. I sifted through them, looking for the symbol, but I couldn't find it. I couldn't match it. Where was Xatrin U3, and why couldn't I recall what it looked like? It had only been half an hour, maybe an hour since I'd seen it.

I fished out the small copier Suma gave me and found

my suit had a built-in arm console. I fiddled with the device and found a way to link them together wirelessly. I tapped through the document, which organized the pages in the right order. There I found Xatrin U3 and the symbol. I looked at it. Three triangles, two wavy lines, and sun rays off the left pyramid. I went to the table to find it.

What had it looked like again? I cursed when I couldn't remember. I found it on my arm screen but quickly forgot it. It was like something magical was wiping it from my memory as soon as I stopped looking at it. No wonder no one had been able to find their world. They'd found a way to keep it hidden. The mind couldn't remember it, even if someone did stumble on it.

My breath quickened as I tried to figure this out. The guards at the end of the hall still watched me but were too far away to have any idea what it was I was struggling with. I was glad when neither of them came to ask if I needed assistance.

I looked around for something to write with. There was a desk nearby, along the wall, but everything was digital. No pens. No paper. Nothing to draw with.

To hell with it. I didn't have time for this.

I kicked the wooden table. This got the guards' attention. I looked at the image and broke the legs into a few pieces. I kept looking at the image on my arm screen while I laid out broken splinters of wood on the ground.

By now, the guards were quickly stalking toward me. I had to hurry. I looked down and saw it was close enough. Once I went to the table, I still couldn't remember the image of the Xatrin U3 symbol, but I glanced to the floor to see three crude triangles. Bingo. As I found a symbol that closely resembled my rudimentary copy of the symbol, the guards closed in on me.

Without hesitation, I tapped the icon, and everything

went white.

TWENTY-SIX

"*W*HO ENTERS OUR DOMAIN?" a voice boomed in my ears.

I was naked, floating in nothingness. A background began to spread across the blank canvas, as if I was watching an invisible artist at work. I spun with the image as it appeared, and soon I understood I was seeing my house and acreage back on New Spero. I glanced down to find Maggie sleeping beside me; the wooden deck boards were under my bare feet. When I looked up again, the picture was complete. It felt like I was home, only there was no scent, no wind, and I still had no clothes on.

"Dean," I said quietly, answering the question before adding some volume to it. "Dean Parker."

"WHY DO YOU ENTER OUR DOMAIN?" the voice asked, but this time, the sound came from around my house. I walked the few steps and peeked over the deck railing. I was walking toward myself, but this version of me wasn't naked. He wore a white jumpsuit, with a gray cloak over his shoulders. He was clean-shaven, his hair shorter than I usually wore it.

"I need your help. The Iskios are back." I followed the other me as he walked around the deck to the stairs and climbed them to meet me in front of my door. Maggie hadn't moved yet, and I was sure she was just there as an imprint of my memory.

"Impossible. They are dead," my alter ego said, this

time at a normal pitch and in my own voice.

There we stood, two Dean Parkers, staring each other in the eyes. His were swirling radiant green orbs of energy and galaxies.

"They've returned." I wanted to be as straight to the point as I could. I didn't know how much time the Theos would give me, and I couldn't mince words.

"How can this be? We sealed them away for eternity," the other me said.

"They left a trap behind. We were tricked into thinking we were finding the Theos, but instead they took a vessel and have unleashed the Unwinding." I watched as the Theos-infused version of me showed his cards. His posture changed, shoulders slumping enough to know he believed me.

"The Unwinding." The words slipped from my doppelganger's mouth, and the image around me began to melt. "Are you worthy, Dean Parker?"

Not this question again. I hadn't passed it the first time.

"Worthy of what?" I asked, suddenly feeling like this wasn't a question to answer while standing naked on my deck. The sky in the distance disappeared, leaving nothing but white light in its stead. The light continued to envelop the rest of the area. My yard, garden, driveway, all dissipated before the power of the bright light. Soon it was just me, once again floating, and facing the other me eye-to-eye.

"Worthy to be our champion?" he asked, his eyes softening.

I didn't hesitate. I knew what I was being offered. "I am."

"Then behold."

I thought about it. How had no one found the Theos before? Or perhaps they had but had failed to get in. What would happen if they didn't find me worthy? Would I just vanish within the stones?

To get here, I not only needed the code to find the hidden symbols of the mysterious Theos Collective, but I also needed to have access to Regnig and Bazarn's concealed library. The odds were stacked against someone trying to find the Theos, but against all those difficult probabilities, I'd somehow accomplished it.

Within a single heartbeat, I found we were in a room, my clothing on me once again. I didn't know if it was another apparition, fueled by the Theos and pushed into my head, or if it was a real space on their planet.

"Is this real?" I asked the figure before me. He had turned away, and something had changed about him. It clearly wasn't my doppelganger any longer. This being was taller and wider than I was, but he still wore the gray cloak, covering most of his back and legs from my vantage point.

"Is anything real?" he asked back in an alien voice, no longer my own.

He slowly turned to me, and my blood ran cold. How long had it been since anyone had laid eyes on a Theos? From all of my readings, there were sightings only a few hundred years ago, but all my experience had taught me those were lies. The real Theos had been hiding away for far longer than that. Longer than most races had existed.

His cloak's hood covered his head, but I could see the green glowing eyes beneath the shadows of the cowl. Gloved hands hung at his sides, strong powerful hands hidden under soft gray material.

"You're real," I found myself saying.

He laughed then, a real laugh, catching me off-guard. "Forgive me, but at times, I wasn't so sure." His arm reached out, tapping me on the chest. "Are you real?" He returned the question, all in my own language.

"I hope so. Otherwise, this is a very strange dream." I smiled, even though my heart was racing as sweat dripped in long lines down my sides and back.

I finally got a look around the room. The walls were smoothed crystal; small stalactites hung from the ceiling with a green tint to them. The floor matched but was a darker tone. "Where are we?" I asked. There was furniture carved from the stone, and stone lanterns glowed along the walls, casting a colorful ambiance over everything.

"You're at your destination."

"Fair enough. Can you help me?"

I still couldn't see his face, but it sounded like he sighed.

"Come, let us talk." He led me away from the edge of the room and through an open doorway that led to a much more inviting space. Wooden floors ran in straight lines across the room. A table carved from crystal sat near what could only be a kitchen; two chairs were pushed under it. "I've not had guests before."

"Then why do you have two chairs?" I instantly regretted my question. He didn't seem to mind.

"For such an occasion." He motioned for me to take a seat. "You can take that off, if you prefer."

I tapped my helmet. "Are you sure?"

"I wouldn't suggest it if I wasn't. If I wanted you dead, I wouldn't have allowed you into my home." His voice was deep, but perfect English spilled from his lips like he'd known it his whole life.

I tapped the release, as Rivo had shown me, and removed the helmet, taking a breath of air. It was perfect – a hint of coolness to it, but refreshing, unlike what I expected from the closed-in home. I saw my own hand shaking as I set the helmet down on the wooden floor. The enormity of where I was finally settled in. I felt like a fly that could be squashed at any moment.

"Don't be afraid. No harm will come to you here," he said, reading my mind. "Tell me all, Dean Parker."

"I don't know where to begin."

"At the start. When you became the man who sits before me. I think you know the exact moment, don't you?" he asked, and I did.

"We don't have much time. I need to find my wife. I need her back."

He pulled back his hood, revealing a long face, two piercing green eyes, and a white mane of hair. He had no nose to speak of, but two nostril holes sat above gray lips; his skin was a pallid ash color. He was striking, and not at all what I expected from the ancient race.

"Here, time doesn't exist. You are free to tell the tale as slowly as needed."

"What then?" Would he help me? Could he even do anything? I saw a man of flesh and blood like myself.

"Then I decide if the unbalance I've felt is possible to fix, or if we stay here and let nature take its course," he said. His face stayed impassive even as mine turned to a scowl.

"We can't let it continue!" I started to shout, but he raised a long finger in the air, silencing me.

"Tell your tale."

"You haven't told me your name," I said, somehow feeling this was important.

"You may call me Karo."

It seemed too simple a name for the being across from me. I calmed, took a deep breath, and started. "The ships came at dawn…"

"Clever. You are the thirtieth being to attempt to enter the portal here," Karo said.

"Thirty! What happened to them?" I imagined them stuck forever in the nothingness.

"They were sent back, with no memory of my questions. They assume the portal is faulty and continue on with their lives."

"Were any seeking you out, or were they random?" I imagined a colorful being finding the ancient portal long ago and ending up being grilled by the Karo-fueled version of themselves.

"Two such seekers have come with the intent of finding us. They were both rejected."

"Why did you allow me in?"

"Because of the history of unbalance you brought with you." Karo stood, moving to his kitchen. "Would you care for something to eat?"

I laughed, wondering where he would possibly get food. I had no idea if we were on the surface, underground, or stuck within projections in my mind. But my stomach growled at the thought of food, so I told him I'd like to eat.

"You've woven quite the tale, Dean Parker."

"Just Dean is fine."

"How is it you go on?" he asked, his glowing eyes swirling as he stared at me from his kitchen.

"What do you mean?" I asked.

"Many through the ages have crumbled at the tasks you've accomplished. How do you go on?"

I thought about it, and it was easy. "I go on because people need me. If I knew someone else could step up to the plate and replace me, I'd happily go back home as long as Mary was beside me."

"And there's the truth of it all. You go on for her, don't

you? It's always been about her, even before you knew it was." Karo lifted a hand, pointed a long finger toward me, and I felt a tug at my head, like he'd plucked a thought from my mind.

"What was that?" I asked, rubbing my hair.

"Food. I wanted to know your favorite dish." I looked over to him and saw him open a door similar to that of an oven. He pulled out a steaming hot pizza, the smell hit the air, and I found myself starting to drool as I saw the melted cheese, the basil topping, and the crispy pepperoni.

"How did you do that?" I got up, crossing the small distance between us. I opened the door and saw an empty opening behind it. I looked inside, then to the piping hot pizza on the countertop. "Are you a god?"

It was his turn to laugh; light crinkles aged his otherwise smooth skin. "Is that what they say? It's been far too long. I've been out of touch for ages."

"Well, are you?" I took an offered slice of pizza, passed to me on a flat, thin green crystal plate.

He shook his head. "No. We are not gods. Our advanced intellect allowed us to create miraculous technology. Many took these as signs of a higher power, but we are flesh and blood."

I was going to call him on it. "Then how have you stayed here for so long without perishing?"

"It would be difficult to explain. It has everything to do with slowing cell disintegration, and some other biological adjustments I won't bore you with." Karo had a vague answer for everything. I suppose it wasn't my place to extract the knowledge of an ancient race when their secret ways were what kept them safe for so long. Still, I couldn't resist a little probing.

"What about that? You picked a thought from my head." I gestured to the pizza. I blew on the slice and took a bite, my taste buds happily dancing at the intense flavors.

"You live long enough, you learn to utilize most of the hidden cognitive functions of the brain. And this" – he pointed at the square box the pizza had come out of – "is linked to my mind through a series of microchips. Saves me time from having to program my meals."

So he could read minds. Regnig had been able to as well, and I wondered how old he was. But he also needed to eat, which meant he was just another being like me. Maybe a little more advanced, but he'd understand the plight I was in the middle of. He could be reasoned with.

"Will you help me?" I asked, knowing this was my last resort. Without his help, I'd have to go back home, see if Clare could pinpoint Mary's location, or wait for word of the Unwinding's destruction to hit the Gatekeepers' network. Then I'd have to make it to her and try to find a way to pull her out of there before I used the Shifter in my pocket.

"You need to see something first. You need to understand." He bit into his pizza and smiled. "This is good. I wish I'd known of it a long time ago. Before you go, do you mind letting me pick a few more from your mind?"

I couldn't tell if he was kidding, but his wry smile made me think he wasn't totally serious. "Show me what you must. I'll do anything to get her back."

"I know you will. But you still need to see." He slid a gloved hand along his clear countertop and walked to the wall, where he hit a series of commands into an appearing keypad. The image of the wall disappeared, showing another room within. Large crystals, each a different color, sat in a circle, breaching from the floor. "Stand in the center."

I set my food down; my plate clanked against the counter as I let it go prematurely. I walked to the crystals without hesitation. If Karo needed me to see this, I'd do it, to find out how they could help me stop the Iskios.

I was in the middle of the circle and looked back, wondering if anything was supposed to happen. "I'm ready, Karo."

"Brace yourself," he said quietly.

Visions from the Theos rushed into my mind without warning.

TWENTY-SEVEN

*W*ind blew through my long hair as I watched the crowd gather below. I was at the top of a hill, the largest near the shuttle zone, and Zall sat beside me, talking nonstop about how excited she was to finally get off this rock.

Thrusters spewed hot red fire toward the ground, and the rocket shook before rising into the sky. Tears I didn't know I had formed along my eyes as I viewed the first flight of exiles to the Iskios colony. We were too different, they claimed. My father told me never to be seen with my best friend. The Iskios were dangerous, too hideous a creature. I disagreed.

Zall held my hand and I leaned in. Her surprise quickly turned to understanding, and our lips met for the first time. They stayed together as the rocket raced into space. Soon only smoke remained, along with two more shuttles.

Zall pulled away. "I have to go. My parents are waiting for me."

"I wish..." I didn't know what to say. Nothing would convey my true feelings. "I wish you weren't going."

"You know there's no other way."

She was right. They'd been banished. My father said they couldn't help it, that they had a compulsion to harm things. Mother was sad for them, but Father was angry we were even letting them go. His eyes spoke the violence he was speaking against.

"I know. Can I walk you down?"

"You'd better not. I'll... miss you." She stood and bent down, holding my face in her warm hands. She kissed me again and turned, walking away from me forever.

I wanted to yell, to tell her I couldn't live without her, but she was already gone before I built up the nerve. It couldn't be. She was Iskios, and I was Theos.

"Captain, this was the work of the Iskios, and the bastards weren't shy about anyone knowing it was them." I looked at the images on the screen. I wanted to scream, to tear my gaze away, but I forced myself to watch them. The Malanzits were a young race, still at war with spears and rocks. They wouldn't have been able to protect themselves from the monsters with bombs and energy beams.

The population of the world was destroyed, this time with a brutality unlike the others. The Iskios had killed on other planets, but not an entire race. They'd also dropped airborne viruses and chemical warfare on unsuspecting worlds, leaving millions of casualties in their wake.

"We have to end this. The Balance be praised," a female officer said. I couldn't recall her name.

"We're picking up signs of an Iskios vessel four parsecs away, sir."

I blinked and turned my head from the horrible images of death from the planet below.

"We've warned them countless times. Seek them out."

"And then?" my first officer asked.

"Then we destroy them."

The chamber was the fullest I'd ever seen it. There wasn't a single seat left empty, and countless Theos were standing on the balcony looking down. Today was the day. The day our fate would be sealed.

And I was the one to give the news.

Balance. I imagined the universe on a scale, the disaster being created by the Iskios far outweighing the kindness and innovation of us, the Theos. We were only a part of the balance, but a large portion nonetheless.

"Quiet!" Hazal called from beside me, striking his gavel down on the table. "Silence for your leader!"

I stood as everyone else sat. A lone cough from the middle of the room echoed through the chamber, and I spoke. "They must perish."

It was as if everyone spoke at the same moment. We knew the Theos' feeling about this topic. It was a mix of reactions. Some wanted compassion, others prison, but more wanted death. A few even wanted us to not intervene at all, but that was blasphemy to a Theos, for we praised the Balance.

I raised a single gloved hand. My cloak opened, and I suddenly wished the evening could have been cooler. I continued to sweat under the clothing, hoping no one noticed my frailty. I wasn't at peace with the decision. It had taken far too many sleepless nights, and even longer to perfect the stones' preparation.

The room eventually fell silent once again, and I waited a moment longer than normal to speak. "We will track each of them down, using our new technology that allows us to identify each living Iskios. The energy output to make this work will be astronomical, but we will harness the stars." Killing a star by sucking the energy out to power the Locator was the least of our concerns, but destroying something so wonderful still hurt me.

"And what will happen when we find them, Governor?" someone called from the balcony above.

"I cannot say. But you will never see another Iskios for as long as you shall live. Their reign of terror is over." I couldn't tell them we would fuse them into the crystals at Elam Four. It was the only way to keep the balance. By killing them all, their energy would cease to exist. We needed it to continue. We needed Balance.

I watched the feeds from *Elam Four*. The crystals began to change colors. How had this happened? None of our scientists could tell us. It had taken centuries to track each and every Iskios down, but we had succeeded. I'd seen the videos of my ancestor making the decree before the crowded chamber but had never imagined I'd be the one to make this decision.

"We cannot continue. The Balance is off. Without the Iskios to offset us, we won't exist." It pained me to say it, but the four Theos around the table nodded in agreement.

Tagu pulled his beard. "Barl, we have anticipated this."

I was flabbergasted. "You have?"

"Yes. We have a solution."

I couldn't believe what I was hearing. Thank the Balance. "What is it?"

"We fuse ourselves as we did the Iskios," Tagu said, eyebrows lifted. His orange eyes shone brighter than normal.

"To what end? Death? What is the difference how we get there?" I asked.

"Come with me. Let me show you the Shandra stones."

I was tired. The tests had gone on for decades, and my patience was at an end. The Balance was deeply disturbed, and we could see it in the universe around us. Unsuspected black holes opened to swallow peaceful systems. A star went supernova in the middle of a highly populated region, with only one hundred years to attempt a relocation. It was time.

"We will store ourselves in the portals, giving the inhabitants the ability to travel. This is innovation we can pass on. Our energy *harnessed. Do you agree, Barl?" Tagu asked. He was wearing down; even though we could live a long life, he'd bypassed the cellular mutation, as had many of our kind.*

"What if a greater imbalance arises in the future? Who will there be to save the universe from destruction?" I asked, not expecting an answer.

A young man stepped from behind Tagu and raised his hand. "I will."

"Ah, yes. Karo here has volunteered to stay behind. He'll act as a guard. We've hidden all traces of ourselves, and we've made it so we'll be all but forgotten. A name whispered on the wind, with nothing solid to remember us by."

"Then how will they know to search us out?" I asked, wondering if we should call the whole thing off. I saw the portal stone, dull and lifeless, and even though I knew my consciousness wouldn't be active inside it, the idea of living out eternity inside a stone caused my stomach to spin inside me.

"They'll seek us out. It is written in the Balance." Tagu always seemed so sure of himself. He had me buying into his rhetoric even when I didn't want to believe him.

"Start the process," I said, feeling the weight of our millions on my shoulders. In the end, we got full support. It was all or nothing, and I cried the night before at the loss. The Theos, my people, were so full of intelligence and life. What kind of universe would allow our existence to be hinged on that of someone as vile as the Iskios? In the end, that was what allowed me to go with peace. I wouldn't have the Balance of the Iskios to concern myself with any longer.

"Very well. Karo, follow the instructions I've left with you. Do not fail our kind," Tagu said firmly.

"I won't, Father," the young man said.

I followed Tagu and touched the Shandra stone.

"We are ready to beam," Tagu said into a mic. We had vessels full of Theos over each world with a portal. From there, they would be lashed into the stone, powering the portals for eternity. Our vessels

were hidden to all sensors and were cloaked from any of the planet's inhabitants' eyes.

A tear slipped down my cheek and fell onto the stone, rolling off and onto the ground. I watched it hit the dust, drying up as it did so. Would anyone remember the Theos? Would they find the hidden portals and use them, and speak the praises of the creators?

My thoughts were cut short as light enveloped the room, and I entered the stone.

TWENTY-EIGHT

I fell down and curled into a ball. The images had come quickly, and I could still taste the lips of the young Iskios girl. I could smell the sweat inside the chamber room, and the fear of Barl as he entered the portal stone.

A shadow crossed over me, and I saw a hand appear beside me. "Dean Parker, I have shown you something no one else has ever witnessed. Do you now understand why we did what we did?"

It was much as Sarlun had told me, but the visceral projection unsettled me more than I could have imagined. The Theos had literally sacrificed themselves to the portals in order to obtain Balance. It was awe-inspiring and overwhelmingly sad at the same time: a balance of its own.

I took his hand and let him help me to my feet. "I understand. How do I get Mary back? And how do we stop them?"

"Some thought we would be able to take our physical form once again, but we cannot. Like the Iskios, we need a vessel."

I cringed, thinking of what he hinted at. "Is that the only way?"

"It would seem so. We will counter their hold on her, and hopefully, their hold on the Unwinding."

"Come with me. You can be the vessel."

He shook his head. "I will come with you, but I cannot be the vessel. I am not of sound mind. I've been here for too long. Though I don't look old, my body would not be able to withstand the energy."

I pictured myself being ripped apart by a force of Theos rushing into me. "And mine would?"

"I'm not sure."

Great answer. "What choice do I have? Show me how." I was resigned to letting it happen. Mary had the Iskios controlling her. I could handle this. I'd save her. I scratched at my beard for a moment and waited for Karo to direct me.

"It won't be easy," he said.

I asked the rhetorical question: "What's ever easy?"

He tapped the top of the red crystal with a finger. "You have two choices."

"What are they?" I asked.

"You can merge with those inside the portal stone here and find Mary, freeing her from the confines of the evil Iskios possessing her." That sounded good. "Or you travel to each stone and gather every Theos to battle the Unwinding."

"That will take too long." I watched my tongue. I knew I had to stop the Unwinding, but selfishly, Mary came first.

"It may. You may be too late to save your Mary and to stop the Unwinding if you delay."

He made my mind up. "Take me to the Shandra."

"I warn you. It will not be easy to control them. The Theos are a strong people. They may try to take you over, much like Mary was." Karo watched me closely, likely trying to gauge my reaction.

"It's a risk I'll have to take. But since you said time doesn't move the same as normal in here, how about another piece of pizza first? I'll need the energy."

Karo laughed and clapped me on the back. "I'll miss having someone around."

"How does that work? If you aren't gods, how do you stop time?"

"We don't. The room just has a field around it that reverses time every millisecond." This seemed like no big deal to Karo.

"You mean we're time traveling?" As if I hadn't been creeped out enough today.

"In a sense, yes."

Suddenly, the pizza wasn't so appetizing.

"In order to access the Theos inside, you must use the table, but not like you have been." Karo showed me how to access another hidden component to it. He explained the order of symbols to enter, ending with the newly found Theos image, which I could now recall, instead of promptly forgetting it like before.

"Show me again, please." I couldn't risk screwing this up. I needed to know the process so I could go gather the rest of the Theos after I had Mary back.

Once I was confident I could do it again, on another world's portal table, he showed me what to do next.

"We must wake them," Karo said. His voice held a tinge of reverence to it. I'd seen him call Tagu "Father" in the vision, and knew it must be hard for him to stand here, where so many powerful Theos had been infused inside the stone.

I touched the gemstone now. It was larger than any from the other portal sites, perfect in its symmetry. This one was wine red, and it stood as a good symbol for the blood the Theos had sacrificed to do what they thought necessary. I wondered if any of the Balance they spoke of really mattered, but I'd tell Karo whatever it took to get the tools to save Mary.

"Are you okay with this?" I asked the gray-faced ancient alien.

"My father trusted me to know what's right, and I feel their energy thrumming to be released. They know something is afoot, that the Iskios are back. They want to fight. I can feel it!" His voice rose, and his eye went wide. "Don't you feel it, human?"

I didn't, but I nodded along. "How do we wake them?" I thought about Barl and the decisions he had to make. Would I ever be able to sacrifice everyone I knew and loved for the sake of others? I knew I wouldn't be able to. He was a much stronger being than I. Maybe his way wasn't right. Maybe you lived with the threat of danger and fought to keep your own safe. In the vision, I'd been inside his skin. I'd felt what he felt, and it was a weight all too familiar to me.

"The code is entered. Take your gloves off. Touch the stone. Feel the Balance. Breathe them in. They will come." Karo stepped back, and he kept walking as I removed my gloves, feeling the dampness of my nervous sweat on my palms. I wiped them on my pants legs and looked back at my host. He was still moving away, as if fearful of what was about to occur.

"Karo, where are you going?" I asked, worried now.

"Touch it!" His voice was ferocious, and I instantly didn't trust what I was about to do. Did I have a choice? Was I being tricked again?

I closed my eyes and pictured Mary in the throne room within the crystal pyramid. She stood there, mist pouring into her beautiful eyes. I saw my wife inside there and knew I had to do this. I had to do something, or she was going to be lost forever.

"Touch it, Dean Parker! Breathe the Theos in, and change the universe!" he demanded, and his last words set a trigger off inside me. I pressed my palms to the cool red stone, and light shot out of it. My teeth chattered with an energy force so powerful I nearly fell off my feet.

I took a deep breath, and another, feeling my head go light with each intake of air. I kept doing this until the energy stopped flowing at me. My eyes were still closed, the light too bright to see anything without damaging my retinas.

I could still hear Karo yelling behind me, a sort of crazed encouragement mixed with sobbing.

When I opened my eyes, I was two feet off the ground, a white light emanating from my body like a mist of illumination. I faltered, but instead of falling, I floated to the ground. My arm darted out, and I rotated my hand to see light lifting from my semi-transparent skin. My bones were visible through the hand, and I closed my fist, trying to catch the light.

I felt the same, but altered in a way I couldn't comprehend, like I was washed away in a river of endless emotions that carried me downstream. Karo was breathing heavily behind me, and I turned to see him staring, tears streaming down his face. "Father?" he asked.

"I'm here," a voice came from within me, not my own. "Son, thank you for your sacrifice. You have done well."

Karo stepped closer and fell to his knees, his white locks covering his face as he bent forward. "What was it like, Father?"

"It was nothing. And everything." I said the words and tried to swallow them away. I blinked hard, willing myself to be in control. I found my own voice. "Karo, there are too many of them." My heart didn't race, sweat didn't pour off my body, but the pressure in my mind was extreme. So many voices trying to shout out at the same time. Everyone wanted to be heard.

Barl came forth; I recognized his emotions as he pushed the others down. "Dean," I said in his voice. "Focus. You can stay in control, this I know."

"I'm trying. What can I do?" I asked myself. This must have looked bizarre from the outside.

"You must remember yourself. Your mission, your drive. Focus on it. Stay in control, Dean." Barl's energy slowly departed, and I pictured Mary in jeans, her hair in a ponytail, digging out the garden at our home on New Spero. The clamoring Theos stilled, and I helped Karo up from his position on the ground.

"Your father is well. Don't worry about him. He loves you very much," I said, and Karo's eyes firmed up, his lips pursed, as if setting a resolve he hadn't had a moment ago.

"Thank you, Dean." He was still looking at me strangely. What did I appear like to him? Was I different?

"You must put one back," Barl said through me.

"Put one back?" I asked, unsure what he meant.

"The portal must function. Put me back," he said, and I understood.

"No," another voice said from inside me. "Let me stay here." Tagu wanted to go back into the stone. I'd happily return them all at that moment if I knew I didn't need them. I felt ready to burst with all of them trapped inside me.

"How?" I asked, unsure who I was even asking.

Karo spoke. "Press your palm to the stone and breathe out. Do you recognize my father's energy now?"

I did. I allowed him to come up from the depth of my mind. *You are returned,* I said, and touched the stone again, feeling a stream of light leave my body and enter the now pale-rouge stone once again. His reunion had been short-lived.

"Karo, I need to leave," I said.

He nodded absently. He was still staring at the stone. "You know how to do this now. Repeat this at any portal, but remember, that portal won't work again after you use it. My father cannot sustain more than one energy transaction on his own. It will be closed after you leave."

I realized then the final sacrifice his father was making. His last energy would be used to power the Theos portal, and none would return here by the Shandra.

I nodded, still feeling the Theos uneasily within. "Farewell, Karo."

"Farewell, Dean Parker."

I hesitated. "Karo, why stay here? Come with me. I have somewhere you might enjoy. They'll keep your identity a secret. They never need to know."

He looked ready to dismiss my idea, but surprisingly, he stalled. "What would I do?"

I shrugged. "I don't know. You could live a life. For yourself, not built on sacrifice and duty. You could live a life you want."

"I don't know if I'm suited for something like that."

I felt the tug of the Theos telling me this was the right thing. "Come with me."

"Go with him, Karo," Barl's voice projected, and I pushed it back. I couldn't let them think they could jump into the pilot's seat any time they wanted.

Karo shifted on his feet before standing up straight. "I'll go."

"We can always bring you back if necessary," I said.

This seemed to solidify his decision.

I moved to the portal table and noticed the lights on it were dim, faded to an outline. I didn't know where Mary was, or how I could stop her, but I had the first step inside me. I had the power of the Theos. And I knew just where to get the latest news of the Unwinding.

Haven.

I tapped the icon, and Karo and I disappeared from the Theos home world.

TWENTY-NINE

*M*ary watched impassively as the Unwinding continued. Forty planets now, not nearly enough. Vessels flew at her, a whole fleet of nuclear attacks and rail guns, firing at will, hoping to end the vortex, to end *her*.

None of it worked. The nuclear devices just added to the destructive energy she was wielding. The fools. She let them unleash everything they had before she waved a hand, shooting green energy at the horde of attacking ships. She latched on to them and pulled them into the swirling maw of the vortex, and felt it grow slightly larger.

She let out a laugh before feeling a shift. She screamed now, a pain ripping through her mind. They were gone! It was all their fault, and now they returned? It couldn't be. The thought repeated in her mind like a mantra. The Theos were back. They were but a glimmer of light in the darkness of her Unwinding, but it was enough to cast doubt somewhere in the depths of her mind.

Another fragment of Mary's mind thrummed with joy. He'd done it. Dean had brought them back. She tried to take the moment of fear in the Iskios inside her and usurp the invaders, but she was shoved back with a ferocity unlike any before. She cowered inside her mind, hiding in the corners, trying to flee their uncontainable anger.

The Unwinding would continue. A star was close, and with that, she would move on. The galaxy was becoming more populated, and she exalted each life she snuffed out with the vortex.

The small part of the woman hiding away kept hope to herself. She wouldn't share it with them. It was hers only, hope that Dean could stop what she was doing.

"*D*ean, I couldn't tell it was you. You nearly had me sending every armed person on Haven to the portal." Leslie paced in front of us, eyeing us both suspiciously. "What happened?"

I still hadn't seen my reflection. What was she so worried about? "I'm fine, Leslie. Meet Karo. He's a friend of mine."

She rolled her eyes. "If you won't tell me what's going on, I'm not sure I can be of much help."

We were outside the caves on Haven, alone with Leslie and a transport vessel. "Where's Terrance?" I asked.

"He's at home, sleeping. We had some unexpected guests arrive yesterday, spinning some crazy tales."

"Did it have anything to do with a large destructive energy force?" I asked, smiling at her.

"I should stop being surprised by you. Yes, they did happen to mention that."

I smiled again, this time for real. I knew this was the right place to come to. The gossip flowed freely here, though a lot of it wasn't factual. I needed to know where the Iskios were last sighted. Then I'd be off again.

"Where are the others? Slate came here looking for you," she said.

"When?"

"This morning! He said you were just with them when you got separated. He also asked me to send a message if you showed up."

I raised a hand, and white mist lifted off it. I tucked the hand into a pocket, but Leslie saw the whole thing. "Don't do that. They're in danger. I have to do this alone."

"Do what?" she asked.

"Don't tell them where I am. Take us to town, and I'll talk to you about what's happening." I started walking for the transport vessel, and Karo stalked behind me. He was still wearing his cloak but left the hood off to reveal his lengthy white hair and big green eyes.

Leslie watched him suspiciously. She sidled up to me and whispered in my ear, so closely I could feel her hot breath on my cheek. "What have you gotten yourself into?"

"Trust me. I don't have a choice," I whispered back, hefting the weight of my borrowed EVA helmet and other supplies from Rivo up on my shoulder. "You'll understand soon enough."

"You better not be bringing trouble to our little Haven, Dean." She looked to Karo, who remained stoic, facing the lander as if he knew he was being spoken about.

"*T*he Jespal system? You're sure?" I asked.

"That's what they told us." Terrance sat across from me at their kitchen table. It felt strange to be going over this information here. Part of me wished I was in a war room somewhere, smelling a freshly polished wood table and pointing at large 3D maps on the walls. This felt too amateur. The whole mission suddenly felt impossible, a task far beyond a simple accountant's skill set.

I saw my reflection in the glass-doored cabinets along the dining room wall and changed my mind. I wasn't just

Dean Parker any longer. My eyes were now pure white. Light misted out of them on occasion, floating drops of energy. My hands shone, and I'd put my gloves on to hide the fact, but Leslie had already seen it. There was no hiding the Theos' effect on my body. I wasn't going to be able to walk the streets any time soon.

"Can you bring up the map?" I asked, and Leslie brought out her tablet. She turned the lights off, and an image of the Jespal system appeared. "And they said it's all gone? The planets, the star, everything?"

"We didn't believe them. Thought they must have been lost, or had an error in their coordinates, but if you're saying Mary did this, then… whoa." Terrance leaned back in his chair and ran his hands through his dark hair.

I stood up, knocking my chair backwards. Karo was the only one who remained unaffected. "Mary didn't do it! She's only the vessel. The Iskios did this!" I yelled.

"Dean, calm down," Leslie said, lifting a hand in the air and pointing her palm toward me. She was right. Shouting at them wasn't going to help anything.

I picked the chair up, feeling sheepish as I sat back down in it. "Where's the neighboring system?"

Leslie zoomed out and showed two options. "They're probably heading for either of these. This one is far closer." She focused in on it, and I couldn't believe my eyes.

"I know that world." I pointed to a planet fourth from the system's star. It was the same world we'd met Suma on. What were the odds? Insurmountable.

"How?" Leslie asked me, and Karo studied me closely as I told them the story.

"That was right before we came to see Kareem, and when you came with us to Earth."

"It almost seems like it was meant to happen, Dean Parker." Karo spoke for the first time since we'd sat down at the table.

"Maybe, or it's a fluke. Either way, it changes nothing, except I know where she's heading now." Butterflies danced in my stomach. It was time.

I thought about my supplies: a box with some concussion grenades Rivo snuck into the pack, a gun, and the EVA from Garo's vessel. I felt my pocket, and the familiar circular Shifter was there. I wasn't sure if it would come to needing it, but I was comforted by its existence.

"We will help you, Dean," a voice said from my mouth. Damn it. The Theos inside me had been silent since the portal room at their home planet. Leslie and Terrance stared at me, jaws open.

"What the hell was that?" Terrance asked quietly. His mouth hung wide open in shock.

"I may have a few travelers in me right now."

"As if we couldn't tell something was off about you. Seeing how you have light escaping your body and your eyes are white and leaking lumens. Who are they?" Leslie asked.

"The Theos."

"What?" It was Leslie's turn to stand up. "How? Why?"

"I needed their help." I explained the Balance as I understood it, and Karo sat quietly, refraining from adding to the story. By the end of my monologue, they were both nervously glancing at Karo, the last remaining living Theos.

"Hello, Karo," Leslie said, then turned to Terrance and said just loud enough for me to hear, "I wish we'd cleaned up a little more."

"Hello," Karo said. "Thank you for taking me in. Do you have any pizza?"

Using the portals felt strange now that I understood how they were powered. If I ended up taking more Theos to help my cause, I'd effectively destroy more portal pathways, and if possible, I didn't want to end New Spero's access to Haven.

"Good luck, Dean. Are you sure we can't help you?" Leslie asked as she gave me a cautious but firm hug. I could tell from her glances that she wasn't entirely sure the new glowing body was actually me.

"It's too dangerous. They said the vortex destroyed an entire fleet from the Jespal system. I'll get her back." The last was said as much for her as it was for me.

I was in my EVA, and I told myself I was prepared for whatever came my way. In truth, I was terrified. The Theos inside me told me they would help, but I still didn't know what that meant, and they weren't handing out answers to my internal monologue.

Karo was with Terrance at the house, and they were trying to figure out a back story for the unique being.

"It's time," I said, and Leslie – looking so much like Mae had, only with a short haircut – smiled softly and walked out of the room, leaving me alone with the Theos in my head.

The portal stone lit up as I found the right symbol. I remembered it from that first trip Slate and I had unsuspectingly taken. How things had changed since that day.

It was time, indeed. I pressed the icon and felt the Theos in me talk to those in the stone for a moment before I appeared in another familiar portal room.

"They're close," Barl's voice said through me.

"I know," I replied. "I can feel them too."

THIRTY

*I*t felt like only yesterday when Slate and I had arrived at the portals on this vacated planet. I hadn't given much thought to that day since, but now it felt odd. The only reason we even found the portal in the first place was because I was drawn to it. I now understood the Theos had been behind it. They had to be. Barl confirmed this for me. It must have had something to do with what Regnig called me: a Recaster.

"If the stones are powered by you, then why did we need to power up the city block to get the portal reactivated?" I asked in the empty room.

Barl's voice replied, "You didn't. You were meant to meet the young Shimmali here."

Suma. All this time, I was drawn to the portal to meet Suma, and of all places, to the same planet where I'd face the Iskios in their full force. It was too much to be a coincidence. I felt the tugging of the puppet strings and didn't like the feeling. What else had been done by their volition? The Event? The Kraski attacking us? The Bhlat attacking them, only to get me to this spot at this time?

I didn't want to know any more than I had to right now, so I let the question sink to nothingness. My stance was blissful ignorance.

I trod down the corridors, walking toward the bridge that would lead me outside. It had been a while, but the lights were still on. It was eerily quiet, just as it had been, with the slightest buzz of power in the walls.

Walking the halls had a sense of finality to it. Not for the first time, I had the feeling I wasn't going to make it out of this alive, and part of me was all right with that. Mary mattered, the lives of those whom the vortex wanted to devour mattered, but I was just a blip on the radar.

"You are more," Barl said, probably trying to comfort me. It didn't work. Instead, I shoved his voice down and kept moving. It wasn't long before I made it to the doors that would lead outside. I prepared myself for anything and opened it.

It was dark and silent. Lava burned red-hot in the distance: an ocean of doom. Thick clouds hung overhead as they had, and thin forks of lightning shot sideways just past the city lines.

She wasn't here, but she had to be close. I scanned the skies. The clouds were too dense to see anything beyond.

"Let's hope this works like she said it would." Rivo had given me instructions on the suit's thrusters, but I still wasn't sure they could get me into orbit. I activated them and was startled at the stream of blue energy that rumbled below my boots. The knees locked, and I lifted off the ground before increasing the output. Struggling to maintain balance, I floated into the air awkwardly at first, but after a few moments of hovering there, I felt more confident.

Before I knew it, I was rising into the sky, higher than the empty skyscrapers of a long-gone race. I still didn't know who'd lived here and wasn't sure I'd ever find out. Wind rushed against me as I rose, and I leveled out my body to counter the opposite force.

The light I was containing pushed out, enveloping me in a sphere. They'd created a shield, protecting me from the crackling lightning around me as I flew into the clouds.

As I lifted, I saw the powerful lava ocean glow red in the otherwise black night. The clouds thickened as I raced through them, breaching the ceiling of them like a seal from the water. I felt free for the first time in weeks but quickly remembered why I was there, and the weight crashed back onto my shoulders, threatening to spin me out of control.

The energy shield surrounding me glowed brighter as I shakily passed through the world's atmosphere. My muscles tightened within my EVA, and I struggled to keep my eyes open as the burning white light around me shone like a beacon of hope.

Then all was calm. I eased the thrusters back, feeling the Theos relax their grip around me, and opened my eyes to see the lightning storm below and the red-hot ocean steam in the distant landscape. There was nothing quite like seeing a planet from above but being outside a ship when doing it was more than awe-inspiring; it was terrifying.

Something buzzed on the side of my suit, and I didn't recall what the sensor was there for. I fumbled my hands to the vibrating section of my flank and found the Locator Clare had made sure was securely clipped in place. In all the rush of finding the Iskios, I'd forgotten about the device linked to Mary's DNA. Clare had said the range wasn't great, but here it was, alerting me Mary was near.

She was here! A cross of excitement and fear at what she may have become filled every inch of me as I saw the sensor lines blink on the Locator's screen. It showed a map, with me blinking red near the planet, and an icon I could only hope was Mary blinking blue at least ten thousand kilometers away. She was getting closer, and fast.

"Here we go," I said to myself as much as to my passengers and looked away from the world below. I could make out a green object in the distance. Each passing minute saw it getting larger. Mary was here, and she'd brought the Unwinding with her.

How was I going to rush toward this vortex? I'd heard the after-effects of its wake of destruction. It left no room for mercy; it just consumed all life and matter in its path. Would Mary even listen to me? Would she be able to stop it, even if she tried?

I hit the thrusters once again and pushed away from the planet, the Theos' gifted shield still burning white around me, just enough to see through it with my visor dimmed.

I flew toward the vortex with trepidation. I hated being out in space, and somehow here I was doing it again. The Theos' voices inside me eased the stress by releasing something to calm my nerves. I wondered if they would take me over, using me as a vessel if they needed to. I assumed they'd do whatever they needed to stop the Unwinding and the Iskios from destroying anyone else.

The planet behind me kept fading further away. I needed to get Mary to the surface, away from the vortex. Another half hour later, it felt like the vortex wasn't getting as close. She must have stopped pulling it.

My earpiece buzzed. "Well, if it isn't the mate. We knew you'd come someday. It was inevitable."

She was near. Where? I spun around, trying to spot her. The icon on my Locator showed the dot right next to mine. "Mary, I know you're in there. Come with me. I can help you."

"She's beyond your help," Mary said in the Iskios voice she'd used back in the crystal pyramid. "Wait." The voice grew in pitch. "What is in you? What have you brought to us?"

I heard something else in its voice: fear. "The Theos are back. I'm infused with their energy. We're going to stop you!" I shouted. "I am Theos!"

She appeared as black mist crept away from her body. It had been hiding her in the blackness of space. The voice that wasn't hers laughed now. "You are a human, and a pitiful one at that. You are no match for the Iskios. Stay still while we devour the Theos energy and become even more powerful. Yes, you've done us a service today. We'll feed on their life force and they can be part of what they resisted so long ago."

"I know what happened!" I shouted. Mary was floating toward me. She wasn't even in an EVA, and as she neared, I saw she was in the same clothing she'd been wearing when I last saw her. I wanted her to get closer. I needed to see she was okay. That the baby was okay.

"What happened?" the Mary-thing asked.

"The Theos. They drove you from their home."

"Our home!" It cut me off. Mary was closer now, maybe thirty yards away. Her eyes were entirely black, and there was no sign of my wife acknowledging me.

"Then when you didn't get the point and continued to expand on your horrible violence, they finally dealt with you. It would've been much easier if they did what they should have done in the first place." I was goading them now.

"And what's that, human?"

"They should have killed every one of you, then and there. Lined you up and ended the monstrosities before you could evolve to...whatever this is." I pointed beyond Mary at the green swirl in the distance.

"You're wrong. We should have turned on them and kept our planet. Either way, our destiny is coming to fruition. And now, there's more life to destroy. More energy. Always more energy." Mary was close now. She floated ten yards from me. I wanted to go to her but couldn't. That was a sure way to get killed before being able to stop anything.

Without knowing how or why, I lifted a hand, and a beam of light shot from my fingertips toward Mary. It hit the barrier around her, stopping dead as the black mist absorbed it.

"Nice try. You really do have Theos in you. Because that was weak," it said through Mary into my earpiece.

The Iskios were trash-talking me. That was new. I lifted both hands, and white energy coursed again, this time not just a dart but a stream. It hit the barrier with ferocity, and Mary screamed. Mist scattered, and she began to fall for a moment. I ceased the flow of energy by closing my fists, not wanting to hurt her out here.

"If you want more of that, come with me!" I shouted, bent my legs, and hit my thrusters. I balanced myself with the rear air thrusts, and soon I was screeching back toward the planet. I didn't have to look at my Locator to know the blue dot was right on my tail.

"You're going to regret being born, human," the voice said, but I didn't react. I just kept flying.

The Iskios floated Mary behind me, and I found they were a little slower than my suit. It was a hectic journey back to orbit, but I felt relief when I finally did look to see Mary's blue icon still beeping toward me.

The Unwinding vortex was a speck in the distance. At least that was a positive.

I turned my communications off for a second. "Okay, boys, if you're going to give me some powers, or whatever you want to call it, now might be the time. Otherwise, we're kind of screwed."

Barl's presence lifted to the forefront of my mind. "Here." I felt a shift inside me. Pressure moved against my legs and extended to my chest and arms. I didn't know what it was they'd done, but everything was clearer. A fog was lifted. All the stress, concern, worry, and anxiety I'd been feeling were gone. This was it.

I turned, seeing Mary float closer. My earpiece back on, they spoke again. "What do you think will be the outcome here? Stop fooling around, and we'll end you quickly."

"Fair enough. Let's just do it on the surface. I have a fear of heights." I spun, shifting my feet over my head. I hit the thrusters again and raced head first toward the surface, this time over the lava ocean instead of into the lightning clouds.

The Iskios-fueled Mary followed me closely as I zoomed toward the surface. Using the thrusters on the suit's back, I cut the ones on the bottom of the boots and rotated, changing my trajectory. With the confidence given to me by the Theos, I raced low to the ground, under the lightning forks bearing down on the unpopulated city.

I weaved between high-rises and through alleyways as I headed back for the skyscraper I'd emerged from. I had to get to Mary, but how? She seemed so far gone, and the brief interaction hadn't shown me any sign that she was still inside her own mind. Damn it. I had to... the crystals.

I needed to break the Iskios' concentration. I recalled the room near the portals where crystals were piled atop one another in a tube: the power source for that building. Perhaps they could break the barrier of Iskios, and I could get through to her again. This time, if she tried to send me home with the wave of a hand, I had the Theos to prevent that.

The building was approaching. I once again changed directions and flew straight up the exterior of the immense vacant high-rise, until I made it to the level I'd come from. I lowered myself down and felt my boots hit the solid surface. I breathed out a sigh of relief as my trek into space came to an end.

Mary floated down on the adjacent building. It was across the street, a lot of air between us, but she felt close enough to touch. I lifted a hand and stretched it out toward her. "Mary, are you in there?"

"Mary is gone. She is a fine vessel, though. As you die, know this. We will take her and the offspring into the final void as we end the Unwinding." Her mouth moved, but the alien voice sent shivers across my neck.

Inky black mist shot from her hand, straight across the open air. I ducked and rolled away from the blast. It hit the wall behind me, disintegrating the exterior, leaving a hole the size of a beach ball. Another came at me before I could dodge it, but my shield held. I saw the black substance get eaten in the light, and I fired back at her.

The gun Rivo had given me was unslung from my back, and I pulled the trigger, seeing red beams cut through the air toward Mary. I didn't want to hurt my wife, but I thought they might help disrupt the shield around her. They bounced off uselessly, and I dropped the gun to the ground before shooting more light at her.

It absorbed much the same as before. She leapt across the chasm, landing sure-footed near me. I had to get her to follow me to the crystals. I turned to run, but a lash of black tendrils swung out from her hand and worked through my shield, grabbing my foot. I hit the floor with a thud, and in an instant, she was right above me.

I thought I saw a flicker of my Mary beneath the black eyes, but I was probably just seeing things. "You are ours," it said, raising both hands toward me.

Black beams hit me, and I screamed in rage. It was primal as the pain racked my body, coursing from my head to my toes. I'd never felt anything quite as excruciating, and I shot back. I willed everything from the silent Theos inside me. They lent me what they could, and Mary was thrown sideways with my last-ditch effort, falling over the side of the balcony. I scrambled over to the ledge. "Mary!" I called, knowing it wouldn't really be her hearing me yell. Instead of seeing a falling body, she floated back up and fired layer upon layer of black mist at me. She was laughing now, a terrible demonic noise.

I fought to get up, to do anything, but it was hopeless. They were stronger than I was. I hadn't harnessed enough Theos for what I needed to do. I would die here at Mary's hands, with the Unwinding heading toward the planet, ready to suck everything in the system into the maw of the vortex. I'd failed.

"Dean, roll away!" a familiar voice yelled, and I looked up to see Mary stumble backwards, screams flowing out of her in another's voice.

Suma was beside me, and the anguished cries became louder when the Iskios realized they'd been trapped. Suma held the same device we'd caged the possessed Leonard inside on the crystal world, and Mary bashed the energy field walls with black mist.

My head fell back in exhaustion.

THIRTY-ONE

"*T*he vortex is getting closer. We have to do something," Slate said. I opened my eyes and tried to blink away the looming headache.

I glanced back to the invisible barrier holding Mary in, and silently expressed my gratitude to my friends, who'd once again come to the rescue and fought by my side.

"What did you fire at her?" I asked. I was sitting down, my back pressed against the wall under the hole Mary had blown open.

"Crystal pellets. Pretty cool, hey?" Slate looked smugly at me. "I remembered the crystals having an effect on Mary when the Padlog dropped stalactites on her, so Clare whipped something up."

Clare was getting good at whipping things up. I'd have to thank her about a million times, for a start.

"Has she said anything?" I asked.

Slate stared at Mary while he spoke. "The usual. We're pitiful. All going to die. Blah blah blah."

"How did you know where I was?" I knew the answer already.

"Leslie. And it's a good thing she told us." Slate broke his locked stare at my wife; his eyes were distant behind his helmet's face shield when he turned to me.

The Unwinding vortex was getting closer, probably being drawn by the trapped Iskios. We had to stop them.

"I'm out of ideas. You're up." Slate helped me to my

feet, and I groggily stood, holding myself up against the side of the building. "Where's Suma?"

"She said something about shutting down the drones. Remember those things? I don't think we want them coming back while we're sitting out here."

Suma was always one step ahead. I was grateful they'd come. Otherwise, I'd probably be dead, and Mary would be devouring the world by now.

I knew she was inside there somewhere. But with her trapped behind the energy field, I couldn't test the crystal theory on her.

"Barl?" I asked, getting a shocked look from Slate.

"What did you call me?" he asked.

There was no reply from the now dormant Theos inside me. All their strength and power seemed to be stunned or gone for good. I shook my head. How could I explain it to him? "Sorry. I should tell you. I found the Theos world."

His eyes went wide. The Mary-thing got up from her crouched position and walked as far forward in her cage as she could, trying to hear.

"You what?" He sounded incredulous.

"I found them. I'll explain later. It had something to do with my little blue friend, and a two-foot-tall bird man named Regnig."

Slate's eyes stayed wide. "This was on Bazarn?"

"Yes. What did you find?" I asked.

"Here, Natalia discovered this in the library. We were each researching different topics, and she found one on transference into stones. This is what you thought the Theos did?" He handed me a small tablet from a pocket.

I flipped through it. "It's exactly what they did. That's how I got them inside me. I transferred their energy."

"Then you'll want to see this. Go to page seven." His voice held an urgency to it.

I did as he requested and couldn't believe what I was reading. There was no mention of the Theos using this technology, but it was implied. If this worked, I could save Mary. It was all theoretical, according to the readings, but I had no choice.

"Slate, you've done it!" I wanted to jump up and down in joy, but I was still light-headed, so a fist pump was all I could muster. "Nat's getting a big fat kiss when this is over."

Slate chuckled. "I'm not sure Magnus will approve."

The whine of the lift carried through the dead air, and Slate grabbed his pulse rifle, getting between me and the elevator. He let the gun slide to his side when Suma's head popped up, her snout crammed into her facemask. She waved at me, and my heart melted. Here were two of my best friends. Slate, who'd been at my side and saved me countless times, and Suma, the Shimmali girl from a different world, who'd become our newest member. I thought back to the idea that we were all guided to this planet a couple years ago. The three of us discovering the portals that day and Suma's never-ending curiosity bound our fates together.

As we stood there with Mary caged behind the energy shield, I knew there could have been no other way. The clouds had lightened, and I could see the green swirling energy force, now the size of Earth's moon in the sky. We had to end this.

"Suma, I know how to fix Mary. We need to bring her to the portal stone."

---

*T*he portal room felt familiar, comforting almost, as we

trudged into it. The Theos inside me remained silent, and I wondered if that was it for them. Slate said my eyes no longer glowed white, and there was an absence in my fingertips where I'd felt them earlier. I didn't know if that was a good thing or not.

The stone glowed as we entered the room. When we dragged Mary in, inside her containment cage, it began to flash quickly and angrily, even more so than when we'd brought Leonard to the crystal world portal with the Iskios inside him.

"How's this going to work?" Suma asked, her tweets and squawks becoming English in my earpiece.

"Essentially, I have to download the life forces inside Mary into the stone." It was going to be a huge gamble, and I suddenly wished Barl were inside me to guide me. I was putting a lot of faith into the tablet's readings from the Bazarn library. The idea was sound. If the Theos had been able to put themselves into the stone and have their life force moved out afterwards, then you could potentially do the same with a single identity.

The readings stated that you could theoretically "download" someone near death and insert them into another body. It referred to downloading one's memories into a clone. This wasn't quite the same as that.

"Are you sure?" Slate asked. His voice was low as he looked at his friend Mary. Her eyes were steaming black, her lips in a snarl showing teeth.

"You will never save this one. The Unwinding is already too far gone. Mary is dead, and so are you," the voice inside Mary said.

I couldn't believe it. I had to try something. I knew my wife was still in there, and I needed to separate her from the Iskios. I found my gaze drifting to the slight bump on her stomach. She couldn't be more than fourteen weeks.

Our baby was inside there. There was no turning back now.

The portal table flashed on and off in warning to the Iskios in the room, but it still functioned as normal as I keyed in the codes Karo had made me memorize. Instead of pulling the Theos out, I'd be putting the Iskios and Mary inside.

I felt my entire body flush in anxiety at the prospect of what we were about to attempt. It was hard to even look at Mary, knowing she was possessed by the Iskios. Her glares and snarls were so alien to her face, it was like looking into a stranger's eyes.

Suma was scanning through the documents Slate had brought with him, translating them with a plug-in adapter.

"She doesn't need to touch it to be absorbed. That's how they worked before. It essentially beams them into it." The portal table said it was ready.

"Then how do we get it to only lock on to the Iskios? If we can do that, then Mary will be left alone in her body with the baby," Slate said.

I couldn't believe I hadn't thought of that. "That's it. We need to isolate the Iskios and beam them into it. But how?"

Suma was still reading, but her snout twitched inside her facemask when Slate made the suggestion. She let out a few squawks, which quickly translated. "I have it!"

I rushed over to her side. "What does it say?"

She looked up slowly from the tablet and walked out of the room, waving me to follow. "We have to isolate one of them. But it will involve opening the shield and shooting at her again with the crystal pellets. When one of them mists off, we pull it into Clare's Locator."

"The one that told me where Mary was?" I asked.

She nodded.

I didn't love the idea, but we were left with few choices.

I pulled it out of my pocket and passed it to Suma, who quickly went to work programming it.

"*A*re we ready?" Slate asked, positioning the pellet rifle in the air, aiming at my wife.

"Ready," I said, and Suma tapped the controls on the shield. We'd spent an hour working out the details in private, away from the prying ears of the Iskios, and we thought it just might work.

Mary's black eyes went wide as the Iskios controlling her realized the energy shield was down. She raced forward, black mist spilling off her hands. Slate shot fast and firmly, hitting her barrier at chest level. The mist shot out, and Suma ran from behind, tapping the Locator. The mist spread until it grazed the Locator, which glowed orange as Suma broke away. I turned the containment shield back on, and the loose mist sucked back into Mary's mouth.

"What have you done?" the alien voice asked.

"You'll find out soon enough," I answered. "Do we have it?"

Suma smiled at us, and Slate set his gun down. "Got it!"

"Now we need to see if the next step will work." Suma went to work at the portal table. I was sure glad to have her there; otherwise, I doubted I'd have been able to pull any of this off. Why had I gone alone? My mind had been so focused on getting to Mary, and I'd thought the Theos inside me would have been able to help more. Either way, it had worked out, or was about to work out. I knew it.

She tapped away at the commands for at least fifteen minutes, while Mary spouted out angry death promises toward all three of us. It was getting easier to ignore, especially since I knew it wasn't her speaking to us. I only hoped she was still in there, undamaged.

"Dean, I think it's ready. The program didn't want to be tampered with, but like anything, there's always a back door open. They were advanced, but a couple of thousand years is a long time for technology. Some of this is actually quite archaic." Suma's noises translated, and I laughed at how confident and smart she could be without coming across as smug.

"Then it's time." Slate pulled the containment field closer to the stone, his forearms bulging as he dragged along with my wife and her "guests."

"We're going to get you back, Mary," I said, looking her in the eyes. The black mist didn't dissipate, but for a second, it felt like she heard me.

"You will all die. Everyone will die. Whatever you do here won't be enough," the Iskios voice said.

I ignored it and spoke to my wife beyond the mist. "I love you. We'll be home soon, honey. Our family will be home soon." I blinked away a forming tear and cleared my throat. "Suma. Let's do this."

She tapped a key on the table, and all of our eyes went to Mary as the shield went down. Black mist raced toward me.

THIRTY-TWO

"*D*ean, look out!" Slate shouted and dove at me, knocking me to the ground. The mist careened over our bodies and was sucked toward the portal stone. The ink-black blotches appeared to fight the pull momentarily, but their effort was futile. They were sucked toward the stone, stopping for a second on the surface of the gem before being absorbed.

Something thudded to the ground behind us. Mary! I pushed Slate's heavy form off me and scrambled over to Mary's limp body.

"Mary, are you okay?" I asked but received no response. She wasn't in an EVA suit, but Slate and I had been able to breathe here before. It was only outside we needed the respirators. Just to be sure, Slate came over and passed me one of the breathing apparatuses, and I slipped it over her head.

Her chest was rising and falling slowly, which was a good sign. Was Mary still inside? And was she alone? "Mary, you're going to be okay," I said.

Suma was looking over from the portal table. "Dean, we have a problem."

"What is it?" We couldn't handle more problems at the moment. I only wanted Mary to wake up.

"The portal. It's dead."

Without the portal, we had no way of leaving the planet. Oddly enough, I didn't even care. If Mary was free of the Iskios, that was all that mattered. "We'll figure it out."

"I'm going to go check on the Unwinding," Slate said. "Maybe it's gone, since the vessel isn't in their control any longer."

I hated the casual way he called Mary *the vessel* but didn't say anything. I was being oversensitive. "Good call."

Suma continued to try to work the portal table, with no luck, but as Slate came back into the room a short time later, Mary's eyes fluttered open.

I'd been through a lot over the last few years, but seeing Mary come to, with no black mist covering the whites of her eyes, had to be the highlight of it all. My heart leapt in my throat, and I broke down then and there. The emotions of the last few weeks came flooding out, and I pulled my helmet off, letting the stale air brush against my wet cheeks.

"Mary, it's Dean," I said through choked coughs. She was looking past me, as if her eyes wouldn't focus on the room around her. "Mary…" My hand touched her cheek, and she finally turned her head, and I saw her pupils dilate as she locked eyes with me.

She tried to speak, but nothing but a low growl emerged from her throat at first. A few more tries, and I made out a single word: "Dean."

More tears fell, from each of us now. Hers fell down the sides of her face, over her ears and to the ground.

"I can't begin to tell you how happy I am," I said, laughing with my tears.

"Are they…?" Mary tried to sit up, her head moving side to side.

"They're gone. Don't worry, they're gone," I assured her.

Her hands went to her face and over her eyes. She

stuck a hand out and gave the tiniest of smiles when she saw no mist attached to any of her appendages. This time, I helped her to sit up, and Slate came and assisted me. She had us lean her against the wall in the portal room. It was silent as Mary glanced around, trying to make sense of what she was seeing.

"What happened?" Mary asked. I set a hand on hers and felt the trembling beneath my palm.

I tried to speak calmly. "We got the Iskios out of you. They won't be bothering you any longer."

She was panicked. "Inside me? What are you talking about? The last thing I remember is being in the crystal pyramid with you two. How did Suma get here?"

"You don't remember anything at all?" Slate asked, crouching down beside Mary.

Mary quickly shook her head from side to side, as if to vehemently deny any recollection at all. "Dean, where are we?"

"On the abandoned world where Slate and I met Suma."

"Why?" Before I could answer, she threw another question out at me. "How long ago were we at the Theos world?"

I didn't know how to answer this without worrying her. "First off, it wasn't the Theos world. It was the Iskios."

Her eyes went wide. She pulled the respirator off her face and touched her mouth, as if feeling the black mist pouring down her throat. "They *were* inside me, weren't they?"

I nodded.

"What did they want? What happened?" Mary's voice was quieter now, less strained, but her hands were still shaking and her eyes were wet with tears.

"They took you from us. You sent us back to New

Spero with some power of theirs. I'm not sure how it worked. The Padlog were there, and they broke the spell momentarily," I said.

"The Padlog?"

"The insectoids. They'd been following us, tracking us to the world. Their Supreme didn't give me much for details on their trip, but they were only trying to stop us from unleashing the Unwinding." I looked up to Slate, who still hadn't told us what the vortex was doing out there. Had it failed after the vessel was gone? I could barely wait to ask him, and his eyes told me he had something urgent to say.

Mary closed her eyes. "I see them now. They fired above me, and I ... I shot them with some black energy. Oh, Dean, what have I done?"

"You didn't do anything. Not a damn thing!" I yelled the last and took a second to compose myself. "They manipulated us to get us there, and they took you as their vessel. It's only been a few weeks. I don't even know how long. Five or six, I think. The days have been a blur."

"Five weeks!" she yelled out in surprise. I glanced down at her stomach, which she caught, and her hand ran down to her belly. "What is it?"

I leaned over to her, our heads were touching. "The Iskios said you were with child. It was one of the reasons they chose you over me as the True."

"I'm pregnant? I'd thought there was a chance but hadn't tested it yet." Her voice started off strong but cracked as she kept talking. "This is unbelievable." Tears flowed freely, and I found myself welling up.

I wanted to reprimand her for not telling me, for going on the quest to find the Theos with the possibility, but it wouldn't accomplish anything good. I bit my tongue, because Mary was here and healthy.

"We're going to have a baby," I whispered, and kissed

her on the forehead.

"Boss, I hate to break up this moment, but we have some unfinished business," Slate said.

I broke contact with Mary and turned to him. "What is it?"

"The vortex is still there, and it's not getting any smaller," Slate said. "I think it's still coming for the planet."

Mary was getting up behind me, and when I went to stop her, she waved me away as she began to stand, using her left hand pressed against the wall for support. "I'm fine. Just a little foggy. What's the vortex?"

She really had no memory of her last few weeks, and that was probably for the best. "The Unwinding is the energy force of the dead Iskios from the crystal world," I said. "We went back, and all the color was gone: nothing but clear crystal the whole world over. It's here now, and from what we've heard, it's devoured entire systems' worth of ships, moons, planets, and even stars."

"And…I was the one leading it?" she asked.

"It wasn't you. It was them using your body."

Mary's arms wrapped around herself, as if seeking comfort. "The distinction doesn't feel as clear for me."

"What do we do?" Suma spoke for the first time since Mary had come to. "The portal is closed, and we don't have a ship. The Unwinding is coming to destroy us." She stood beside Mary, and now it was my wife who put an arm around the small Shimmali girl.

We stood inside the dead portal room, each looking at one another for answers we didn't have. There had to be a solution, but what was it?

"Let's go outside. I need a clear perspective." I let Slate and Suma go ahead and paused to turn to Mary. "I'm so glad you're back."

My hands gripped around her tightly, and her head

nestled into my neck. "Dean, thank you."

"For what?"

"For finding me. For getting me back. I don't know how you managed this, but I can't wait to hear the story when we're back home." She slid her hand into mine, and we walked down the corridors. She looked around, seeing the inside of the building Slate and I regaled in our tales about the place.

"I would have done anything."

"Is everyone okay?" She was obviously asking about the rest of our friends.

"Yes. Oh, and we now have a robot in our crew." I smirked as Mary eyed me suspiciously.

"I'll want to hear that story too." Her hand went back to her stomach. "Dean, do you think she's okay?"

"She?" I asked, wondering why she chose a sex.

"I can feel her down there. It might be a boy, but I don't want to think of her as an *it*." It made sense to me.

"I think *she* will be just fine." I winked at her, and we made it past the corridors, bridges, and the exterior doors where Suma and Slate stood, propping the door open.

"Look, boss." Slate pointed toward the sky, where we could make out the swirling vortex even from way down here. The cloud cover was lighter than it had ever been, but winds blew heavily around us as we stepped onto the platform high above the city level.

"Is that it?" Mary asked.

"That's the Unwinding. The destructive force they'd been waiting a long time to unleash on the universe. We'd hoped that freeing you from their grasp would have been enough to stop it, but evidently, it wasn't. For all we know, it'll move without rhyme or reason now." I stopped talking and watched it a moment longer before speaking. "Or maybe it was programmed by the Iskios that had been inside…" I hesitated, knowing it would sound insensitive. Mary didn't seem to notice.

"We need to stop it."

I knew that, but I just wanted to escape it. Then we could get the collective knowledge and power of the Gate-keepers, or the Planetary Alliance I'd heard Rivo's father mention in passing and let them deal with the problem. Sadly, there was no way around this.

We couldn't leave the planet, and it was about to be destroyed by the Unwinding.

"I didn't come here to save you only to have us be eaten by an energy vortex." I hated the option, but it was the only one we had. All the pressures of the last few years, starting with the moment James was ripped from my living room, to the search for the Theos, then Mary, exhaled with a deep breath.

It was my only possibility.

"Boss, why do you have that look on your face again?" Slate asked, picking up my vibe.

I squinted at Mary. She was so wonderful. Even now, with tangled hair and dirt-stained cheeks, she was the most beautiful woman I'd ever laid eyes on. She was my every-thing, and she was carrying our child. The irony of my decision pained me to no end.

"Dean, what is it?" Mary asked, grabbing my hands in hers. She felt like home.

I looked away, unable to watch her eyes as I said it. "I know how to stop it. But I think it's a one-way trip."

THIRTY-THREE

"*W*hat do you mean, one-way trip?" Mary pointed toward the powerful vortex, high above in space. "How can you stop that?"

I patted the Shifter in my pocket. "Garo Alnod."

"Who, or what, is a Garo Alnod?" she asked.

Of course, she didn't know anything about Bazarn, or Rivo and her father. "Without getting into all the details, Garo is one of the wealthiest beings in the universe. One of his companies was trying to create something called a Shifter. You'd be able to transport anything to another dimension."

"Why would anyone do that?" Mary asked.

"Let's say your star's about to go supernova, and you have a system with a hundred billion lifeforms nearby. This would allow you to transport a whole world away. Believe me, I don't understand the science behind it at all."

"Okay, well, that makes some sense," Mary said, probably still wondering what this had to do with me.

"His nemesis, Lom of Pleva, a bad dude who was behind the hybrid creation, wanted the technology for war."

Mary's interest was fully piqued. "He created the hybrids? Like Bob and Janine?"

"Yes. The very same."

"Wow. I've missed out on some important things, haven't I?"

"We'll get to that. He wants the tech, so Garo sets up

for his nemesis to die in a freak accident while Lom was visiting one of his very own mines. Everyone thought he was dead, but Rivo swears he's not, and he's coming for Garo and the Shifter." My hand still rested on the pocket.

"What does this Shifter have to do with our situation?" Slate asked. He didn't know any of this, since we'd been separated on Bazarn.

"I have it, or one of them. The last true device with the ability to shift something to another dimension, or so Garo claimed. He was freaked out, and I offered to take it from him." I didn't know what the others would think.

"You took the Shifter? Is that what that battle on Bazarn was all about? We barely made it out of there alive!" Slate shouted.

Mary raised a hand, taking the conversation back to her. "I'm not even going to ask about Bazarn or the battle there. What are you saying, Dean? You want to use this technology on the Unwinding? Great, let's do it."

I didn't want to say it out loud, but I had to. "I can't use it from here. I have to be… up there." I pointed to the vortex.

"What do you mean? Dean, how are you going to get up there?" Suma asked, finally chiming in.

"I'm wearing Garo's suit. It has built-in thrusters. I've already been there. I goaded the Iskios down to the surface."

"I was floating around in space this whole time?" Mary asked, her expression saying she found the whole thing unsettling.

There was no point in keeping it from her. "Yes. As far as I know, you were."

She didn't comment further on the subject. "Is there any other way?"

"Not unless you can think of anything." I'd run

through options in my mind for the last half hour, but nothing else would work.

"Dean, this is a planet with lots of technology. I bet we can find a ship. Use it to shoot the Shifter into it." Suma stood straight-backed, proud of her idea.

"The vortex is getting closer by the minute. I don't think we have much time, and it needs to be tapped manually. Garo showed me how it works, and he was clear about the details." I brought the compact disc-shaped device out.

Suma stuck her palm out, and I handed it over. She fiddled with it, and I showed her what I knew about the Shifter.

"Here's where we select the dimension to send it to. How will we choose?" Suma asked.

I hadn't thought about that quite yet. "There's no way of knowing what's there. I mean, even Garo made it sound like theory at this point of their research. It didn't sound like they'd had anyone return once they dimensionally shifted."

"We'll be sending it into another dimension?" Slate asked. "There could be millions or billions of lifeforms on the other side, being sent to their deaths."

"Or there could be nothing but empty space." Mary was getting behind me, and that made me grateful for the support.

"Guys, it's either we get devoured by the thing, and let it continue on until it reaches countless other planets, including New Spero, or we toss it away and let some other parallel universe deal with it. I know where my vote's going." I tried to sound confident, but the idea of making it someone else's problem didn't sit well with me. My stomach flopped inside.

"The odds of finding a dimension with life are low. I

studied a theoretical class on the subject," Suma said.

"Fine. Let's say we're doing this. How do you get to it?" Slate asked, frowning at me. He already knew the answer; it was written all over his face.

"I use the suit, fly up there, use the Shifter and fly into it, taking it with me wherever we're going." As soon as I said it, Suma's hand wrapped around the device as if she intended to keep it away from me.

"Dean, no," Mary said. "There has to be another way."

Slate started to undo his own EVA. "Give me the suit. I'll go."

"Stop!" I shouted over them. "I've made my decision. I'm going. Slate, it's too small for you. Suma, it's too big. I've already flown in it, and it's tricky. We can't risk anyone else doing this." Mary wouldn't look me in the eyes.

Suma passed the Shifter over to me. "I'm sorry, Dean." She turned around and walked away. Slate mopped his mask with a gloved hand and joined her, leaving Mary and me alone.

"Dean," she said, her voice light, yet heavy with sadness, "maybe we can get away. Suma thinks there could be a ship nearby."

"Then what? How do we stop it?" I asked.

She refused to look up as tears fell onto her flushed cheeks. "We can find another way, get help."

"You know that's not in our cards. I can't let anyone else deal with it. Just like the Event, or Mae going to the Bhlat, or finding a way to keep everyone we could alive and bringing them to New Spero. We don't have anyone to do this for us. We never have." I hugged her close to me.

"What about our baby? She needs you."

That brought out the tears I'd been trying to hold back. All I'd wanted was a quiet life. I'd become an accountant knowing I could do my work, be my own boss eventually, and watch baseball games on Sunday afternoons. When I met Mary, I wanted nothing more than to have a family and just *be* on our acreage on New Spero. While we'd had a few months of that over the past couple years, it wasn't enough. It was just a tease of what could be. Now it would never happen, and I already mourned for the life we couldn't have together.

"I know…and I need her too. I'm sorry it's come to this, Mary. If there's any way I can make it back, I will." The words were fruitless, said for her sake more than anything. I didn't think it would be possible.

Storm clouds thickened as if to set the mood for my task, and lightning began to flash across the cityscape once again, leading toward the lava ocean.

"I need more time with you," Mary said. Her grip on my hand was tight.

The vortex was closer, the wind stronger over the platform on which we stood, high up on the building. "Time is something we don't have." After all the fight to get Mary and our baby back, I had to leave.

Change the universe. Kareem's words echoed in my mind. Was this my task? To save our universe from the Unwinding? Did it all lead to this moment? The Kraski, the hybrids, the Delta, Patty, Ray, and all the others who'd lost their lives along the way? Was it all so I'd be here with the Shifter in my hand as the Iskios energy vortex threatened everything in the galaxy?

Regnig had called me a Recaster. I had the power to change things. I hadn't found Mary so she could stay under duress. The vortex was the ultimate stress, and I could change that. I would.

I took my helmet off once again and coughed as the harsh air hit my lungs. I didn't care. It was worth it. Mary slid her respirator off her face, and our lips met. Her hand pulled me in closer, the moment intimate and raw, lust and love intertwined as we stood there, lightning cracking in the sky around us. Wind gusted heavily, and we ignored it all, and for a short time, there was nothing in the world by the two of us.

Eventually, we broke our contact. Both of us had tear-stained cheeks. "I love you, Mary. I always will."

"I love you. Come back to us." She rubbed her belly, and my heart shattered.

I wiped my eyes before getting my helmet back on. I tried to firm my resolve and push it all down. My reservoir was getting full of the pain and angst, but now wasn't the time to let it out. It was time to save my friends, and most importantly, Mary and our baby.

"Dean…" Slate pointed to the sky, where we could see the large vortex above the world, even through the clouds where we stood. It was closer. That made it time.

"Slate, I can't begin to say…"

"Then don't, boss. Just do what you have to do. Finish the mission and come home to us." He hugged me and fired off a salute.

Suma ran to me, wrapping her short arms around my waist. "What he said." Her squawks were deeper than normal.

The three of them stood beside one another, watching me as I moved to the edge of the balcony. I checked to make sure the Shifter was ready and tapped on the thrusters. I'd just done this, but the Theos had been inside, guiding and helping me when I needed it. Now it was just me, one human trying to make a difference for many.

This was it. I'd never see them again, and I didn't even know how to feel about any of it. There was no choice now. I was committed. Much like every other adventure leading me to this point, I was going in head-first, but this was the only time I assumed there was no coming out of it alive. The other times, I'd done what needed to be done, but somehow thought everything would be okay. This was different. It felt...final.

I waved to them where they stood, a handful of yards away, each of them clearly upset. I couldn't look at them anymore or I'd lose my nerve. I spun and accelerated away, not looking back.

It was one of the hardest things I'd ever done.

THIRTY-FOUR

*W*ith less control than before, I raced toward the looming vortex. I was above the clouds, each breath coming quickly as I pushed through the world's atmosphere. The suit's built-in energy shield kept me safe as I bucked to and fro crossing into space. I had to straighten using the thrusts on the back of the suit a few times but quickly found the hang of it again.

"Barl?" I asked, hoping something from inside would answer. No one did, but for a moment, I thought I felt a tugging on my mind. "If you're still there, now would be a good time for some help."

The vortex was huge now, the swirling mass compiled of emerald green colors, dancing as they moved. If I didn't know how deadly the thing was, I'd have thought it beautiful.

I kept away from it, seeing small space debris being sucked toward it from a distance. As soon as I got closer, there would likely be no turning back from the power it held. I'd be committed. I looked around, hoping for some sort of intervention from the outside, only there was nothing else near us. I checked the suit's map, and nothing but the anomaly showed on the sensors.

The world below was quite the sight, and I stared at it momentarily. The red lava was visible even from this distance. Mary and the others were down there with no way of getting home. I could only hope they'd find a way off the vacant rock. Leslie knew where they were and would find a way to get to them. She wouldn't leave them behind, especially after the portal showed as dead.

The Shifter was tethered to my arm, and I opened it, seeing digits glowing on the screen. These were the coordinates for some other time and place. I wondered if I'd be consumed, or if I'd live long enough to see where we ended up. I wasn't sure I wanted to.

It locked in on the target. The image of the vortex appeared on the screen now, and the Shifter estimated the size and trajectory. It was now or never.

"Goodbye, Mary," I said, knowing she wouldn't hear me. I hit the thrusters on the back of my suit, pushing me slowly toward the center of the vortex. The power of its pull quickly grabbed hold, and I moved smoothly through space directly at it.

The fear that had threatened to overtake me earlier was gone now as I neared my goal.

I was moving faster, directly into the singularity of the vortex. The Shifter was held tightly in my left hand, and it was flashing red. The lock had failed.

"Come on, come on!" I cheered it on, watching it flick from red to green as I got closer to the center. I was moving quickly and almost lost my grip on the device. I was running out of time.

"Work, damn it!" I shouted at the top of my lungs, and it flicked to green, staying there for a second. I hit the button and everything came to a screeching halt. Nothing moved at that split second, and inside I felt the Theos come to life. Barl whispered something to me as they came alive; a brilliant white light shot me away from the vortex and the shifting dimension. The Shifter snapped from my wrist as my neck cracked from the force, and everything turned black.

———————

*E*verything hurt, and I struggled to open my eyes. When I did, I almost passed out again. I was in space! What happened? It slowly came back to me. The vortex, the Theos spewing from me into the singularity as they pushed me out of danger. I spun around now, using the thrusters on my back, looking for any sign of the massive green energy, but it was gone.

I looked down, expecting to see the planet below, but it wasn't there either. All I saw was a gray moon a few thousand kilometers away.

"That can't be good." If the mass was gone, and so was the planet, that could mean a couple of things. Either the planet had shifted with the Unwinding vortex, or I'd shifted with neither of them. Dread seeped in fast and hard, and I found myself unable to move. Was I in another dimension with nothing but a flying EVA? The Shifter was gone. The Theos were gone. I was alone in empty space.

It was at least ten minutes of me assuming the worst and trying to determine where I was, when I finally noticed the star in the distance. If that was the same star, then I might only have been pushed away a short distance – "short distance" being a relative term in space.

That would put the planet on the other side of the moon that was taking up all my viewing range. Relief inundated me. I hit the thrusters on the bottom of my boots and made for the moon. It took me an hour or so to rise over the moon and finally get a glimpse of what I was looking for. The planet was there. I cried in joy as I sighted it. Even from this far, I could see the lava and clouds. It was perfect.

"I'm coming back, Mary. I'm coming back."

———————————

*T*he suit, as advanced as it was, fed me with some intra-venous nutrients as I moved through space. The needle poked my skin, and I could feel the liquid enter my blood-stream. I instantly felt better. Likely there was something healing and rejuvenating in the blend.

I'd been traversing space for a couple of days now, and I could only begin to imagine what was going through Mary's, Slate's, and Suma's heads. I slept sparingly, worried something terrible would occur if my eyes were closed. The suit kept going, though. No fuel gauges beeped, and my oxygen hadn't depleted. Garo Alnod had the best EVA money could buy.

So many thoughts coursed through my brain in those two days. If I was still in my own universe, would they be waiting for me at the portal's high-rise? What would our baby look like? Would she, or he, have Mary's eyes and my hair color? What kind of future could we give a child? Dreams for New Spero lingered after an unfocused day-dream session. As much as I'd stuck my head in the sand about our new planet before, seeing that girl on the street before I left had really hit me hard.

There were things we needed to do. It wasn't always about what was happening out there in space; we had to take care of our own planet first and foremost. I didn't want to raise a child only to have the same issues that Earth had suffered as they grew older. I wouldn't let that happen.

Dozens of these topics internally battled back and forth as I flew toward the world where Mary would be mourning my death. Memories of her face kept me going in those two long days, and eventually, I was there above the planet, right where the Iskios' final attempt at destruction had been a short time ago. There were no signs it had ever existed.

With a spin, I changed trajectory, and raced head-first toward the world below.

———————

The platform I'd left them on was empty, devoid of any evidence of my friends. I ran inside, hoping to catch them staying close by. My legs pumped, the feeling odd after being in space for over two full days. I stumbled as I passed by rooms, checking the inside of each for Mary.

Chiding myself for being foolish, I tapped on my earpiece and scanned for an active line. It scrolled through twice, not discovering any. After finding the portal room empty, I hurried back out to the platform and scanned again. Still nothing.

It was dark out, and I turned the light on my suit. The elevator lift wasn't there. "They must have taken it down!" I shouted in happiness to myself. Remembering I had the thrusters on the suit, I lowered myself to the surface, a cloud of dust puffing up at my landing.

The same streets we'd trodden through a couple of years ago led me toward the building where we'd started this section of the city's power again. I don't know why I went there, other than it was the only place Slate, Suma, and I had visited that first time on the planet.

I scanned for an open line again. This time, a faint signal stretched to my earpiece. "Mary! Slate! Suma! Anybody, come in! It's Dean!"

Maybe they weren't there. Conceivably, I'd been

blasted to another dimension by the Shifter, and this was an alternate reality.

A response came, a distant whisper in my ear. "Dean…i…n't be."

"Mary?"

"Dean!" Her voice came in clear as I crossed the street. Lightning lit the dark road, and a building boomed as one of the forks struck a lightning rod rising ten feet in the air above it.

I ran now, and the signal got stronger. Another lightning flash, and I saw the silhouette of a person a block away. My legs propelled hard and fast as a surge of adrenaline hit me, and I shouted out as I lost balance, skidding forward on the hard ground, coming to a halt.

"What an entrance," Slate's voice said in my earpiece. I felt a strong hand turn me over, and I lay there smiling at Mary and Slate, who were leaning over me with concern.

"How?" was all Mary could muster as she knelt beside me. I unlatched my helmet and let it fall to the stony ground.

"Divine intervention."

THIRTY-FIVE

"Do you think it'll ever run?" I asked Suma. She'd been in the hangar two days now, with nothing to show for progress.

She let out a series of chirps and tweets, which translated to something about it being a rust bucket.

"That's a no, then?" I asked with a laugh. She threw a dirty towel at me, and we walked out of the hangar together. It was afternoon, and the storms had eased up the last couple of days. The whirring of an engine approached us. At least we'd been able to salvage some sort of all-terrain vehicle. Slate and Mary were back from an excursion.

The vehicle resembled the rover we used on missions for the Gatekeepers. It sat two, one behind the other, and had large wheels, bringing the height of the unit to about six feet. Slate poured out of the driver's cockpit with a big smile across his face. He threw off the respirator he was wearing and tossed something to me.

I caught it deftly and regarded it in my hand. It was the shape of an apple.

"As good as the ones from Grandma's backyard," Slate said, taking a bite out of another one. Mary came out with a second load.

"Five kilometers from the city. There's some water and a patch of vegetation on this unforgiving planet. If anything, we'll have food and water," Mary said. I went to the vehicle and unloaded a bucket with water, and a crate of similar fruits.

"How do we know it's edible?" Suma asked.

"We don't, but I've put back about four of these so far, so you can wait and see if I croak, I suppose," Slate said. His humor was back, and that was a good sign from the big guy.

"They'll come. Leslie knows where we are," I said for the tenth time since I'd come back.

The others nodded in agreement.

"I'm going to look for other ships tomorrow. Dean, are you in?" Suma asked. We'd spent the better part of each day scouring for a ship we could use to get off-planet. So far, none had been close to functional.

"I'm in." Risking it, I took a bite from the piece of fruit Slate had tossed my way. It was tart, and the juices dripped down my chin.

Mary smiled at me before we made our way to our temporary home on the vacant world. "They'll come," she said, mirroring my own uncertainty.

Whatever happened, we were together. We were survivors.

The End

ABOUT THE AUTHOR

Nathan Hystad is an author from Sherwood Park, Alberta, Canada. When he isn't writing novels, he's running a small publishing company, Woodbridge Press.

Keep up to date with his new releases by signing up for his newsletter at www.nathanhystad.com

Sign up at www.scifiexplorations.com as well for amazing deals and new releases from today's best indie science fiction authors.

Printed in Great Britain
by Amazon